lake monsters

Also by Joseph Citro

The Gore, 2000

The Vermont Ghost Guide, 2000

Guardian Angels, 1999

Green Mountains, Dark Tales, 1999

Shadow Child, 1998

Passing Strange, 1996

Green Mountain Ghosts, 1994

Deus-X, 1994

Vermont Lifer (writer/editor), 1986

Hardscrabble Books—Fiction of New England

Laurie Alberts, *Lost Daughters*

Laurie Alberts, *The Price of Land in Shelby*

Thomas Bailey Aldrich, *The Story of a Bad Boy*

Robert J. Begiebing, *The Adventures of Allegra Fullerton;
Or, A Memoir of Startling and Amusing Episodes from Itinerant Life*

Anne Bernays, *Professor Romeo*

Chris Bohjalian, *Water Witches*

Dona Brown, ed., *A Tourist's New England: Travel Fiction, 1820–1920*

Joseph Bruchac, *The Waters Between: A Novel of the Dawn Land*

Joseph A. Citro, *The Gore*

Joseph A. Citro, *Guardian Angels*

Joseph A. Citro, *Lake Monsters*

Joseph A. Citro, *Shadow Child*

Sean Connolly, *A Great Place to Die*

Dorothy Canfield Fisher (Mark J. Madigan, ed.), *Seasoned Timber*

Dorothy Canfield Fisher, *Understood Betsy*

Joseph Freda, *Suburban Guerrillas*

Castle Freeman, Jr., *Judgment Hill*

Frank Gaspar, *Leaving Pico*

Robert Harnum, *Exile in the Kingdom*

Ernest Hebert, *The Dogs of March*

Lake Monsters

A NOVEL BY THE AUTHOR OF *The Gore*

Joseph A. Citro

University Press of New England

HANOVER AND LONDON

University Press of New England, Hanover, NH 03755

© 2001 by Joseph A. Citro

Originally published in 1991 by Warner Books, Inc.

Printed in the United States of America

5 4 3 2 1

LIBRARY OF CONGRESS CATALOGING-IN-PUBLICATION DATA

Citro, Joseph A.

Lake monsters : a novel / Joseph A. Citro.

   p.   cm.—(Hardscrabble books)

ISBN 1-58465-110-5 (pbk. : alk. paper)

1. Vermont—Fiction. I. Title. II. Series.

PS3553.I865 L34 2001

813'.54—dc21   2001002087

To the memory of my friend,
Dr. Loren Connelly Bronson.

Contents

lake monsters

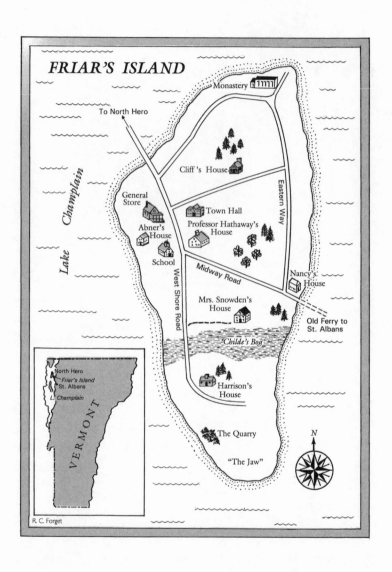

Prologue

A scream echoed in the granite hallway. Abrupt, sharp, tense with pain.

The tall man flinched, turned his head away, pressed his back tightly against the cold stone wall. He listened, motionless but for the glistening beads of sweat sliding down his face. In his black suit he was almost invisible among the shadows in the passageway. His long, pure white hair was like a mist in the half-light.

The screaming stopped.

He listened, inching closer to the open door. Across from him, candlelight flickered on the wall, projected from inside the room. Now he could hear something else. A painful sobbing came from within, a melancholic contrast to the pizzicato dance of the flames.

The man's face wrinkled, as if his thoughts pained him. He was undecided. Should he enter the room? Would his own pain fuel the relentless crying that came from beyond the open door?

On the previous evening he had stood on this same spot, contemplating these same questions, experiencing the same indecision.

But tonight he would not run away.

With an effort of will he flattened his features into an emotion-less mask, and, before he could change his mind, stepped into the room.

The perspiring girl looked up at him from the bed. Her pale face brightened as a faint smile stretched her quivering lips. She is so young, he thought, so very young. No more than a child.

"Mr. Dare," she said weakly, as if the simple words emptied the last breath from her lungs. He saw her round belly straining tight against the heavy comforter.

"And how is our princess tonight?" His voice was deep, steady. He hoped it would bring her confidence and strength.

Mrs. Putnam, the midwife, cradled the girl's face against her breast. Using a folded cloth, she bathed the girl's forehead with water.

"She's feelin' the life," Mrs. Putnam said to Cortney Dare.

"The pain is awful," whispered the child. "It don't go away." She lifted red-rimmed eyes and looked at him plaintively.

"It'll go away soon," said the man. "All the pain will be gone soon."

The child smiled weakly, proffering her scarred and trembling hand. Cortney Dare stepped near enough to take it, but not near enough to hear what she whispered.

"She said she hopes it'll be a boy," Mrs. Putnam told him.

"I think it will be," said the man. He seemed about to say something more, then stopped. He left hurriedly, as if the child's agony were his own.

The girl gasped as a strong fist of pain clenched her insides. Mrs. Putnam held her tighter, stroking her matted hair. "There, there," said the midwife. "There, there."

The child seemed to relax a bit as the discomfort passed. She breathed easier; there was more strength in her voice. "Will you tell me a story, Missus?"

"My goodness, child, I think you've heard all my stories."

"I know. But maybe you could tell me one again . . ."

"I could do that, if there's a special one you'd like to hear. Or," the midwife smiled as if an idea had come to her, "I could tell you a new story, a story that an Indian boy told me a long, long time ago, back when I was a girl like you. It's the story of a big eel, a giant, that lives out in the lake."

"Is it a scary story?"

"Oh, no, my darlin', it's not a scary story at all . . ."

Vermont

The Present

The Monster Hunter 1

Bored and aching from the long drive, Harrison Allen passed the big green sign that announced:

BURLINGTON 62 MILES
100 KILOMETERS

He fidgeted in the seat, tapped his fingers on the top of the steering wheel. He'd been on the road heading north from Boston for the last three hours; it would be at least another hour before he arrived at Mark's house.

Harrison had never enjoyed driving. It was usually his practice to speed, to get where he wanted to go as fast as possible. Today, however, he had broken his habit by holding to a conservative—and legal—sixty-five miles per hour. The way his luck had been going lately, he knew better than to tempt a speeding ticket.

After three hours in the car, with no diversion but the mindless music on the radio and the uncomfortable chaos of his own thoughts—which, lately, had been running all too frequently toward self-pity—he became irritated at the prospect of another hour of driving.

Another hour!

A bit of additional pressure on the accelerator and the speedometer needle climbed to seventy. That makes it under an hour, he thought. Then—*what the hell*—he accelerated to seventy-five.

Angry at himself for his restlessness, and in an effort to avoid yet another bout with self-pity, he concentrated, working hard to take pleasure from the scenery while contemplating once again the real purpose of his trip.

He felt funny, in a way, returning to Burlington, Vermont, after all these years. It was as if he were trying to return to the past, to rediscover the point at which things started to go wrong. How foolish. Did he really expect he could make a fresh start?

It wasn't as if he had outgrown Burlington; no doubt there were still lessons to be learned there. He realized that during his four years as an undergraduate at the University of Vermont, he must have overlooked many things.

The monster was a case in point.

It was odd, he thought, four years living right on the shores of Lake Champlain and never once hearing about the monster. Of course he had been younger then, his mind had been on loftier matters: girls and beer and parties. And occasionally, when he was too tired for anything else, his studies.

Harrison's mind reviewed the years since graduation, the images like slides flicking rapidly on a screen: travel in Europe, an attempt at writing a novel, an impulsive, quickly broken engagement, an English teaching job in Rhode Island, and the last five years in marketing for a computer manufacturer in Boston. Rather an unremarkable biographical sketch, he had to admit.

And now what?

When MeisterData went belly-up not three months after Leading Edge, the job was gone. The company was gone, and what were the prospects for a marketing executive whose product had failed in the marketplace?

Suddenly all Harrison had to look forward to were a few months of unemployment checks. And then?

Then what?

Then it was back to square one with his life.

Again Harrison forced himself to be optimistic. Six months of unemployment checks would certainly buy enough time to do what had to be done. He could slow down, stretch out. Relax.

Take some kind of psychic inventory, get to know himself and maybe simplify his life to the point that he could start all over again. Do things right this time.

And better yet, he'd be living rent-free in Vermont! It would be like a long vacation. An opportunity to see what it was like to be independently wealthy.

Smiling with a momentary satisfaction, Harrison turned his attention to the Vermont landscape. Assuming a deep, well-modulated voice, he pretended to be a tour guide, "Interstate 89, bisecting Vermont as it connects White River Junction with Burlington, is one of the most scenic stretches of highway in the country. Designed to complement the beautiful land that it crosses, I-89 offers the traveler a delightful excursion through the magnificent Green Mountains: quaint white villages, ponds like silver mirrors, rivers and streams that decorate the hillsides like tinsel on a Christmas tree . . ."

He chuckled softly, embarrassed by the sound of his voice in the empty car.

Near Waterbury, with Camel's Hump on his left and Mount Mansfield—Vermont's highest peak—on his right, Harrison easily remembered why he had once vowed never to leave the Green Mountain State.

Fifteen years. He had been away for a long time. The mountains looked good to him, like the welcoming faces of old friends.

How easy it was for good friends to lose touch. He and Mark had been like brothers during their college years. And now? Sure, they continued to write—one, maybe two letters a year. But they'd seen each other only once since the '81 wedding. That visit had been almost five years ago, when Mark and Judy had come to Boston for a long weekend. How quiet Mark had seemed then, how docile in the presence of his vivacious wife.

But Mark and Judy were still together after nine years. And Harrison Allen was still very much alone.

He could not have felt more unattached at that moment, his belongings in storage, his apartment in Brookline sublet to a stranger. No job and no reliable prospects for the future. The only things he felt belonged to him were the car he drove, the portable typewriter—there was no electricity where'd he'd be living—the camera equipment in the back seat, and the two bulging suitcases in the trunk.

No fixed address, he thought, as he shifted into fifth, crossing Bolton Flats toward Richmond. He felt as if he were riding a time machine into the past, toward his old college town, toward his old friend.

And what was drawing him back into the past? Just an idea, really. An idea worthy of an eighteen-year-old. But it was an idea that gave him the only direction in his life. He was going to become a monster hunter.

Absently, Harrison pushed the cassette into the player.

"Now let me see if I can get this just right. It was in late August, early September. It was after work, early evenin'. Me and my boy, Cliff—I guess he was about fifteen at the time—we was out in my boat, little aluminum twelve-footer from Sears. We was in the bay—

"What's that? Oh, it was St. Albans Bay, just east of Friar's Island. The lake was real calm an' dark, just like a big sheet of black ice. Anyways, it was startin' to get dark out, and I could see red in the sky. They was thick black clouds overhead, an' they was somethin' about that calm, like any second them big clouds was gonna pucker up and let loose one helluva rainstorm. There wasn't no wind to speak of. The clouds weren't movin', neither was the water. Everythin' was real calm. Somethin' about that kind of an evenin' makes you want to talk in whispers, makes you feel real close to whoever you was with.

" 'Course that's the best time for fishin'. All around us, and off in the distance, there was little boats with fellas settin' in 'em, just like me an' Cliff. Some had just one fisherman, some had more. Nobody was payin' no attention to nobody else. Fishin's kind of a private thing that way, you know?

"Well sir, everybody was just watchin' their lines, lookin' at the little spot where it disappears under the water, waitin' for it to move, waitin' for some fish to take it.

"Now, it's this next part I want to get just right for you. I want you to see it just the way I done.

"I already told you how quiet it was. And Cliff, well, he's a quiet boy. Oh, he's got his share of the devil in him, same as any boy. But Cliff's devil's a quiet one. Anyways, he says to me, 'Dad, I got somebody!'

"Well, sir, I figger he's kiddin', havin' a little joke, that is until that fishpole of his bends jest about in half, bends nearly to breakin'!

"I can see he's hooked into somethin' pretty big, walleye, most likely, or maybe a big-ass bass or somethin'.

"'Let up on yer drag!' I hollers at him. You could hear that drag screechin' as the thing pulls out line. No point tryin' to reel in, too much fish headin' for deep water.

"The tip of the boy's pole is vibratin' like the tail of a rattler, and ol' Cliff, he's gettin' scared.

"'What is it, Dad?' he says. There's a look on his face like he's tryin' to cover up how scared he is. I see him sweatin' and shakin', an' I know how he feels.

"'Let her take line,' I tells him. 'Let her have all she wants!'

"Right now I'm thinkin' maybe he's hooked into one of them salmon. Or maybe a big laker.

"Cliff's pullin' real hard and the thing's still takin' line, an' that ol' pole of his, why it's bent around like one of them divinin' rods over a spring.

"We're both anxious to see what he's got there, and Cliff, he keeps lookin' at me, then at the water. He's sweatin' more and more, and lookin' more and more scared.

"Finally he says, 'Here, Dad, you bring him in.' And he starts to hand me his pole. Well, I figure it's his fish, so I says, 'No, sir. You play it out,' but before we can argue about it, the fightin' stops.

"If you ain't a fisherman, you don't know that feelin' of terrible calm right after your line goes limp and your fish gets away. It's a lonely feelin', a feelin' of failure.

"Well, Cliff, he's lookin' broken-hearted as can be as he's windin' in line. I don't know how many feet of it.

"And me, I don't know whether to say let's go home or let's try a few more casts. I mean, we both know there's somethin' pretty goddamn—excuse me—somethin' pretty awful darn big out there. But common sense tells us we won't get another crack at it tonight.

"So Cliff's reelin' in, and I'm tryin' to think of somethin' nice to say to him, when all of a sudden somethin' hits the boat!

"Ka-thunk!

"Sounds as though we bottomed-out on a submerged log. But the thing is, we ain't movin' at all. Plus, why cripes, we're way the heck out in the middle of the lake! I mean, any logs or stones or anythin' like that would have to be thirty, forty feet straight down!

"I think both of us got real scared then. I could see Cliff a-shiverin' jest as though the vibration from whatever hit us was still shakin' inside him.

"Then Cliff lets out a holler, like the devil hisself had jumped up and bit him on the ass—oh, sorry—on the behind. His fish-pole jumps right out of his hands! Then it dives right into the water and heads down in-underneath the boat!

"Well, heck, I figure whatever he's hooked into never really got away, she jest doubled back and swimmed right in-under the boat! An I'll tell ya one thing, mister, no fish I ever seen will do that!

"So I makes a grab for Cliff's pole when she comes out the other side, but, hell, she's movin' way too fast and I cuts my hand on the monofil'ment.

"So we're jest sittin' there, lookin' out over the water, tryin' real hard to see what it was that's playin' with us. An' we looked down, trying to see if it swum under the boat again.

"But for a long time nothin' happens. It keeps gettin' later. And darker. Some of the other boats had gone in. You could see one or two was still out there with Coleman lanterns, way off in the distance. I remember how you could see their lights reflected in the water along with the reflection of the moon. No mirror was ever any smoother than the surface of that lake.

"Anyways, just then I seen somethin' kinda movin' off on the right side of the boat, off towards Melville Landin'. The water starts ripplin' and churnin', and then it's like one of them logs that ain't supposed to be there's a-comin' right out of the water, bobbin' up to the surface.

"And all of a sudden — and Cliff seen it too — this black, pointy head comes right up out of the water! The head and neck is kind of juttin' out on an angle, like the blade of a jackknife openin' up.

"I can see the water drippin' off it as it comes higher and higher out of the lake. I'm thinkin' to myself, why Godfrey-mighty, this can't be real. But it keeps comin' and comin', like a snake a-crawlin' out of his hole. It's all black, don't ya know, and shiny. An' it's evil lookin', like somethin' out of one of them old, scary movies.

"And in the moonlight I can see Cliff's nightcrawler, all white and puffy lookin', hangin' out of its mouth, and the monofil'ment line, jes' like a long strand of silver thread, trailin' off into the lake.

"There must've been six foot of head and neck juttin' out of the water, and I'll tell you, mister, I wasn't interested in seein' what sort of body that neck was hooked on to!

"But you know, the funny thing . . . I mean the thing I'm always gonna remember jest as long as I live, is the way that head turned, slow and easy-like, jest like a lighthouse or . . . or maybe the periscope of a submarine. It kept on turnin' till its eyes locked right tight on to me and my boy.

"I tell you I looked right into the eyes of that thing, and it looked right into mine. It didn't act scared or nothin'. We just kept lookin', eye to eye, as if the thing was tryin' to remember me, like it was tryin' to memorize everythin' about me so it wouldn't never forget.

"You better believe I'll never be able to forget it, though I'm here to tell ya I sure as hell want to.

"Anyways, after a while it just slides back into the water without a sound, just as if it had never been there. And me and Cliff, well sir, we hightailed it for home . . ."

. . .

Harrison ejected the cassette from his player and tucked it into his shirt pocket. He liked to listen to it now and then, whenever he wanted to reaffirm his purpose. He'd recorded it several months ago from a public-radio broadcast about the Lake Champlain Monster. It was an old interview, recorded back in 1968, but it was this actual eyewitness account that had inspired Harrison's interest in monster hunting.

The speaker, Oliver Ransom, had since died, but Harrison knew he would be able to locate other witnesses that he could interview. He was especially eager to find Cliff, Oliver Ransom's son.

Harrison felt confident that his research would lead to a definitive study of the monster. Hopefully, he would be the one to document the creature's existence once and for all. Perhaps he'd become famous as a result.

His friend Mark's enthusiasm about the search—at least judging from his latest letter—seemed to match Harrison's. Mark had sent him some recent clippings from the *Burlington Free Press*. One said that the monster had been sighted 134 times since 1980.

One hundred thirty-four times!

And it was back in 1981 that Sandra Mansi's famous, though somewhat questionable, photograph—taken in July 1977—was finally released to the media. Since then, Lake Champlain had become known as America's Loch Ness.

Two months ago Harrison had joined the American Cryptozoological Society. He'd quickly learned that sightings of "monsters" in North American lakes were not uncommon. Indeed, in various parts of the United States and Canada, all sorts of creatures were routinely reported: lake monsters, vanishing cats, giant unknown birds, and fearsome man-beasts covered with fur yet walking on two legs.

But in every case there was one maddening detail: the absence of proof. There was no proof of any of them.

Still, Harrison found the topic of monsters endlessly fascinating. It was as if these elusive oddities were placed among us deliberately, as reminders that we don't know all there is to know. To

Harrison, they suggested that our science, our space program, and especially our high-tech computers, were little more than modern forms of hubris, ways of distracting our attention from the natural world.

Harrison was convinced that one need not be an expert or even a scientist to study these phenomena. After all, one cannot earn a degree in the mating habits of the yeti.

Indeed, Harrison smiled, the credentials of an out-of-work marketing executive were every bit as solid as those of a university professor when it came to stalking the monster of Lake Champlain.

A Change of Scene 2

I

In the late afternoon darkness, Harrison climbed the steps of the old brick building on Union Street. The heavy wood and glass door to Mark and Judy's condominium opened almost too quickly when he knocked. Then, for the first time in nearly five years, Harrison Allen and Mark Chittenden stood face to face.

The balding head was new to Mark's bearded, ascetic-looking face. He seemed much thinner than Harrison remembered, almost drawn and sickly. *Probably jogging too much with the rest of the faculty members*, Harrison thought. God, he was so sick of exercise and gyms and fitness programs and—he caught himself, recognizing envy for what it was.

Mark stepped away from the door, allowing Harrison room to enter. "Welcome," he said, offering his hand, his smile placid and uncharacteristically reserved.

Judy Chittenden entered from the kitchen, her long black hair in a tight braid. "Well, hello, stranger." She beamed. "Come in, Harry, sit down!"

She took Harrison's hand and they exchanged kisses on the cheek. With smiles and great animation, Judy led him to the living room.

"You guys sit down. Harry, please, make yourself at home. I'll get us some drinks. What's your pleasure, stranger?"

"A beer would hit the spot."

"Should have known. You'll never change." Judy turned with the grace of a dancer, her long braid swinging.

Maybe you're right; maybe I won't change. It was a discouraging notion.

He looked around the room: large old building, fourteen-foot ceilings, white plaster walls, prints—Picasso and van Gogh—in metal frames, light oak bookshelves, green plants in the windows. Hanging ferns. Things looked tidy, orderly, as if all had been made clean and comfortable for the expected guest.

"Nice place," said Harrison, still glancing about.

"Yeah, nice," said Mark, "if you don't mind living in a woolen mill."

"They did a beautiful job of renovation. Looks great!"

"It's home." Mark's face sank into a comic frown, as if to say, Okay, so I did it, I'm a card-carrying member of the great American middle class. Then, the frown broadened into a beatific smile that said, But hey, so what? The middle class ain't such a bad place to be.

Both men started laughing, and the tension passed. They hadn't lost their knack for nonverbal communication. For a moment it was as it had been many years ago in college. Harrison knew the undergraduate was still alive in both of them.

"It didn't take you two long to start acting foolish," said Judy, returning from the kitchen with three bottles of Molson ale. "At least you could have waited for me. Would you like a glass, Harry?"

As the empties piled up, Mark was saying, "Actually, Harry, I'm not much of a believer in the thing. When that Mansi woman's photograph came out in the *Free Press*, back in—when was it? 1980 or so?—there was quite a bit of interest in the monster. It was big time. I mean we had TV crews up here and everything. Some people even managed to get it placed on the endangered

species list. So if it turns out to be real, it will be illegal to catch it
or kill it. Right now interest has pretty much died down. People
either accept that it's out there or they don't give much of a shit.
You can bet the local merchants are getting their pound of flesh,
though. We even had a Champ Car Wash open up on Shelburne
Road, and there's a local potato chip company making Champ
Chips."

"Are you saying you don't believe in it at all?" Harrison heard
the disappointment in his own voice.

"I don't rule out the possibility. I mean, it's a goddamn big
lake. One of America's great lakes, really. Over one hundred miles
long, eleven miles wide in some places. And four hundred feet
deep, or so I'm told by my learned colleagues at the U of VM.
That's a pretty big body of water. I wouldn't go so far as to say the
monster's definitely not out there. It could be there and I've just
missed it. Me and a shitload of other people. I might add that I
don't personally know anyone who's seen it."

"And you wouldn't admit it if you did, right, dear?" Judy
laughed.

Mark gave Judy a comic scowl over the top of his eyeglasses.

"So what about the photograph?" Harrison pressed. "How do
you feel about that?"

"Oh, God," said Judy. "Now you'll really get him going."

Mark's eyes flicked toward his wife, then back to Harrison. "It
makes me think of Conan Doyle and his fairies."

"Fairies? What do you mean?"

"A put-on. Flimflam. A hoax. To me, Mansi's photo looks like
a picture of a swimmer in a wetsuit. Look at it this way: The
woman allegedly took the photo in 1977, right? But she didn't get
around to releasing it to the press until '81. Now she can't even
produce the negative, and she can't remember just exactly where
she was when she snapped it. 'Somewhere north of St. Albans,'
she says. Christ, do you realize how much shoreline there is north
of St. Albans?"

"I agree the picture could be a hoax," said Harrison. "And it
shouldn't be used to prove or disprove the monster's existence.

But what about the hundreds of other sightings, starting with Champlain himself back in 1609?"

"Who knows what he saw. We can't conjure him up to ask him. To the best of my knowledge, the monster has never been spotted by anyone trained in scientific observation. I'll go this far, Harry. I'll admit it has to be one of four things—"

"Watch out," said Judy, "he's getting behind his podium again." She winked at Harrison, saying, "You and I will definitely be needing more beer. I'll get them."

Harrison watched her leave the room, admiring her pretty bottom as it moved beneath snug denims. Self-consciously he pulled his attention back to Mark. "You were saying you'd narrowed it down to four possibilities?"

"Right." Mark held up an index finger. "It's either a hoax, the work of generation after generation of *organized* tricksters over the last *four hundred years.*

"Or, two"—another finger—"It may be honest misinterpretation. For example, many people have seen sturgeon 'porpoising' —you know, breaking the surface of the water, then diving again —and thought they saw the monster's humps. Big carp will do the same thing in the late spring, while sturgeon do it in the hot weather. A family of otters might do it anytime at all."

Harrison nodded.

"A third possibility, of course, is illusion. Out-and-out seeing things. Hallucinations. You know as well as I do, Harrison, 'the sea plays strange tricks on a man.'"

"Or a woman," added Judy, coming back with three more green bottles of Canadian ale. "So," she continued, lowering her voice, "you've got one guy playing a trick, another who sees a family of otters swimming single file, and a third guy who's tripping or something. What have you got? Three sightings and no monster."

All three chuckled at Judy's imitation of Mark.

"After ten years, she knows all my rants."

Harrison smiled. "But you said there were four possibilities. So what's the fourth?"

Mark lifted his eyebrows. "Reality. The fourth possibility is that the monster's really out there."

ONE A.M.

Judy, relaxed from the effects of the alcohol, rose from her cushion on the floor. She stretched languorously, announcing through a yawn that she was going to bed. She kissed her husband somewhat awkwardly and walked over to Harrison, where she stood in front of his chair. She bent forward and kissed him, too. "We're happy to have you with us, Harry," she said. "And you're welcome to stay as long as you want. Let me leave you with something to sleep on: Maybe going to the island's not such a good idea. It's a creepy place, not the idyllic little vacation spot that you probably imagine. That's why we left. You're better off here in Burlington. There's more to do, lots of people to meet, better opportunities to find work. And you can stay right here with us until you find a place of your own. What do you say, Harry?"

Harrison smiled warmly at her. He was touched by her offer. "I say I'll sleep on it. Thanks, Judy."

"Well, guys, I'm done in. Good night." She excused herself and was soon snoring drunkenly in the next room.

In the living room the men continued to talk quietly. The air was saturated with Mark's cigarette smoke; Harrison's eyes watered from irritation and fatigue.

Mark was half reclining on the couch as Harrison slid from the chair to the soft, thick carpet on the floor.

Their conversation rolled like a great wheel, from monsters to careers to marriage to women to politics . . . to the old days, and back again to monsters.

"Somehow I still get the feeling you're not sincere about this, Harry. That it's just a lark, or a whim." Mark crushed out the last Marlboro from the last pack. The conversation had leveled to an intimacy only possible between old and partially drunken friends.

"Sincere? Shit, what's sincere? You go to Egypt, you dig for ruins, you're doing archaeological research. Fine. That's respectable; it's even encouraged. But if you go to Vermont to look for a lake monster, you're some kind of crank, right?"

"Now come on, Harry, don't get defensive. I'm just wondering, what's in all of this for you? I wish you'd level with me."

Harrison closed his eyes and thought. He took a deep, slow breath. Then spoke softly, "I don't know. I really don't. I mean you gotta be someplace, right? And I had to get the fuck out of Boston. Look, I'm thirty-five years old. I got no job, no house, no family. Most people my age have their mortgage nearly paid off, are department chairmen, and are failing at their second marriage. Christ, I don't even have a girlfriend!"

"That's crap, Harry, and you know it. Look at me—I'm still an assistant professor of English, I live in a condo with my wife of nearly ten years. And you and I are the same age. I mean, what have I got if I give up teaching? What salable skills do I possess? I'd very likely end up working for the government, or maybe in public relations or marketing. And you've already outgrown that kind of thing. You see? You and I aren't in such different boats. You think I'm the picture of educated middle-class contentment? Hell, I fight with my wife, we threaten to leave each other, we make up, we get sick of work, we consider career changes, we consider not changing careers. Christ, Harry, I still wake up in the middle of the night sweating, teeth clenched, wondering where's the fucking payoff."

"I know, I know."

"So what's with the monster-hunting crap? Even if you photograph and identify it, what have you got? It's still not going to make you rich and famous. It's not as if you invented video games or compact disc players, or something like that. The only people who'll get rich are the ones selling monster T-shirts, and monster stuffed animals, and McMonsterburgers at the neighborhood McDonald's. You're not even going to get it named after you. It's already been dubbed *Belua aquatica Champlainiensis* after our old pal Samuel de."

"Okay, okay, so call it a vacation. I've got six months of unemployment checks coming to me. If I'm careful with my money I can be completely self-indulgent from now until midsummer of next year. I'll read, write, look for the monster. Drink. When I get bored I'll look for a job. Talk about a case of arrested adolescence . . ."

"Ah, that's my old Harry! And again we're very much alike. Look at me; I've never even gotten out of school. But I'm not running away from it, either."

Harrison looked up, startled by the sudden turn of the conversation, his drunken nonchalance penetrated by the sting of Mark's verbal rapier. "Is that what you think I'm doing? Running away?"

"I don't know, Harry. Are you?"

It was a fair question. Harrison thought a moment. "I don't know either. I mean, I'm not sure. It just seems as if things have suddenly started to fall apart for me. Nothing seems solid. Nothing seems in place with my life. Maybe it's always been that way, but I guess I've finally reached an age when it's starting to bother me. It's as if I'm in the center of something confining, watching the various pieces of my life floating away like balloons out of reach. I have this nagging feeling that I'd better get things squared away quick, before time runs out, before something goes irreparably wrong. Do you have any idea what I'm talking about?"

Mark nodded sullenly. Neither man spoke for a long while. They were out of cigarettes, and there was no more beer. It was time to sleep.

2

MORNING

Mark unfolded a large, awkward road map of Vermont. It covered the dirty breakfast dishes on the table.

"Judy may be right about the island—it really is no place to be unless you're completely comfortable with yourself. There's not much of anything to do there. Not even a bar or restaurant. Maybe it's a good place for couples—"

"Or hermits," added Judy, trying to extract the empty coffee mugs from under the map.

Mark ignored his wife and continued to speak as if lecturing a class. All he lacked was a pointer in his hand.

"The house is here," he said, tapping a spot near the southernmost part of the island. "It's the only house south of this marsh" —he tapped again—"which, as you can see, completely bisects the island. Childe's Bog, it's called. The town, the bridge to North Hero, and all the other houses and camps are north of the bog. So your only neighbor is an abandoned granite quarry a little bit southwest of the house."

"I think you'll prefer it to your other neighbors," said Judy.

Harrison smiled. "I keep getting the feeling you're not too fond of the island, Judy."

"As always, Harrison," said Mark, "you have a firm grasp of the obvious."

"It was like living in a Bela Lugosi film," said Judy, frowning.

"Judy was never much of a rosy-cheeked country-girl type."

"That's right, none of this back-to-nature shit for me. I like my eggs from the supermarket and my bathroom indoors. I also like neighbors who speak the same language. That is, if they talk at all."

"She's right about that," said Mark, chuckling. "The islanders could never be described as talkative."

"Did they ever tell you why it's called Friar's Island?"

"Good question. Apparently no one is quite sure, but I've heard several possible explanations. For a while—well, more than a hundred years ago—there was a group of monks living there. There's a creepy old monastery on the northern part of the island. It's deserted now, of course, and it's kind of ignored by the islanders."

"Shunned," said Judy, her voice falsely tremulous.

"Also," Mark continued, "you'll notice the island is shaped a little like a monk's head. You can imagine this top part as his cowl and this"—Mark pointed to the southeastern promontory—"as his chin. The islanders call it 'The Jaw.'"

"So my new home is between Childe's Bog and The Jaw. Quite an address!"

"Well, it's easy to find, anyway. Just point your car south and drive till the road ends. The road stops just beyond your dooryard."

"How long has it been since you folks were up there?"

"Judy and I took a ride up in the spring. Checked it out for damage and stuff like that. We don't get up there too often anymore."

"Once a year is too often for me."

"Why don't you rent it out?"

"We probably could, but we'd have to fix it up a lot first. We used to rent it two or three months during the summer to a couple of families from Quebec. But they stopped coming and, frankly, renting it got to be too much of a hassle. It was easier just to decide I wasn't cut out to be a landlord."

"But didn't you live there yourselves?"

"Oh, sure. We moved in right after we were married. It was the cheapest thing to do at the time. But commuting to Burlington every day got to be a real pain in the ass. You can't imagine what those roads are like in winter! So there it sits, empty, collecting dust and taxes. I can't even sell it, the way the market is today. Besides, I'd have to install plumbing, electricity, and central heat even to make it viable as a rental property. And then there's the problem of finding someone who'd rent it. Some inheritance, eh? So, honest to God, Harry, you're welcome to it for as long as you want. It would probably be a good idea having somebody up there to look after it."

"But who's going to look after Harry?"

"Will you get off it, Jude!" snapped Mark. "You've made your point, okay!"

There was a frozen moment of uncomfortable silence. Mark blushed, Harrison felt embarrassed.

"Sorry," said Judy, clearing her throat as if to disguise the tremor in her voice. "I just can't imagine Harry holing up there all alone. You've got to admit it's creepy, and the natives are . . . unpleasant, to say the least."

She looked Harrison full in the face. "So if you change your mind, Harry, you're always welcome here. I mean it."

"I appreciate that. Thanks. Maybe I need to sleep on it a couple nights up there."

"Well," said Mark, tapping his Rolex, "I gotta go. I'll be late for school."

Islanders

I

Two children crouched behind the stone wall, their backs to the marsh, watching the '86 Saab move slowly along the dirt road toward the house.

"Stay down," commanded Bobby Capra. "Don't let 'em see ya."

Bobby was the leader. He was a gaunt, earnest-looking boy of twelve, with defiant, cold gray eyes in an otherwise expressionless face. Bobby was used to giving orders to his friends, and equally accustomed to having his orders obeyed. One long-standing command was that everyone call him "Cappy" or, less formally, "Cap." He wouldn't answer to Bobby.

Every summer Cappy came to the island for two tedious weeks and altogether too many weekends. His father, who owned a building-supply business in Plattsburgh, New York, referred to the cottage as their island hideaway. Cappy referred to it as the pits. He hated it. Nothing to do. No video arcades, no pizza shop, no television. Nothing. And if he wanted to blow some weed, he had to bring it with him. The island kids probably didn't even know what it was. Bunch of stupid woodchucks.

But what the hell, there wasn't anybody on the island

worth hanging out with anyway. That's why he put up with that wimpy Brigitte Pelletier, whose parents owned the place down the road. "Bree-sheet," her mother called her in that stupid-sounding French-Canadian accent.

Younger by two years, Brigitte was fat and didn't know anything about music or drugs. She tagged along after Cappy as if she were some lost mutt that nobody wanted—and Cappy could see why. She looked like an ugly little boy. In her loose-fitting shorts, her chubby legs resembled boiled hot dogs about to burst, and her floppy T-shirt hung on her like elephant skin. She could easily pass for a boy, too, if her mams hadn't started to grow. They poked at the front of her jersey like she was hiding a couple of Hershey's Kisses underneath.

The only dependable break he got from her boring presence was when her parents carted her off to church. Christ, they drove all the way over to Isle La Motte because there was some big-deal Catholic church—a shrine or something—over there. Probably they did it to pray for a miracle, hoping their daughter would come back looking like Kim Basinger instead of Freddy Krueger. "Dat man, who you t'ink he is?" asked Brigitte, her face a pudgy study in perplexity.

"Dunno. Never seen the car before," replied Cappy, without moving his steel-cold stare from the Saab with the Massachusetts plates.

The kids watched the car come to a stop in front of the old building, and saw a man get out. The stranger stood by the driver's door, just looking at the house.

Brigitte and Cappy looked at the house, too. For Cappy, it was a grand and mysterious place. Though somewhat sinister looking, it nonetheless held all the enchantment of a Christmas gift begging to be opened. Its wooden walls had weathered to a dark gray; the slate shingled roof was like a steep cobbled roadway leading to the sky. And it was old, astoundingly old. Cappy and Brigitte couldn't guess exactly how many years—though they'd tried often enough. Still, it was easy to see that it had stood solid and still through many fierce Vermont winters, withstanding countless killer storms off the lake, enduring every bit as well as the many stone buildings that dotted the island.

The strange man approached the front door, fumbling a key ring from his coat pocket, never taking his eyes off the building. His apparent fascination with the house was shared by Cappy, who had done a little research on the place. It had been built by a ship's captain not long after the surrender of Cornwallis at Yorktown. That meant it was constructed sometime in the late 1700s.

According to local legend, there was a treasure buried somewhere on the island. Probably French gold and silver. Maybe a million dollars' worth. And, so the story went, the map was hidden someplace in the old house—the captain's house, as the islanders called it.

Cap's house.

Cappy eyed the man, the intruder, as he wrestled with the ancient lock. In a moment he pushed the door open and stepped slowly into the interior darkness. But he didn't close the door behind him.

"Umm . . . ummm, maybe we should just leave now," suggested Brigitte, a flickering of fear in her soft voice.

"*Ssssssh,*" snapped Cappy. "He can't see you if you stay still and stay quiet."

"But he is da guy who own dis place?"

"How the fuck should I know. Shut up, will you."

2

Harrison Allen filled his lungs with the scents of the old house. There was a mustiness in the air, the kind that comes when old buildings stand closed and empty for too long. A dampness and a raw chill filled the place, and only a fire would dispel them. Mixed among the profusion of odors, almost hiding, there was a faint suggestion of smoke, a remnant of the many wood fires that once had warmed the ancient rooms.

He stepped to his right, crossing a threshold into the living room (was that what they had called it in the old days, he wondered? maybe a parlor?). The windows were shuttered, closed to a view of the road and lake beyond. He noted a fireplace, shallow and tall, with an old shotgun mounted on the wall above it. There was a table made from two wide oak timbers (he'd move that to a place in front of the window; it would be his desk), a sofa, and an easy chair, both covered with yellowing linen sheets.

His first thought was to find a bed and move it in here, to live in this one big room as if it were a cabin. Such an arrangement would make the place easier to heat in the cold months ahead.

Harrison walked out and across the little foyer from which he had entered. He stuck his head through the doorway opposite the living room.

This room was empty but for a pair of broken wooden chairs that looked as if they had once been part of a set. No doubt this had been the dining room. The walls were a dull, faded brown. Occasional rectangles of brighter, more colorful fleur-de-lis patterns disclosed where pictures must have hung. In the corners of the room, near the plaster ceiling, the faded wallpaper peeled and curled like scrolls of antique parchment.

After crossing the dining room, Harrison passed through a door that opened into the kitchen. Here he discovered the dining room table with two unbroken chairs. There was an old cast-iron wood stove, once no doubt used for cooking. Fastened to its side was a complex but ingenious contraption for heating water. Beside the stove, and looking very much out of place, was an apartment-sized four-burner gas range. *Probably easier than firing up the wood stove every time you want to heat a can of soup*, he reasoned.

The kitchen sink was a real museum piece. It was of a preporcelain vintage, made of metal (iron, maybe?) that was corroded and flaking. Next to the sink was a hand pump—the water supply.

As he observed all this in the strange half-light from the open front door and shuttered windows, he felt a small, tight smile curling his lips. He folded his arms across his chest, looking around with a discriminating eye.

"Home," he said to the cold, plaster walls.

"Well," he chuckled, "at least the price is right."

3

From where Cappy and Brigitte crouched, they could see the man come out of the open door and begin to turn back the shutters from the windows on the front of the building.

"Shit," said Cappy.

"Eh? What da matter?"

"He's opening up the place, dummy. That means he's stayin'."

Stung sharply by the unkind word, Brigitte's eyes darted from side to side as if searching for something to say. "M-My fa'der say dere's no map in dere."

"And what makes him such a goddamn authority?"

Brigitte looked down at the ground, hoping Cappy would not see the film of tears in her eyes.

Both of them watched, waiting in silence.

4

Cliff Ransom's family had lived on Friar's Island since long before it was chartered as a town. In fact, Ransoms had lived on the island when Vermont was still part of the New Hampshire Grants.

Now Cliff was the last of a long line of Ransoms. He had distinguished himself by becoming the most highly educated person in the history of the family. Cliff had completed eight years in the Island's school system. Then he had been bussed to Swanton for his two unsuccessful attempts at high school. He quit school when he was sixteen to go to work in the quarry, which was within walking distance of his house.

The quarry, a rare source of black marble that shipped its product all over the world, was still owned by an island family, but now the family leased it to a company from Proctor. During the summer months, it still provided jobs for several of the islanders. Cliff had been with the company since 1968.

Cliff didn't get off the island much, and really didn't want to. He liked the island and the islanders, and he resented the influx of new residents and summer folk. He especially disliked out-of-staters—"flatlanders," he called them—and Canadians. He had a name for them, too.

Saturday afternoon found Cliff in the center of town, sitting on the stone steps of the town hall. Beside him was his friend Bill Blood. There was a six-pack of Bud on the steps between them.

Cliff was contemplating a minor change of routine. "Ya know, Bill, I been thinkin'. I might jest hafta take me a little trip down to Burl'ton one of these days."

"Gettin' to be that time of year again, is it?" inquired Bill.

"Yep. It pains me, though. It's a hell of a long way to drive for a little bit a ginch, don't ya think?"

"I guess prob'ly." Bill sniffed mightily and spat beside the stone steps. "Tell ya somethin', son: I think it's high time you done some serious thinkin' 'bout gettin' married. Cuts down on travel, ya know."

"Like you done, huh?"

"Well, no. If I'd *thought* about it, I prob'ly wouldn't a done it."

"Mebbe so, mebbe not," said Cliff, and he took a long, contemplative swig of beer. "Least you don't need to drive down-country to get a piece of ass."

"Sometimes I like to make the trip anyway, jest to avoid it."

Both men laughed conspiratorially.

"Whatever happened to that little piece a tenderloin you was tappin' over to Hero?"

Cliff smiled slyly. "She got herself knocked up. Had to git married."

"Who knocked her up?"

Cliff smiled again.

"Too bad you can't locate yerself a little somethin' a tad closer to home, like right here on the island."

"Mebbe a little too close for comfort," Cliff answered sagely as he rolled down the sleeves of his flannel shirt, finally admitting the air had become a bit too cold for him. He adjusted the yellow knitted toque that he had worn every day—except when he wore his John Deere cap in the summer—since he had discovered the thinning hair at the top of his head.

Looking up at the line of dark trees to the west, Cliff stared at the red sky where the sun was beginning to disappear. After taking another pull from the bottle, he swished the beer around in his mouth as if it were mouthwash.

"But you know," he said, half to himself, "that new school-teacher looks pretty damn good to me."

"Jesus Christ, Cliff," taunted Bill, "she's way the fuck out of your league. Why, she ain't even from around here! I bet she's even from outta state!"

Cliff snapped out of his reverie, slapping his friend on the back. "That don't mean she ain't good enough for target practice, now do it?"

They bellowed rowdy laughter until their attention was caught by a car approaching from Bridge Road. A blue Honda passed the town hall and pulled up to the general store.

"Speakin' a the devil," said Cliff.

"There you go, boy, signed, sealed, and delivered," said Bill, watching Nancy Wells getting out of the car. "Let's see ya do yer stuff."

"Shit," said Cliff, and he took another swig of Bud.

5

Nancy Wells slammed the door of her Honda and locked it, a deeply ingrained habit, but needless on Friar's Island. When she realized what she had done, she reversed the key in the lock and remedied the situation.

She paused before entering Mott's General Store, surveying the center of the tiny island town. *Her* tiny island town. She smiled and sighed happily. What a peaceful place it was! Romantic, like something out of a dream.

Here she could live as she wanted to live. She could keep things simple, avoid difficulty, and—for the most part—ignore the world's unpleasantness.

From where she stood, right next to the gas pump, Nancy could see the town hall, the library, Professor Hathaway's house, and just a littler farther down, her pride and joy, the school.

A one-room schoolhouse! It was ideal, a dream come true. It was part of a vanishing America that reminded her of simpler lives in a simpler time.

She turned slowly and walked up the wooden steps of the general store. Her intention was to check the mail—both her own and the school's—and pick up some groceries for tomorrow.

Abner Mott, white-haired and as clean looking as a doctor in his spotless butcher's apron, smiled at her from across the counter.

"Afternoon, Miss Nancy Wells."

She liked the way he always addressed her by her first and last names, as if they were one name.

Since she had arrived on the island some three short months ago, Abner Mott had always made her feel welcome. Of course, as a businessman it was only good practice to make his customers feel liked and respected, but Mr. Mott seemed to go a little beyond the call of duty. He always had a smile for her, an observation about the weather, and perhaps a question or two about the state of education on the island. He unfailingly made her proud to be the schoolteacher, and he communicated that, at least here on Friar's Island—if nowhere else in the country—folks still looked up to educators and still valued learning.

Sure, that was a romantic notion in the late 1980s, but it was romanticism that had attracted her to the island and its school. She had hesitated only slightly before accepting the position.

Even if the job itself hadn't been enough to convince her, the "teacher's cottage" that came with it would have been. It was a rustic four-room house made from gray island marble and situated on the eastern coast, the "sunrise shore," as the islanders called it.

At the library she had read all about the cottage's role in the island's educational history. Until 1935, when ferry service to St. Albans had been discontinued, her cottage had been the boatman's house. Then the town took it over to be rented to the schoolteacher. A twenty-year-old Miss Deborah Swain, from Hyde Park, Vermont, had accepted the teaching post and had rented the cottage for ten dollars a year. The rent had crawled steadily upward to twenty-five dollars a month by the time Miss Deborah died last spring.

Now that teaching post was filled by Miss Nancy Wells, from Albany, New York, and she was charged fifty dollars a month for the teacher's cottage, utilities included.

"I'm sorry, Miss Nancy Wells, but there's not a thing for you today."

No mail. It made her feel a little lonesome, reminding her of how cut off she was from the rest of the world. But then again, what had she expected? Did she really think she'd hear from Eric again? Surely not after the way she'd left him. He probably didn't even know where she was. And if she *did* hear from him, what then? She had no intention of seeing him again, that was for sure. The whole thing had lasted too long, had been too crazy; it was a part of an unwholesome past that had nothing to do with her new life on Friar's Island.

But sometimes she did get lonely . . .

Nancy felt ashamed of herself. How could she think so self-indulgently while in the pleasant beam of Abner Mott's smile.

"Guess I'm a miserable failure as postmaster," Mr. Mott chuckled.

She looked timidly at the storekeeper, feeling a little less than pure. If Mr. Mott were to find out about Eric, what would he think of her then? Would he dismiss her as a woman with a past? A scarlet hussy, perhaps not fit to teach the island's young?

She shook away the notion with a little toss of her head. "I can't imagine you failing at anything, Mr. Mott."

She'd think no more about it. By God, she had better things to do than feel sorry for herself on a Saturday afternoon. Right now she had groceries to buy, and—as usual—it would be fun to take a look around the store.

"Anything I can help you find, miss, just give a holler." As with many of the island's residents. Nancy's daily stops at the general store were a sort of ritual.

"Thanks, Mr. Mott. I just want to look around."

"You go right ahead."

In spite of her frequent visits, she remained fascinated by the store's atmosphere and inventory. In her mind, Abner Mott and his general store were the same thing, manifestations of the same personality, one that—like her schoolhouse—was part of an older, better time.

The store's interior was not large, but it was crowded with shelves and displays. Because of the island's small population, it was rarely necessary to accommodate crowds of shoppers—a good thing, because some of the aisles were so narrow that two grown people could not pass without bumping into each other.

Abner wrote signs that he placed here and there around the store. Some were on pieces of brown paper bag; others were written on white paper plates. The intent, of course, was to impose a rude order on the crowded chaos. But—Nancy smiled—the intent was often lost because of the signs' lack of specificity. The one in front of her, for example, was written on the rectangular cover of a shoe box. It said ODDS 'N' ENDS, and was tacked above a section of shelves containing lamp chimneys, rubber seals for canning jars, flashlight batteries, a bag of golf tees, and an open shoebox full of belt buckles.

Nancy remembered the first time she had seen the oldest and most controversial sign in the store. It was thumbtacked right below the countertop where Abner transacted his business at an ornate mechanical cash register. The sign read: NO OUTSIDE PAPERS.

What it meant, of course, was *No out-of-state papers available.* This wasn't quite true, because Abner did carry the *Union Leader* from Manchester, New Hampshire, and the *Weekly World News,* but, as Abner explained, he made the rules and they were his to break.

Actually, NO OUTSIDE PAPERS was the storekeeper's quiet rebellion. He got sick and tired of tourists and summer folks stopping in—especially on Sunday—and asking for those damn New York papers that weighed more than a bale of hay. Who could possibly read all that trash anyway? Abner refused to carry them. What's more, he got sick and tired of saying no to people who asked for them. His solution was to put up the sign. Now he'd say, "Nope, can't you see the sign?" And he'd point down to it and tap his finger on the countertop. Nancy had seen it happen more than once; people would read the awkwardly scrawled lettering and walk away looking confused.

Smiling again, Nancy remembered the time she had fallen into the same trap. Abner Mott had explained his rationale, carefully assuring her that the sign wasn't intended for her or the other islanders.

She wandered past the white, glass-fronted meat counter at the back of the store, through rows of canned goods and cosmetics, nails, ammunition, toys, clothing, rubber boots, cold soft drinks and beer. Abner was even licensed by the state of Vermont to sell alcoholic beverages. Until three years ago one had to drive all the way to the liquor store in Grand Isle to pick up a fifth of Seagram's or some ginger brandy.

Nancy stopped at the magazine rack. It was positioned at the front of the store, with its back nearly resting against the big display window that looked out on the street. As she scanned the titles, she noticed a silver Saab pull up near the gas pumps. She had been on the island long enough for an unfamiliar vehicle to stand out as dramatically as a fly in a glass of milk.

A tall, handsomely built man got out of the car and stood looking around. Nancy watched him with great interest, automatically falling into the familiar pattern of island natives appraising an outsider. The man had a lost look about him; he was probably stopping to ask directions.

She began flipping through a copy of *Newsweek* as the man entered the store. Peeking over the top of the magazine, she saw him stop short inside the door. Now he looked not only lost, but completely perplexed.

She was amused by the expression on his face, recalling the first time she had set foot in Abner's establishment.

The man saw Abner. He walked directly over to where the storekeeper stood behind the wooden counter, poised between the cash register and three-quarters of a wheel of white cheddar under a clear plastic cover.

"Hep ya?" inquired Abner Mott.

"Yes, sir, if you're the postmaster."

"I believe I am."

"Then I've come to the right place. My name's Harrison Allen. I'm moving into Mark Chittenden's place down on the other side of the swamp. Can I pick up my mail here?"

"Hafta. No delivery down that way."

"Fine. I take it you're also the storekeeper?"

"Yup. I pump the gas, an' I do the clean-up work, to boot."

"Speaking of clean-up work, that's the other reason I came in. I need a broom and a bucket. A mop. Stuff to clean the place up with."

"Bet it could use some cleanin'. You buy the place, did you?"

"Oh, no. I'm a friend of Mark's. He's letting me use it for a while."

"Zat right? Haven't seen them folks in a month a Sundays. Still teachin' down there to the college, is he?"

"He's still at it."

"I kinda hoped them two would settle in over the house. I liked 'em. Don't think the wife had much use for the island, though."

"I guess the drive to Burlington got to be a bit much."

"A shame the way that ol' place is goin' all to sin. Ain't nothin' right about that."

"I'll try to keep it under control. Maybe I'll even fix it up a little. But first I've got to clean it."

"You'll prob'ly find everything you need right over there by that sign that says, 'Godliness.' The cleanin' stuff's right next to it."

Abner's eyes twinkled mischievously. He winked at Nancy.

Harrison smiled wanly and moved away, still looking rather

puzzled. Nancy tried to stifle a laugh as she stepped up to the counter with a loaf of Fassett's Oatmeal Bread, a quart of milk, and a box of Nutri-Grain. She had traded the copy of *Newsweek* for *Redbook*.

"Your Sat'dee-evenin' readin', Miss Nancy Wells?"

"I'm afraid so, Mr. Mott."

She paid for her groceries and walked out of the store. As she got into her car, she felt a kind of envy for this newcomer, who was lucky enough to live alone in such a fine old house.

She found that she continued to think about him as she drove home.

6

Bill Blood hitched up his trousers, nodded stiffly, and started home for supper, leaving Cliff alone on the steps of the town hall.

Cliff polished off the last of the six-pack, wiped his mouth on his sleeve, and butted his Marlboro against the stone slab on which he sat. With the intent stare of a hungry eagle, he watched the schoolteacher as she left the store and drove away. After rolling up the bottoms of his blue jeans, he creased the cuffs neatly. Then he stood up, belched with great authority, and walked down the road toward his place.

7

Cappy Capra and Brigitte Pelletier decided to go home. It was very tempting, the way the guy had left the place wide open. It was unlocked and everything! Very inviting. But it probably meant the man would be coming right back, and Cappy didn't want to risk getting caught inside. Okay. No problem. There would be another time.

As they skulked along the edge of the marsh, they saw the silver Saab returning. Quickly they moved out of sight.

"See, I told ya he'd be right back," said Cappy. "You gotta learn to trust your instincts."

Brigitte nodded.

Two weeks later...

Dark Reflections   4

NIGHT ON FRIAR'S ISLAND

Abner Mott stood by his living room window, looking
out at the lake. He could feel the pulse of the water as it
throbbed against the cliffs and sands like a great heart
beating. Along the rocky shoreline, silhouetted ever-
greens twitched and shivered in the wind's arctic breath.
In Abner's dooryard, towering hardwoods, Bible-black
and ancient, surrendered the last of their autumn leaves
to a passing November wind.

Abner thought of the neglected orchards—once the
life's blood of island economy—where scattered apples
blushed like faded rainbows atop the brown and brittle
grass. Today the fallen fruit would rot and vanish, forgotten by all but the hungry deer.

He looked up. The November moon was full, snow-
cold, and majestic. It hung like a frosted mirror on the
ebony wall of the sky.

Nine o'clock.

No traffic moved on the narrow island roads; the general store had been closed for an hour. Faint lights burned
in the far-off windows of neighboring homes. Inside each,
Abner pictured quiet families sitting before television
screens or nodding by warm hearths.

He shuddered.

Somehow he knew that even in the warmest home there was something in the air. A chill, perhaps, or something like a chill. It caused collars to be buttoned and sweaters to be donned. It was more, he knew, than the simple coming of winter, more than the clear, crisp air that seemed to freeze, shatter, then fall to the earth as snow.

No, it was more than temperature. It was tension. It beckoned solitary figures to their windows to watch the lightless streets, or to stare transfixed at the thick and somber shape of the forest where it waited motionless as a sleeping animal on the edge of civilization, just outside their tiny island town.

Abner blinked at the churning, glimmering dance of moonlight on the surface of the lake. With a sigh, he turned from the window to meet the eyes of his wife. Then, furtively, each looked away.

There *was* something in the air, something foreign yet familiar, something—Abner was sure of it—that all the islanders could feel. It didn't have a name like "heat" or "cold," yet it was tangible, sensed in an indefinable and alien way.

Sensed but not recognized.

Sensed but never discussed.

To Abner, it felt as if a balance had been disturbed, as if something fundamental were just a little out of alignment. And there was no one who could say just what it was. And no one who knew how to correct it.

Abner had lived among the people of Friar's Island for a good many years. He was sure every one of them knew, intuitively, that something irreversible was taking its course.

And everyone, except perhaps the newest among them, had felt this thing before.

2

By ten o'clock only one light burned on Friar's Island. It was on the table by the window in Harrison Allen's house. With a fan of yellow lined paper spread out in front of him, Harrison stared past the soft orange glow of the kerosene lamp, eyeing his dark reflection in the night-filled windowpane.

Harrison was aware of the early-to-bed tradition of the islanders; he was almost used to it. But still, he thought, sometimes a man likes company.

Especially tonight.

Harrison felt tense, oddly restless, yet he couldn't put his finger on why.

Maybe he should take a drive up to the general store. There was a pay phone outside; he could call Mark and shoot the shit for a while.

He walked away from the window and sat heavily in the armchair beside the table that held his Jack Daniel's and water.

Hell no, he thought, *I've been enough of a burden to Mark and Judy already.*

Besides, hadn't he come here to be alone? Wasn't that the whole point?

Sipping his drink—too bad there was no ice—he let his mind rove back to his last days in Boston. He had been sitting with some co-workers from the plant. It was an Irish bar near Government Center. . . . Shortly after they're received word about the bankruptcy . . . shortly after they're learned there would be no more jobs.

Across from him, sipping white wine, was Andrea. She was laughing and speaking disparagingly about the Bush Administration. She had the attention of everyone at the table.

Ever since she'd been hired—less than three months before the closing—Harrison had developed a respect for Andrea, a respect tinged with fear. At first her agile mind and verbal precision had made him feel that he was in the company of a fearsome adversary. Perhaps to ensure that those sharp words would never be used as weapons against him, he began to cultivate her friendship.

In time, through casual conversations, she had become very important to him—not as a woman, really, but as a symbol.

Harrison had never been a Don Juan; he always approached

other people—especially women—with a great deal of caution. And with caution uppermost in his mind, he had wanted very much to approach Andrea, elevate their friendship to the level of a relationship. But somehow he always lacked the nerve. He repeatedly told himself that the proper occasion had not yet presented itself.

Then, when Harrison learned their jobs were about to end, he almost panicked. He felt as if his whole life were a fast train speeding toward a derailment. What would he do? Where would he go?

And what would become of Andrea?

Office gossip informed him that she had secured another position in the public relations department of a ski resort in Colorado. He knew she would be leaving soon; he knew she was lost to him.

Harrison sipped his Jack Daniel's, swirled the liquid in the glass, listened for the nonexistent ice cubes, and remembered.

Andrea.

She was so damnably self-sufficient, so independent. She challenged him in ways he could not bear to be challenged. Yet, in those rare blissful moments when they were alone together, by the water cooler or in the cafeteria, she had always seemed so interested, so curious and uninformed about topics he thought were important. So many times he had found himself caught in those wide brown eyes as he prattled on about his plans, aspirations, and his trivial achievements. He even shared with her his secret ambition—at the time little more than a whim—of searching for the Lake Champlain Monster. Her praise for his idea was gratifying enough to make the search itself almost unnecessary. Harrison remembered wondering, how many other men's plans and ambitions had been born, matured, and died in those wonderful brown eyes?

He squinted into the dim glow of the kerosene lamp, letting his head rest on the back of the chair. The glass felt solid, somehow comforting, as he held it in both hands on his lap.

Was it fear or envy that had made him turn from her, made him resent her intellect, poise, and effortless success? Or was it anger? Anger at himself for his timidity, his lack of resolution? *No,* he thought, *it was simple childishness.* And it was this childishness, this immaturity, that made him run away from her as he had run away from so many others.

His colleagues at the Irish bar must have thought him insane when, without a word, he had slammed down his glass of stout with vicious finality and left the room. They, and Andrea, had watched, open-mouthed and silent.

Harrison felt his face redden in the chill air of the living room. Even now, so long after seeing her for the last time, he felt angry at Andrea for her competence. But he was more angry at himself, because he had avoided her. He'd retreated, a frightened child in a man's aging body.

Perhaps Mark had been right; perhaps he *was* running away.

The word "coward" came to mind, jabbed at him like the point of a dagger. He quickly suppressed it. No, now he had to be objective, honest. Christ, he should *thank* Andrea for the challenge. Because of her, Harrison understood he had to be successful at this one thing. He couldn't back down or turn away. He *had* to find the monster.

Willing his mind away from painful recollections, he moved back to his desk and his notes.

He had spent the day researching at the town library in St. Albans. Before him on page after page of yellow paper was the product of his efforts.

It was difficult for Harrison to become enthusiastic about his random collection of monster sightings. Which among them had scientific value? There was a lot of theory, a lot of speculation. He had even discovered the names of a few "eyewitnesses" that he might later interview.

Most promising was that he had located a man from New York state, a schoolteacher named Joseph Zarzynski, who'd been chasing the monster for more than ten years. Mr. Zarzynski was considered an expert on the beast.

Even at monster hunting, Harrison had a rival.

The recorded sightings of the creature started in 1609, when Samuel de Champlain, the French explorer after whom the lake was named, saw "a great long monster, lying in the lake, allowing birds to land on its beak, then snapping them in whole."

Harrison chuckled; he hoped his quest would not prove as fanciful as Monsieur Champlain's description.

Monster sightings continued with persistent regularity. Many lacked the drama of the Oliver Ransom encounter, but the sheer frequency of reports made the beast come slowly to life in Harrison's imagination.

It must also have come alive in the imagination of the famous nineteenth-century showman, P. T. Barnum. Barnum had offered $50,000 for the monster's carcass—a tidy sum for 1877.

Then, one hundred years later, the famous Mansi photograph was taken. After being thoroughly checked, analyzed, and authenticated, the picture was released to the media in 1981. With this first photographic evidence, the monster had come out of the closet. People began to talk about it openly, without fear of ridicule. It was discussed at cocktail parties with the same enthusiasm as periodontists, cholesterol levels, and baseball. Someone nicknamed it "Champ." Others called it "Champy." It was cute. It was E.T.

It had become a friend!

But, Harrison thought, it had not always been a friend . . .

More contemplative now, Harrison sat back, eye to eye with his reflection in the dark window glass. Why, he wondered, have tales of the monster so frequently inspired fear?

Walter Hard, former editor of the prestigious *Vermont Life* magazine, once spotted the creature off Appletree Point near Burlington. Subsequently, he kept track of sightings through the years, speculating that hundreds of people had seen the monster but refused to report it. "They're afraid of ridicule," he said.

Ridicule—was that it? Was ridicule the source of people's fear? Or was there something else? Something darker, more sinister?

Long before Walter Hard or Barnum or de Champlain, the Indians near Split Rock—which once divided Mohawk and Algonquin territories—believed something dangerous lurked in the invisible depths. They dropped offerings of food from their canoes, a kind of toll to guarantee safe passage on the lake.

Harrison knew that the Split Rock waters were the deepest part of the lake, measuring more than four hundred feet. Only God knew what could be down there. What kind of fear was it that had caused Indians to make their edible offerings?

And the photograph? Sandra Mansi's color picture seemed to depict exactly what so many witnesses had described. Harrison picked up his August 1982 copy of *Life* magazine. The Mansi photograph was reproduced on page thirty-four, much larger than it had been in *Time* magazine, or *The New York Times*.

He looked at the details of what seemed to be a head and long neck protruding from the lake's calm surface. Where the neck joined the submerged body there seemed to be a hump just below water level. The dark image looked for all the world like some kind of dinosaur swimming away from the camera. It was in a small bay, with bushes visible in the foreground, and on the shoreline across the bay, trees and nondescript vegetation.

Was the fear experienced by Sandra Mansi during her sighting similar to that experienced by Oliver Ransom?

Was it an instinctive fear of the creature itself, or simply humankind's atavistic fear of the unknown?

And if someday the unknown became known, what might the monster turn out to be?

Skeptics said it was Dino the Dinosaur.

Scientists said it was most probably a plesiosaur, a large marine reptile thought to have become extinct seventy million years ago. Or maybe a zeuglodon, an ancestor of the whale, extinct for twenty million years.

And for me, what is it? thought Harrison. *Just exactly what is it to me?*

Still feeling a restlessness that he was unable to channel into research or even concentration, Harrison rose from his desk, pulled on his parka, and left the house by the front door.

He stood on the step a moment while his eyes grew accustomed to the night. Then he crossed the road, making his way the short distance through thorny bushes and over nearly invisible out-croppings to the rocky, wind-blasted western shore of the island.

The moon was high and bright; in its pale brilliance the shore-line looked like a black-and-white photograph. Before him, across two or three miles of churning, breathing water, Grand Isle lay upon the horizon like a long, sleeping serpent.

The icy wind combed his hair tight against his head as he squinted at the water, straining his eyes to see movement—any movement—that was not tide, not wind, not the white-capped waves nor the undulating reflection of the moon.

Just what is it to me? he thought.

Harrison quickly became cold. The rock he was sitting on drained the heat from his body, and his parka was no match for the relent-less wind. He stood up, thinking of the warmth in the bottle of Jack Daniel's that waited for him on the kitchen table.

Stepping gingerly from rock to rock, he climbed to the top of the bank that sloped upward from the water's edge. From there he could see the house, a massive silhouette in the clearing across the road. Behind it, the gnarled shapes of apple trees, unpruned and long abandoned, stood in military formation in the moonlit orchard. It was like rediscovering some moment from the past, some ruin that asserted: Once men lived here, once all of this was important.

Now only the lake was unchanged, only the wind and the wild berry bushes that grew along the shore.

And the monster? What of the monster? How long could it swim undisturbed, surviving on fish or vegetation, eluding all cameras and guns?

As he walked toward home, Harrison felt his unease growing. There was nothing welcoming about the house; there was no real sense of home. The building was distant, ominous, cold. He had never opened the shutters on the upstairs windows. Now they made the place seem secret and remote. The lower windows re-flected the moonlight like staring eyes.

Harrison knew that something was wrong.

Hadn't he left the kerosene lamp burning in the window? It was out now. The house was dark. Could the kerosene supply have run out?

Harrison laughed at himself. Was his melancholia turning to dread? Was he working up a good fright? He felt as he had when he was a child sitting around the campfire in an unfamiliar wood, telling tales of ghosts, and purple hands, and trees with strange Indian names that walked and killed by night.

Thorny bushes tugged at his corduroys as he stepped onto the road and crossed it to the gravel yard in front of the house. As he reached for the door handle, he felt something odd on the slate step beneath his foot.

He jumped, gasped in surprise, feeling something where nothing should have been.

Looking down, he saw an indistinct cluster of small objects. Apparently they had been placed carefully on the step until his foot disturbed their symmetry.

The moonlight wasn't strong enough for him to make out what he was seeing. He opened the door and reached for the flashlight that he kept on a table to the right.

With light in hand, he was able to examine the objects on his step. There was an ear of dried corn, its spiraled kernels dull red and brown in color, three acorns, a polished white stone the size of a pocket watch, and a tiny rusted frame that might once have contained a picture or mirror.

Harrison's forehead tightened, wrinkling into a puzzled frown. He gathered up the objects and brought them to the kitchen, where he arranged them on the table beside his bottle of Jack Daniel's.

Had someone left these for him while he was at the lake? They definitely had not been there when he walked out of the house; he would have stepped on them. But who would call on him after ten o'clock at night?

And who would leave such a peculiar assortment of objects?

Were they some kind of joke?

Did they mean something?

And if so, what?

Or perhaps there was some kind of animal that would do such a thing. A pack rat maybe, or a squirrel.

But a squirrel wouldn't put out the kerosene lamp.

Harrison took a shot of whiskey to fight the chill that pulled his muscles tight against his bones.

And another for the lesser chill that came with his strange discoveries.

The Lord's Day   5

On Sunday mornings Nancy Wells liked to sleep late. Sunday was, after all, a day of rest, and resting on the Lord's day was perhaps the last vestige of strict Congregationalist upbringing that she willingly carried with her into adulthood.

She rolled over groggily, stretched, yawned, and squinted at the drawn shade outlined by brilliant bars of sunlight. A golden beam fell across the face of her alarm clock.

Nine forty-eight.

It's late!

Getting out of bed was an effort. When she tossed aside the covers, her soft flannel nightgown offered little insulation against the crisp morning air. She crossed her arms over her breasts and shivered, saying, "Brrrrr."

She couldn't see her breath, but when her bare feet hit the cold wooden floor she snapped awake with a painful jolt.

After her anxious feet found their slippers, she rose and plodded toward the kitchen to heat water for coffee. Then she headed into the bathroom, trying to decide whether to take a shower. The chill morning air made the decision an easy one—she'd stay grubby.

She was carefully placing her contacts into her eyes when the kettle began to whistle.

Soon, stirring instant coffee, she smiled at the informality of her lifestyle. Living alone, she had become . . . what? Careless, maybe? Certainly not sloppy—that was too strong a word. But she was, she had to admit, careless.

A flannel nightgown, for God's sake! How perfectly unsexy! And not showering? Downright bestial. Then, to complete her battery of sins, *instant* coffee.

She remembered mornings with Eric in Albany. They'd race each other to the shower. Their daily competition had become a private joke. God, what would Eric say if he saw her in a *flannel* nightgown? Or—heaven forbid if she had dared to serve him instant coffee? Why, he would have been outraged!

She smiled, amused at the thought. But smiling wasn't right.

Fuck him. What difference did it make what he might have said? Or what he might have thought, for that matter. Eric was as much a part of the past as her Congregationalist upbringing, both relegated to the status of slightly embarrassing memories. Youth. Innocence. All of it gone.

But in a way, Eric was partially responsible for her being here today. Perhaps, at the very least she should be grateful to him for that.

"Why in the name of the merciful Christ would you want to hole up on some godforsaken island in Vermont? An *island* in Vermont, for Christ's sake!" Eric was waving his wineglass around, working himself up to one of his fire and brimstone rants.

"Because it's my job, Eric, my own job. I've *got* to get started on my own. Please try to understand."

"But you can get a job right here. Just wait awhile. I can probably talk to Ed Whalen, get you something at the library. A few hours a week, anyway. Maybe full-time. And you can move in with me. Take courses toward your master's."

"How would that be, Eric, shacking up with my psych prof?"

"We're practically living together now."

"I just can't do it, Eric. Can't you see that?"

"You can. You just don't want to."

"That's right. I don't want to."

That stung him, and he was silent. He looked blankly at her, all motionless and quiet. Then he took three unsteady steps to the sofa, where he sat sullenly. Nancy watched him as he studied his wineglass, swirling the red liquid and staring as if hypnotized.

He spoke all too calmly, almost in a whisper. She knew his trick and resisted the temptation to move closer so she could hear him better. "You were just using me," he said. "Toss the prof and prove what a sophisticated girl I am."

Nancy didn't rise to the bait. She went to him and sat beside him. He didn't say anything, just cried softly as she held his bearded face to her breast.

They had made love that night, but it was forced, mechanical, a practiced merging of familiar bodies. It was their physical alternative to continuing a discussion that had already ended.

She had left in the middle of the night while Eric slept. After that, they never saw each other again. She wasn't even sure that he knew where she was.

2

The shotgun screamed!

Pellets tore noisily through dry leaves overhead.

High above, a mallard squawked; feathers flew. The duck dipped in its straight-as-an-arrow course. Then, seeming to recover its balance, it tore like a zipper across the blue sky and vanished out of range.

"FUCK!"

Cliff Ransom emerged from the marsh empty-handed. He'd got off a couple of shots at some ducks, and another at a partridge, but he'd missed every friggin' time. That pissed him off. *Can't even fuckin' shoot straight no more*, he thought in a rare moment of self-criticism.

He resolved he'd better at least get a squirrel or he'd have to buy something at the general store for supper.

And that reminded him: On Sunday the general store closed at noon. He dug his father's watch out of the pocket of his green woolen pants and checked the time.

Eleven thirty-three. Christ, better haul ass.

He charged back to his pickup, placed his shotgun in the rack over the rear window, and started the engine. *Runnin' kinda raggy,* he thought. *Better tune her up 'fore snowfall.*

Tires squealed. Gravel sprayed.

No speed limits were posted anywhere on the island. Even if there had been, Cliff would have ignored them. They'd be for off-islanders.

His engine roared.

3

Over a breakfast of orange juice, Nutri-Grain, and instant coffee, Nancy planned her activities for the day. First, she would take a brisk walk around the island. The fresh air would help her to wake up, and a little exercise wouldn't hurt her one bit. And then? Well, really the place could use a good cleaning. There were two days' worth of dishes in the sink, and God knew what under the chairs, the couch, and the bed. Maybe she would see if she could borrow someone's vacuum cleaner.

No. Too complicated. She wanted to keep things simple. Broom and dustpan had been good enough for Miss Deborah Swain, and by God, they'd be good enough for her.

And that reminds me, she thought, *I'd better get in a bit of wood for the stove. I'll need it if it gets as cold as last night.*

Toting wood seemed like a lot of work. At the library she had read how in the old days each pupil was required to give the teacher half a cord of firewood. A custom well worth reviving.

There I go, thinking of school again. The thought of all the papers waiting to be corrected intruded on her Sunday morning reverie, giving her a kind of sinking feeling. *I can't put them off another day.* The English, math, and social studies papers were hidden somewhere in the clutter on the coffee table. *That's okay, I'll find them when I clean.*

"Oh, come on, Nancy," she said aloud, "don't be so lazy." Maybe that was the word: lazy. Not sloppy. Not careless. Lazy.

Okay, so I'll get in the wood and clean the house and do the dishes and correct the papers and . . .

And what?

There was something else.

"Oh, God, how could I forget?"

This was the evening she was supposed to go to Professor Hathaway's house. Tonight was the night they had to plan his visit to the school.

How could she have forgotten? She had been looking forward to their meeting all week. Her respect for the delightful old man bordered on adoration. A genuine old-fashioned educator, the real thing! His conversation was always amusing and instructive. She couldn't wait to share his scholarly yet always entertaining approach to education with her students. It would be like showing them a little bit of history.

How could she have forgotten?

The memory lapse worried her. Did such forgetfulness mean that *it* was coming back? She knew it was possible; it really could come back again. Anytime.

When she was a kid, the doctor had asked, "Now, Nancy, I want you to think real hard. Can you remember anything strange or unusual that occurs just before it happens? Anything at all?"

"Like what?" the frightened little girl with the black eye had whispered.

"Like anything, honey. Do you get itchy? Do you get nervous, maybe? Or sleepy? Do you see little specks of light or spots? Anything like that you can think of?"

She had pushed her lips very tightly together, squinting her eyes to show him how hard she was thinking. "I think . . ." she began.

She struggled painfully with whether she could come right out and tell him.

"Don't be afraid, honey. I want to help you."

"Go ahead, Nancy." her mother urged.

"Well, sometimes . . ."

He smiled down at her. Then he bent forward, placing his big, soft hands on her trembling arms.

"Well, some . . . sometimes I forget things . . ." Before she could say more, she started to cry and fell against the doctor. He hugged her and he smelled good, like soap and pipe tobacco.

"Don't be afraid," he said softly, gently.

But she had been afraid then, and the idea frightened her now. Forgetfulness had been her signal, her warning sign. The doctor had told her that many people experienced something that would alert them when an attack was coming. He called it an aura. If she could learn to spot it, it would give her a few moments to prepare.

She had outgrown the attacks, which, the doctor said, was normal. But they could return. And that was normal, too.

NO! She was being silly. She hadn't had an epileptic seizure in maybe fifteen years.

Surely she was overreacting to a little lapse of memory.

4

Cliff sped along, bounding violently over the dips and potholes of West Shore Road. His theory was that if he took the bumps fast enough his tires wouldn't have a chance to hit bottom; that way he'd get a smoother ride.

Between the schoolhouse and the general store, he saw a woman walking along the side of the road. She sure was classy looking. To Cliff, she seemed as out of place on the island as a speed limit sign, though she had greater effect in getting him to slow down.

She was tall and poised, moving rapidly with long, purposeful strides, her jet-black hair bouncing and blowing in the breeze.

From this angle, Cliff was able to judge that there was a substantial quantity of breast between her coat and her rib cage. Nice.

Slowing to a near crawl, Cliff stared at her unabashedly, while she hardly took notice of the pickup or its appreciative driver.

The schoolteacher, he thought. *Stuck-up bitch.*

Speeding up, he recalled that he had to make it to the store before closing. The growl of his perforated muffler would tell her he was there, even if she pretended she didn't want to notice him.

The bouncing pickup roared up to the gas pump in front of the general store, then screeched to a stop. Cliff jumped out and filled his own tank. He knew the NO SELF SERVICE sign on the pump didn't apply to him. Like the nonexistent speed limits, it was for the flatlanders.

When the thirsty truck was satisfied, Cliff went inside, paid Abner for the gas and for a case of Bud. He lugged the beer outside and threw it into the bed of the pickup, where it would stay nice and cold. After grabbing one for the ride, he started for home.

Cliff lived alone. His house was on one of the connecting roads between the eastern and western shores. It was the family place, the place where he had been born and raised.

Wilma, his mother, had died here in 1960. His father, Oliver, had hung on for another ten years, wearing away from the skin cancer that dried his flesh and made it peel grotesquely from the bone. Cliff had grown to hate his father, quickly losing patience with the old man's increasing pain and irritability. Cliff hated the sight of the discolored skin as it peeled off in ugly layers like the rotting hide of an onion. And it smelled a hundred times worse. But most of all, Cliff hated the additional chores he had to do as his father slowed and wasted. He was glad when they carted Pa off to the hospital in St. Albans, where Cliff visited him only once before he died.

Since then Cliff had done very little work around the place. He ate from dirty dishes; he wore dirty clothes. The sheets on his bed had discolored and turned to rags long before he discarded them. Now he slept on a soiled mattress under his sleeping bag.

At first Cliff had lived mostly in the kitchen and living room. During his second winter alone, he'd dragged his bed into the kitchen and closed off all the rest of the rooms to save heat. When spring came, he didn't bother to open them up again.

Yanking the refrigerator door open, he inspected its contents.

He took out a slightly withered hot dog, rolled it in a stiff slice of Wonder Bread, poked around for some mustard, found a beer instead, and sat at the table to eat his lunch.

Goddamn but that's a prime piece of woman, he thought, smacking his lips and reflecting on the schoolteacher. *Definitely not Vermont-grown. Gotta be imported. City stuff, prob'ly, with her snooty airs and her black spiky boots.*

He belched.

One thing sure, he thought, *she ain't seen the last of me, no, sir, no way.*

His mind swept back to the ducks he had missed, and the excitement—yes, the power that always surged each time he pulled the trigger of his shotgun. It was such a kick to blast a deadly hail of BBs into the autumn sky.

Cliff could feel himself becoming a little aroused. With a sudden impulse he hurled his empty beer can into the corner, where it clanked and bounced and finally settled among its clones in and around the overflowing plastic garbage can.

That was his savings account. According to Vermont law—the so-called bottle law—he could redeem his garbage for five cents a can at the general store. Someday he would do just that.

Yup. Someday.

Cliff decided to do a bit of planning. He wanted to decide what he would do this afternoon. Go back out hunting? Tune up the truck? No—maybe he should fill the pickup with a load of firewood and take it over to Mrs. Snowdon.

Maybe he could ask her about the schoolteacher. She'd know. Besides, he hadn't brought her anything for quite some time. And she might be wondering . . .

Cliff decided to have another beer and think about it. There were no more cans or bottles in the refrigerator so he had to go out to the truck and get his case. First thing he'd do was make a couple more deposits into his savings account.

5

Sunday's a good day for a walk, Harrison thought as he carried an armload of firewood in from the shed. He felt well today, clear-headed and alert. The fresh air filled his lungs and came back as a tune on his lips. Perhaps he was adjusting to the solitude. On a day like today, he could almost enjoy being alone.

He pulled on a red woolen jacket over his Greek fisherman's sweater and lit up the corncob pipe he had bought yesterday at the general store.

There had been an amused twinkle in Abner Mott's eyes when Harrison paid for the pipe. "You'll look just like an islander with that thing stuck in your teeth," Abner said with a chuckle.

Harrison had never smoked a pipe before, and Abner's comment made him a bit self-conscious. Was there a critical edge to the innocent-sounding remark? Both of them knew the pipe was an affectation. So what? Was Abner telling him he shouldn't try to look like an islander?

Ah well, nothing to worry about . . .

He set out, puffing his pipe nonetheless. Clouds of thick gray smoke obscured the vapor of his breath in the crisp November air. He walked along the road that passed through Childe's Bog, continuing north toward the village.

It occurred to him that he didn't know what time it was. He'd gotten up, dressed, eaten breakfast, and completed his chores without even glancing at a clock!

It was great not having to watch the clock, not having to be at any particular place at any particular time, not having anything competing for his attention. For once in his life, all his activities were self-directed.

So this is what a life of leisure is like! More and more he was certain that he should have been born rich, free to pursue whatever interested him. Monster hunting was definitely a pastime for the independently wealthy; too bad he hadn't been able to start his search for Champ a long time ago.

He continued walking and humming his tune, looking around with half a smile on his face. Harrison felt a kind of pride in Friar's Island. He felt almost—and he considered this with great caution —at home.

As he passed through the marsh, he was startled by gunshots. Duck hunters, he guessed. Briefly he entertained the idea of buying a hunting license. Maybe his new, more primitive lifestyle should include hunting some of his own food. Harrison remembered the old shotgun hanging on the wall back at the house. All he needed was the license and some shells. He bet the marsh was full of birds. And it was, after all, a lot closer to his house than the general store.

Just ahead, on the town side of the marsh, he noticed a narrow footpath branching perpendicularly from the road and running along the edge of the bog toward the center of the island. He'd be sure to explore that someday. He wondered where it might lead. An abandoned quarry, maybe? Someone's hunting camp? Maybe even a garbage dump.

A feeling he'd lost many years ago was returning. The thrill of his monster hunt was amplified by the prospect of exploration. And there was so much to explore! The little footpath, the marsh, the quarries, the lighthouse, and the hundred other roads and paths and buildings, all of which were new to him yet full of history and very much a part of his new home. In his mind's eye, as in the imagination of a child, he saw how the island must have looked in the early days, when French and English troops fought for possession of the territory that was now called Vermont.

It was all very exciting to him. And it was mysterious; it was like stepping across time and into another era. There was so much he wanted to find out, so much he wanted to do.

Maybe I really can go back, he thought. *Maybe I can find the place where things started to go wrong. Maybe it's even possible to make a new start.*

By God, it was worth a try!

His reverie slowed, his thoughts became less fanciful, his mind took a leap. Again he recalled the puzzle that had been nagging at

him for days: Who in the world could have put that strange collection of objects on his front steps?

An ear of corn, a half-dozen acorns, a stone, and a rusty metal
frame.

Who could have put them there?

Why?

And what the hell did they mean?

Explorers

6

I

It was completely by coincidence that the children got together on that November weekend. Both their families—the Capras and the Pelletiers—had made a final trip to the island, intending to lock up their camps and secure them against another long Vermont winter.

This chance encounter gave Cappy and Brigitte one last opportunity to go treasure hunting.

Now, crouching behind an outcropping about one hundred yards from the captain's house, Brigitte watched Cappy as he studied the stranger. The man was moving logs from the woodpile to the front door.

"Let's go get out of here," said Brigitte. She could hear her accent thickening, as it always did when she was nervous. "I t'ink he going to make da fire, stay home all day, dat man."

Cappy didn't say anything. With a terrible concentration, he fastened his cold, gun-sight stare on the front door.

After several minutes, the man left the house. Now he was smoking a pipe and striding rapidly up the road toward town.

Like her companion, Brigitte kept very low for fear of being spotted. The act of hiding and the unrelenting suspense made her more nervous. "But Cappy," she whispered, "how do you t'ink we find dis map? Even da man who live dere can't find map?"

"Well, of course he can't find it if he don't even know it's there. He ain't *lookin'* for it.

As soon as the stranger was out of sight, Cappy set out toward the house with Brigitte in tow. Moving slowly through the tall brown grass, they looked from side to side. Brigitte imagined snipers hiding behind every tree.

"Where you t'ink we should look?" Brigitte asked, her voice uncontrollably high-pitched, her chubby fingers laced tightly together and pressed against her heaving chest.

Cappy ignored the question, so Brigitte asked again, timidly, fearful of being ignored a second time, "Where we go to look, eh?"

"Attic or cellar, prob'ly."

Again Brigitte hesitated, held back as if her legs were getting fatter, growing enormously heavy. Suddenly it was nearly impossible to move them.

"I'll stay outside, keep watch," Cappy said. "I'll yell at you if the man comes back."

Brigitte looked into Cappy's cold, confident eyes. She *couldn't* go into that old house alone. She just couldn't.

An almost imperceptible flexing at the corners of his mouth— Cappy's approximation of a smile—suggested that he was only kidding. He turned and made off for the house, never glancing back.

Breathing easier now, Brigitte followed the boy silently, obediently. She couldn't help herself.

Just as Cappy had said, the man had not locked the front door. In fact, no doors were kept locked on Friar's Island. All summer long Cappy had led her into any house or camp he pleased almost anytime he wished. But today the challenge was here. She knew this house held a special fascination for him; he had never entered it before.

But there had always been something about the place Brigitte simply didn't like. Of all the buildings on the island, this was among the most isolated. Its remote location and stark aspect frightened her very much. Unwilling to examine the feeling too closely, Brigitte wanted to toss it off, dismiss it as merely the fear of being discovered. But she knew it was more than that. She could tell by the way her body seemed to take on weight and move more slowly as they got closer to the front door.

Brigitte's heart pounded like a mallet against the inside of her chest. No, this was far more than the fear of being discovered. She'd never felt anything similar when they'd explored all the other houses and cottages. Voices in her head seemed to whisper in English and French, "Stay back. Stay away . . ."

If she could only be more brave, like Cappy. How come boys were always the brave ones?

"Wait a minute, Cappy. I don't like dis. Dis . . . what we do . . . it is not right."

Cappy turned on her, his face livid, furious. "Come on *Bree-sheet*, don't be a *sheet*. You gettin' an attack of the guilts, or what?"

Brigitte looked down at the ground, intimidated by her confident companion. Yet she had that feeling, that intuition: *She should proceed no farther.* Under Cappy's stolid gaze, she felt suddenly conspicuous, as if she were fatter, uglier, stupider than she really was.

"I . . . I just have dis bad feeling," she mumbled.

"Feelin', shit!" said Cappy as he led the her through the front door and into the dim foyer.

Brigitte surveyed the interior, which for some reason seemed darker than it should have been. Directly before her there was a stairway leading up; to the right, the door to the living room.

They went right.

The room was generally tidy except for the scattering of newspapers, magazines, paperbacks, and notepaper that covered the floor in a kind of half circle around a comfortable-looking red leather chair. Next to the chair, a small table supported an empty glass and a half-finished bottle of whiskey.

Cappy, intrepid as ever, walked right over to the table. He picked up the bottle, removed the top, and lifted it to his lips.

He drank. With great satisfaction he aspirated, "Aahhh," and wiped his mouth on the back of his hand.

His expression never changed as he extended the bottle toward Brigitte.

"Oh, no, better not," said Brigitte. "Da man, he'll see it is gone, no?"

"Don't be a *sheet*," said Cappy, shaking the bottle. The amber liquid swirled and splashed within.

The muscles in Brigitte's legs tightened, starting to cramp. With difficulty, she walked over and accepted the bottle. Little bubbles had formed on the surface of the liquor. She watched them, fascinated for a moment, then raised the bottle, letting the tea-colored fluid run down the bottle's neck, stopping against the dam of her tightly closed lips.

She didn't take any into her mouth. Lowering the bottle, she licked her lips. The bourbon stabbed at her tongue like a million tiny needles. It tasted awful!

"We better get upstairs," said Cappy, his eyes resting a little too long on Brigitte.

He knows, thought Brigitte. *He knows I did not drink.*

The stairway to the attic was directly above the stairs to the second floor. Cappy paused at the foot of the attic staircase to examine a shutter-covered window. Through its wooden slats they had a good view of the front yard and road. It was a perfect lookout; it would be easy to spot the man if he came back.

Brigitte waited for Cappy to lead her up the narrow stairs to the attic. Cappy didn't move.

"You go," Cappy commanded.

"*Pourquoi moi*? No! You go! You da one who know about da map!"

"But you're more sober than I am, aren't you, *Bree-sheet*?" Brigitte knew there was no more to be said. In spite of her growing revulsion for the house, she knew she would have to do as instructed. She would have to climb those dark stairs to the mysterious attic.

She felt trapped within her humiliation. She knew Cappy had

seen that she didn't drink. Now she was afraid he would believe she was a coward. A stupid fat girl coward.

"You tell me fast if you see him come, eh?" she said tonelessly.

Turning and looking up, Brigitte studied the long, narrow passageway to the attic. It seemed like a dark tunnel with walls that were uncomfortably close together. For some reason she had the strange feeling that the tight, dark tunnel led down instead of up.

The increasing weight of her legs made the climb almost impossible. She pictured herself as a very small child climbing stairs that were way too big for her. She climbed step after agonizing step, the boards groaning under her feet.

All the time she groped along the powdery plaster wall, looking for a light switch that wasn't there.

When she finally reached the attic, she found herself in an unsettling half-light. It was bright enough so she could see, but everything looked indistinct and far away. The light came from sunshine pouring down in little strips from between the hundreds of slate squares that made up the roof.

Brigitte wondered why the roof didn't leak when it rained.

Massive hand-hewn beams were dense shadows overhead. Dust coated everything. It rose like tiny conjured ghosts each time she took a step. Her footprints on the floor told her no one else had been up here for a very long time.

The floorboards, fifteen-inch-wide pine planks, creaked menacingly under each hesitating footfall. The dust, dancing now in the pillars of sunlight, made her want to sneeze. She fought the urge; she was afraid to make a sound.

Through squinting eyelids Brigitte surveyed the unpartitioned expanse of loft. Piles of sagging cardboard boxes formed rickety towers beside worn leather trunks and wooden crates. A rusty metal file cabinet, its side dented, lay on its back. One drawer had been removed; it stood on the floor alongside. Yellow papers were chaotically piled in the drawer. They overflowed, littering the floor all around.

Everything was as quiet as dust and shadows until she heard a faint scratching somewhere among the dark, indistinct shapes at the far end of the house.

Brigitte looked up.

Was it rats? Maybe a squirrel?

Then all was quiet again.

Brigitte found herself frozen, standing perfectly still, holding her breath. Furtively her eyes sought motion, probed among the shadows in the darkest corners, under the eaves, around the old brick chimney.

Sensing nothing, she relaxed a little. She forced her mind to return to the treasure map.

Where could it be?

Cautiously, she looked around again. To her left she saw a basket of mummified apples. They looked like tiny brown withered faces. Shrunken heads. Beside them, a canvas bag.

Brigitte knew better than to begin rummaging through these things. The map would not be in any of them—too obvious, too new. But where should she start looking?

She moved to where the cobweb-shrouded chimney came up through the floor. Her eyes followed it upward to where it exited through the roof.

Ah, maybe behind a loose brick?

God! It could be anywhere! Behind a brick, under a floor-board, tucked into some hidden knothole in one of the ancient timbers. Or— *mon dieu*—it could be stashed in any of a thousand other places. A thousand thousand! The task seemed monumental! Before she'd even begun to hunt, she was ready to give up. The feeling of frustration made her pulse quicken and her lips purse tightly together.

What's that?

She heard the sharp scratching sound again. This time it sounded almost like a hiss.

She gasped. Breath followed breath, rapidly, loudly. She tried not to exhale but couldn't stop. She wanted to hold perfectly still, keep absolutely quiet.

More than that, she wanted to cry out to Cappy. But her pride prevented it.

Brigitte's eyes still probed the eerie half-light. She thought she could see more airborne dust than she had stirred up.

Trying not to concentrate on her fear, she decided explore a bit, then get out fast.

But what if, just by chance, she happened to look in the right place? What if she actually found the map?

Eh bien, maybe she just wouldn't tell Cappy she'd found it. That would show him. Maybe she'd just remember where it was hidden, then come back for it later. After all, why should she share it with Cappy? She had nothing to prove to the boy. Besides, Cappy was mean to her.

Now, feeling more resolve, Brigitte took another step toward the chimney. Her eyes locked on one single brick that was slightly askew, no longer held snugly in place by the dry, cracking mortar.

All at once she felt cold.

A sensation of nausea sloshed in her stomach. Acrid-tasting gas escaped through her mouth and nose. She felt as if she were about to vomit. A horrible stench, like sewer water, filled her nostrils. Brigitte held her breath and jerked her head around, trying to see everywhere at once. Her body remained rigid, her pudgy fists clenched in tight sweaty balls; her nails dug into her palms.

Was it getting darker? Was the attic filling with dust, making the light fade between the slates of the roof?

Again she heard what sounded like the scampering of tiny clawed feet. Louder now. Brigitte tried to concentrate on the sound, to identify it. It was like hearing noises during a dream: the sleeping mind struggling to ignore sounds that might wake it.

It seemed more rhythmic now—*swish-swish swish-swish*—almost like an engine. Yet it didn't sound mechanical. It sounded more like . . . breathing.

Labored, congested, asthmatic breathing.

Something was in the attic with her! It made low, hoarse, animal sounds. Rasping. Obstructed.

Getting louder!

Getting closer!

Why couldn't she move? Why couldn't she run? Brigitte closed her eyes as tightly as her lips and fists. Her teeth clenched together like a vise. Her legs were columns of stone.

If she could only cry out to Cappy . . .

But she could not.

All she could do was say over and over in her mind, *Oh God, oh God, oh God* . . .

Then she felt something touch her cheek.

On the floor below, Cappy ground a cigarette butt under his heel. He picked up the telltale bit of evidence and placed it in his pocket. Then, from the floor above, he heard the soul-splitting scream.

"AAAAAAAAGGGGGGGGGAAAAAAAAAHHHHHHHHH!"

He froze. The scream continued, frantic, tortured, garbled, as if his friend were gulping in air so that her scream might continue.

For a fraction of a second Cappy thought Brigitte might be playing a trick.

But then he knew.

All his stoic coldness left him. He was suddenly a frightened little boy whose playmate was in trouble.

Cappy started up the stairs to help, but the paralyzing fear that seized him allowed only a couple of steps.

He turned quickly, almost diving down the noisy wooden stairway.

Cappy ran, driven down the stairs by a single compelling instinct. He found more speed when his eyes locked on the front door and the freedom of the afternoon.

Almost flying now, he prayed to escape this dreadful house that was crowded with the grisly sound of Brigitte Pelletier's tortured, dying wail.

2

The sun had completed its slow flight to the western side of the sky. It sank with almost discernible speed into the glowing horizon.

Harrison watched it vanish.

He felt as if the afternoon had passed too rapidly. Though he'd broken his habit of wearing a watch, he guessed it must be around four o'clock.

Had he squandered the day wandering around the southern half of the island? He'd crossed Childe's Bog and walked along Midway Road to the old ferry dock. There he found a seat on a stool-sized tree stump. He'd been sitting for quite some time, probably more than an hour, his binoculars scanning the slate-gray surface of the lake between Friar's Island and St. Albans Bay. All the while he hoped for a glimpse of that sleek serpentine shape gliding through the heaving waves.

Harrison lifted his eyes from the glasses. High in the sky he saw a large bird, probably a hawk, soaring and circling, never moving its wings yet lifting higher and higher on a rising blanket of warm air. What was it called? A thermal, he remembered, pleased with his recall and his observation.

He stood up and began to move north along the shore, alternating his attention between the changing surface of the lake and the jagged rocks on which he walked.

It was time to call it a day. He turned around and began to make his way back along Midway Road, past the mid-island hills covered with apple orchards and on toward town.

As he passed the schoolhouse, he thought about the local economy. Until recently, he supposed, apples and quarried stone were the island's major products.

He wished he knew a great deal more about Vermont history. There were probably hundreds of interesting stories about this island alone, tales of the monster comprising only a small percentage of them. Harrison smiled; at least now he had plenty of time to study.

Tomorrow, he decided, he would begin a series of interviews

with the islanders. Some of them no doubt had stories about the monster.

Motion caught his eye. He noticed the schoolhouse door opening.

Harrison had seen the woman a few times before. At least once at the general store, and from time to time driving her blue Honda. She must be a schoolteacher.

He found he was gawking, but couldn't pull his eyes away. She was tall, graceful, with long night-black hair that hung freely down her back. She wore a coat and a gray woolen skirt. Harrison liked her knee-high black boots with high heels. The footwear looked strangely out of place in the rustic surroundings.

She hugged a pile of books and papers against her chest. As she left the school, she pulled the door closed behind her. Harrison watched as she groped in her coat pocket, probably looking for the key to lock the building.

Fumbling awkwardly, she dropped her armload of books. Loose papers, belted by the wind, scattered like leaves in a dozen directions.

Harrison watched, transfixed. The young woman scrambled after the airborne sheets, moving with difficulty as her high heels punched into the damp schoolhouse lawn.

"Help me, can't you!" she cried when she noticed him.

His trance broken, Harrison dashed after a drifting paper, thinking how silly he must have looked grinning vapidly as he watched her.

With half a dozen papers in his hand, he trotted over to her like an eager student with a late homework assignment.

"Thank you," she said breathlessly, taking the papers and smiling broadly, revealing bright, near-perfect teeth.

"Thank *you*," said Harrison, "for reminding me of my manners."

"Look, I'm sorry about that. I didn't mean to yell at you. Sometimes I panic over little things."

"No problem. I'm just happy I was here to help. My name's Harrison Allen."

"I'm Nancy Wells," she said, switching books and papers to her left hand and extending her right. "You know, if it weren't for you, Harrison Allen, I'd be spending the rest of the day chasing these damned things all over the island. As it is, I spent half the morning looking for them before I remembered that I'd left them here at school."

Harrison grinned. "The absentminded professor."

Her smile faded as if it were a bright light suddenly extinguished. "I'm afraid I *have* been a little absentminded lately."

Harrison realized he had said something wrong. Shifting his weight uncomfortably from foot to foot, he smiled again, unable to think of anything more to say.

Nancy seemed to pick up on his hesitation. "You're new on the island, aren't you?"

"Yes. I just moved here from Boston. I live—"

"I know where you live. The old captain's place down by The Jaw. Did you buy it?"

"I—"

"Oh, listen to me. I'm sorry. It's none of my business."

"That's okay, I don't mind. The house belongs to a friend of mine in Burlington, Mark Chittenden. He inherited it."

"It sure is a handsome old place, isn't it? It's independent and proud. But it's kinda spooky, too, way off by itself like that. I heard it was built by a sea captain. Somebody told me the floors are tipped or slanted or something so that when he walked around it would feel like he was on board a ship. Is it true?"

"I'm sorry to have to report that it is not. It's too bad, though. That would be neat."

"Ah, well, another legend dies. How do you like living on the island, Harrison?"

"It has its drawbacks."

"For instance?"

"Well, it's kind of difficult to invite a lady for a drink when there's not so much as a bar or café."

"Ah, I see what you mean." She squinted at him and her nose wrinkled prettily. "But what about when a lady has never seen the inside of the captain's house?"

"Oh, I'd be proud to give you a tour sometime. But you'll have to settle for the pride of occupancy rather than ownership."

"I'd love to."

"And we might discover a place where the floors are a little slanted, but it'll be from age rather than design."

"Sounds great!"

"How about right now?"

"I'd like to, Harrison. Really I would. But I have something else to do now."

Harrison felt his smile vanish. He shouldn't be too aggressive or persistent, but he didn't want to miss an opportunity to see Nancy again. His mind raced to find another bit of conversation. He wasn't ready to say good-bye just yet.

"Which way are you headed?" he finally asked.

"Upstreet. I'm on my way over to visit Professor Hathaway. Have you met him yet?" Harrison shook his head as Nancy continued, "He's going to visit school tomorrow to tell the kids about the Indians that used to live on the island. He's probably the closest thing we have to a local historian. Hey! Why don't you come with me? He'd love to meet you, I'm sure, and I'll bet you'd enjoy meeting him. Would you like to?"

"It would be a pleasure. You say he knows a lot about local history?"

"More than anyone else around. Or at least he's the only one willing to talk about it. Are you interested in the history of the island?"

"Very much so. Maybe he'll be able to answer some questions for me on some work I'm doing."

"Sure, if anyone can. What kind of work do you do, Harrison?"

Harrison paused, thought about it, then took the plunge. "I'm a monster hunter."

Lessons

7

I

Robert "Cappy" Capra ran like he had never run before.

Brigitte Pelletier's dying cries bounced inside his head like echoes in a canyon. He had no time to feel guilty about running away, no time to wonder if his friend was safe or hurt or dead. He had just one driving thought: to get away from that house, away from that banshee howl that made his flesh tighten and his nerves feel like high-tension wires with a million volts coursing through them.

He never slowed down, he never looked back. He ran faster than he would have believed. Faster than that time when kids with bicycle chains and knives had sworn to cut him. Faster than when the cops chased him for stealing a tape player from the K-Mart.

He ran faster and faster. Sweating. Heart pounding. Eyes wet and stinging. He ran knowing with greater certainty than he had ever known anything in his life that something awful was after him.

And it was gaining.

He allowed himself to slow down, just a bit, confusion replacing his terror.

The marsh! He was running through the marsh!

Already the ground was damp under his feet, sucking at his sneakers, slowing his progress. Bushes tugged and

77

clawed at him, scratching his flesh and tearing his clothing. He stumbled blindly ahead, searching with hands and feet for some dry clearing in this pathless bog.

Could he trust his sense of direction? If he could just forge straight ahead, he should be able to quickly traverse the bog. That would get him to Eastern Way, and home.

Suddenly a new panic bound him like a straitjacket. He froze, motionless as the dead amid the leafless trees. He snapped his head from left to right, eyes darting all around, looking for a passable route. He knew he couldn't go back; something was after him. But surely whatever it was wouldn't follow him into the bog. No way!

That's it! Deeper into the marsh; he'd be safe there.

Again he bolted, tripped on a root, and pitched face first into cold, foul-smelling mud.

He spat.

As he picked himself up, he heard sounds all around him: the scratch and hiss of the wind in the trees, small animals scampering invisibly, the croak of frogs, the buzzing of insects. And the sound of a branch breaking.

A cold bolt of fear shot into him. He was frantic now, crying loudly, nearly hysterical.

Totally lost, unself-conscious in his fright, Cappy began to sob, "Mommy, Mommy."

Then the haze began to come.

The marsh began to take on a new brightness, as if the sun, now kissing the profile of the western horizon, had magically become brighter.

A calmness settled over him; he was like a lazy animal basking in that impossible sunlight.

Out, he somehow knew, was straight ahead. It was so simple. No, he wasn't lost. There were dry rocks and fallen trees to walk on; he wouldn't have to get any wetter.

He looked around. The brilliant marsh seemed alien and unfamiliar.

Why was he here? Why had he ventured so deeply into Childe's Bog?

To watch the animals, he guessed. To listen to the frogs and birds, and to try to see some ducks—or maybe geese—flying above in vee formation.

Everything was beautiful in the marsh, so calm and still, with earthy scents and soft, musical animal sounds and pretty red light that softened and beautified the trees and grasses and pools of still water.

Yet he knew there was something he had to do. He remembered that he was on his way to do . . . something. What? There was a thought, a purpose that scampered around in his mind like a squirrel in a tree, always just a little bit out of sight.

He felt funny not being able to remember, but it didn't frighten him. It was a little like smoking pot and starting to say something, then getting distracted and forgetting what he was talking about. Or maybe it was like trying to remember a dream when he was almost awake, but lying relaxed and comfortable in his bed, too warm and content to get up and start the day.

What was I just saying? Cappy thought. *Mom. I was saying, Mom. That's it, I have to get home. Mom and Dad're probably waiting for me so they can leave. I'm probably late. Probably going to catch holy hell.*

With his new purpose firmly fixed in his mind, Cappy walked out of Childe's Bog as if he knew it as well as he knew his own backyard. Automatically, as if from memory, he stepped sure-footedly over logs and stones without even seeing them.

Then he began running again, not wanting to keep his parents waiting. Finding himself on Midway Road now, he knew it was just a short walk to his home.

2

Professor Hathaway served tea from a fine silver tea set. He was a charming host, hospitable and enthusiastic. He warmed the room with his comfortable smiles and animated gestures. Harrison could see the old man was delighted to be entertaining guests.

The professor wore a rumpled Harris tweed jacket of indeterminate age, a wrinkled red flannel shirt, and a thin black necktie, loosely knotted. He gave the impression that this was his normal mode of attire, whether he was with company or passing long days alone.

Though quietly amused by the professor's fastidious informality, Harrison fell quickly under his charismatic spell.

The professor's house cast a spell of its own. It was as if their host had set up housekeeping in a library. Every room was lined with shelves crammed full of books in horizontal and vertical formation. The floor, the tables, even the chairs had collected the overflow from the shelves. The professor had had to clear a place for his guests to sit, and another for the tea tray.

The large oak desk by the eastern window was curiously uncluttered, Harrison noted. It had nothing on it but a pad of yellow lined paper and a pewter mug full of pens and pencils.

"So you like our little island, do you, Mr. Allen?"

"Very much, yes. And please, call me Harry."

"Well, I'm not surprised that you should," said Professor Hathaway, settling into a thickly padded chair that seemed almost to swallow him. "Friar's Island has a unique history, or rather, histories, as I'd prefer to say. Our island, like any town, I suppose, actually has many histories: each resident's, each building's, each outcropping of stone's. Tomorrow I am pleased to go to Miss Wells's school to talk about the history of its Indians. I'm afraid, however, that the children will be disappointed to learn that there is very little evidence of any permanent Indian settlements on Friar's Island. Probably they just visited here on explorations of one sort or another—hunting, fishing, that sort of thing. And then only in the summertime. Bones and other artifacts have been found that seem to have belonged to a glacial culture dating back to, maybe, one thousand B.C. There were beads and pottery, and an adze or two from more recent peoples. And, I mustn't let you forget, a fascinating fragment of a clay sculpture that some folks speculate was a model of our infamous Lake Champlain Monster."

"That's great!" said Harrison. "I think you're anticipating my next question."

The professor raised his eyebrows. "You're interested in the monster, are you?"

"I'll bet the kids would love to hear about that, too," said Nancy, smiling first at the professor, then at Harrison. "They're very interested in that sort of thing."

"Of course they are, and they should be," continued Professor Hathaway, "because it's a most thought-provoking subject. The very notion that receding glaciers carved out lakes and deposited sea creatures, abandoning them to adapt to fresh water, truly titillates the imagination. It happened to landlocked salmon, so why not to something bigger but possibly less prolific, like some variety of prehistoric whale? The fact is, there were whales around here some twelve thousand or so years ago, you know. The skeleton of one was found in a gravel pit in Charlotte not so very long ago. Its remains are now in the geology museum at the University of Vermont in Burlington.

"Another possible victim of landlocking could have been the long-lost cousin of the most famous of all elusive water beasts, the Loch Ness Monster."

"Why not?" agreed Harrison. "From what I've read, all the alleged eyewitnesses describe the Loch Ness Monster and the Champlain Monster in pretty much the same way."

"Indeed." Professor Hathaway nodded. "There could be a family resemblance."

"Have you ever seen it, Professor?" asked Nancy.

"I? Heavens, no. I've never been fortunate enough. But it has often been sighted up here in the islands, or so I understand."

"Do you know of anyone who's seen it?" asked Harrison.

"My experience with the local folks is that they'd rather not discuss it . . . or much of anything else. You can't get them to say yes or no. But in a four-hundred-ninety-square-mile body of water, it's kind of difficult to prove that it *isn't* out there."

"I'd sure like to prove that it is."

"Well, you're in an ideal spot to try." The professor smiled at the couple. "As a matter of fact, the state of Vermont is full of in-teresting lore and legends. Have you ever heard of Chester's Jekyll and Hyde burglar? Or the elves of Montpelier? Or perhaps that strange 'Devil's Triangle' at Glastenbury Mountain near Benning-ton where people have been known to vanish without a trace?"

Harrison and Nancy traded glances.

"Oh, and don't forget, there was a vampire in Woodstock. And of course, the famous freezing of old people to keep them over the winter, then thawing them out in the spring. That mysterious practice occurred in central Vermont and was actually covered in several newspapers, including the *Boston Globe* and even *Yankee* magazine. As you've no doubt guessed, the story was later proven to be apocryphal. But what about the hundreds of other ghosts, and treasures, and bugaboos of one kind or another? The state's full of that kind of thing, Harrison. But those tales are all written up here and there. The stories that interest me the most are the ones that probably have never been recorded. Would you like some more tea?"

"Come on, Professor, you're not going to leave us hanging there, are you?" said Nancy, smiling the eager, inquisitive smile of a schoolgirl.

"What's that, dear? The unrecorded ones?" His face wrinkled into a cherubic smile as he peered at her over the top of his glasses. "A local example might suffice. The name 'Friar's Island' probably comes from the shape of the island itself, which is said to resemble the head of a hooded monk—a friar—with rather a prominent jaw. But there's a far more interesting explanation: it could also have been named for what seems an excessive amount of religious activity that has always taken place here. You might be interested to know that until nearly the end of the eighteenth century that old monastery near the northern point of the island was still in use. There was a group of French Canadian monks—friars—in residence there. When they abandoned the place—I'm really not sure when or just exactly why—it stood deserted, just as it is now, until right around the turn of this century. It was then occupied by a commune of spiritualists throughout the heyday of the American spiritualist movement, up until around the time of the First World War. These spiritualists lived there until, I imagine, local pressure inspired them to move on.

"Spiritualism was a common enough religious affiliation in those days, but the group here was apparently a good deal more secretive than many. Apparently they believed that this island, and the northern part of it specifically, was a good vantage point from which to communicate with the other world, or whatever it was that they wanted to communicate with. Perhaps they actually made contact—who knows? Anyway, to this day the old monastery has the reputation of being haunted. And, at the risk of sounding like a stereotypical character in a gothic novel, the old place is shunned by the locals. I don't find that my neighbors are too eager to talk about the monastery, or the groups that used to live there."

"What do you know about these groups, Professor?" Harrison asked, thinking he should be taking notes.

The professor's eyes flashed, then dropped to his teacup. "Not much of anything at all, I'm afraid. From the bits and pieces that I've picked up over the years in my studies, it is the land itself that has been of interest to the various groups. It attracts some, repels others. This island has always held a kind of occult fascination for those schooled in the arcane sciences, Native Americans and Europeans alike. So you can see that the tradition predates the spiritualist group I just mentioned. The Indians that I'm going to talk to your class about buried their dead here. But the land, though fertile and rich with game, was avoided by the living.

"Some of the earliest French settlers referred to the land on the northern part of the island as *la mauvaise terre*, literally, 'the bad land,' but it meant more than 'bad' to them; it meant the evil, or the wicked, land. They, too, stayed clear of it. It was the groups with an active interest in otherworldliness that sought the place out. Why did those renegade French-Canadian monks come all the way down here to build their monastery? Why were the turn-of-the-century spiritualists so desirous of that specific property? Why is that area of the island still totally unsettled, even today?"

"Do you have a theory, Professor?" Nancy asked.

"I think the Indians left their dead here because they believed it was somehow closer to the spirit world, that leaving their bodies here would somehow give their spirits a head start on their journey from this world to the next. Likewise—and this is just conjecture—I believe the monks, and later the spiritualists, believed that there are, in this world, certain gateways to the next. There are actual geographic locations where the fabric of the first, second, and third dimensions—what we think of as 'reality'—is very thin. With the proper combination of words and rituals, some believe that border or gateway can be crossed. I believe Friar's Island is considered such a place. Especially the northern end."

"Wow!" said Harrison. "So the Indian burial ground you spoke of is, or was, on the north end?"

"Of course."

"And the monks who built the monastery," asked Nancy, "what do you know about them?"

"As usual, nowhere near enough. The original monks, back in the late sixteen or seventeen hundreds, were French. It was presumed, of course, that they were Roman Catholics, and perhaps their roots actually were in the Catholic Church. But apparently it wasn't a Christian God that they worshipped. There was evidence found in the monastery of the black mass, devil worship, or something of the kind. Although the evidence was attributed to the later colony of spiritualists, I am convinced that the relics predate them by quite a bit.

"It is said that the mainstream Catholic Church forced them away from the island and into hiding during the eighteenth century. All the relics and writings that they left behind were confiscated, either by the Church or the townspeople. Some items, however, fell into the hands of the spiritualists and have since been lost. What those writings and relics might have included, we can only guess. I'd love to know . . .

"Anyway, slightly more is known about the next occupants, the spiritualist colony. The group continued into this century and therefore is a bit easier to research. It is that group that interests me the most.

"You see, some of their papers were kept by the island community. Now they're the property of the island's historical society. They're on file at the town library. I have read what there is of them, and it is clear to me that they are incomplete. Where the rest have vanished is another of the island's mysteries. They may have been destroyed or removed. They may have been hidden. Or maybe they are packed away and forgotten in somebody's attic someplace here on the island."

"Is anyone on the island old enough to remember those days?" Harrison asked.

"I think so, yes. Old Mrs. Snowdon, for one. But I understand she won't talk to anyone about much of anything."

Nancy looked puzzled. "I don't think I know her."

"No?" The professor looked at her with mock surprise. "She's probably Harrison's nearest neighbor. She lives in a cabin just this side of the marsh. There's only a path leading to her place—no road. I'll bet you've seen her in town once in a while. Dresses strangely, like a European peasant woman. And that's her son you see in the village now and then. An unkempt, uncoordinated lad who looks about thirty or thirty-five years old. Lots of folks think of him as the village idiot. Always has a faraway look in his eyes, and he mumbles as he walks. The townspeople seem fond of the Snowdons, however. They cut wood for them and bring them clothes and food. I've seen her in the store, and never saw Abner charge her for a thing.

"I think the Snowdons are—"

The professor stopped abruptly. A look of distress shaded his face, then quickly vanished. "I have been going on, haven't I? Sometimes I forget my manners; it's so rare I have company. I guess being with a couple of young people like you made me think that I was back in the classroom." He chuckled self-consciously. "But there'll be time enough for that when I come to visit the wee ones at school. I hope they'll be as tolerant of my ramblings as you two have been."

"It has been fascinating," said Harrison, realizing that the evening was coming to an end. He glanced discreetly at Nancy's watch; it was eight o'clock.

Nancy, too, picked up on the hint. "It's getting late for this working girl."

She stood up. Harrison and the professor followed her lead.

"I want to thank you both for sharing your evening with me. Harrison, it was good to meet you. Tell me, I wonder if you've heard the story about the treasure that's supposed to be hidden in your house?"

"Is that right? Really?" Harrison felt as eager as a boy.

"Well, if I can prevail upon you to join me another evening, I'd gladly tell you everything I know about it. And perhaps we can discuss that elusive *Chaousarou* that seems to interest you so much."

"The what?"

"*Chaousarou*. That's what the Indians called the Lake Champlain Monster."

"It would be a pleasure, sir."

"And Miss Wells, I'll very much look forward to seeing you tomorrow in school."

3

Gaston and Michelle Pelletier, Brigitte's parents, were angry. Neither was speaking.

Michelle made frequent trips to the window to watch for Brigitte, but the only thing she saw was the soft afternoon light turning much too rapidly into evening. The girl was very late. She knew well enough that they had planned to leave the island a long time ago.

All the packing was done, the windows were sealed, and the water and electricity were turned off. Their camp was closed up tight for the winter.

As soon as Brigitte returned, they would spank her for the inconvenience she had caused. If she would act like a child, they would treat her like a child. Perhaps the indignity of a spanking after so many years would remind her of her obligation to her parents.

The girl had been making them angry more and more lately. Especially since she had teamed up with that Capra boy. Right now the two of them were off somewhere together, mindless of the delay and the worry they were causing.

Gaston didn't like to drive after dark. The way it looked now, the family wouldn't get back to Montreal until very late. And tomorrow there would be work for Gaston, and school for the girl.

"Shall I light the kerosene lamp, my dear? That would be pleasant," said Michelle.

"You might as well put the fuses back in," said Gaston, not picking up on what had been intended as a peace offering.

Michelle sighed. She lighted the lamp with her Bic lighter. "I should go and call Mother from the pay phone at the general store. She'll worry if she calls the house and we aren't there."

She crossed the room and sat on the arm of her husband's chair. Michelle was an attractive woman in her late forties. Her firm plumpness recalled what had once been a fine, full figure; her graying auburn hair remembered an exciting fiery red. As her hand found the back of Gaston's neck, she began to massage the tense muscles there. His irritation passed, as it always did.

"Let me get you a drink," she whispered. "I know just where I packed the scotch."

"That would be good."

She unpacked the bottle and a glass, all the time worrying about Brigitte. She *was* getting to be a problem lately. They both knew it, but neither liked to speak about it. They only discussed it when they were angry, vowing to start doing something about it. But their anger would pass, and with it their resolve. They'd do nothing.

Neither wanted to admit that Brigitte was a flaw in their otherwise perfect marriage. For ten years they had been blessed with a rare happiness, a perfect togetherness, needing nothing, wanting nothing—or so they had assured each other. Each, for the sake of the other, had tried to minimize the disappointment at not being able to have a child. Each lied to the other, saying a child was not necessary to fulfill their perfect union.

And then, as if in answer to their prayers, Brigitte came. And things were complete.

But the years passed. School, television, friends, and a thousand other temptations had beckoned their daughter away from the protection of the family.

Lately Brigitte was often rude, headstrong, and arrogant. Except around that Bobby Capra.

Cappy.

Thank God she wasn't around Cappy too often. It wasn't healthy the way Brigitte seemed to fear, idolize, almost worship the Capra boy. It was her first love, a puppy love, as the Americans called it. When Brigitte was with Cappy, it was as if she had no family at all.

Just like now, the child expresses total disregard—

"It is raining, my dear?" asked Michelle, walking back to the window with Gaston's drink in her hand. "I thought I heard it raining."

Looking out the window, she saw no rain, and no Brigitte. The reflection of the kerosene lamp in the dark glass made her think of another era, a time before electricity had come to the island, when nighttime meant isolation, not a two-hour automobile trip to Montreal.

Her eyes fixed on the flame in the window. Somehow it seemed very far away. Too far to touch. Her mind seemed to swim in the window glass as if the panes were made of water. She could feel the glass all around her. It was cold. The glass was cold. She felt it, yet she was not touching it. The reflected flame fascinated her, called her, irresistibly beckoned her into the reflecting, churning glass sea.

She thought she could take a step and pass right through the windowpane and into the more comfortable world beyond.

Wait! She shook her head.

Part of her mind knew that something was wrong. Why was she thinking so strangely? Her mind grasped frantically for explanations. Had her husband somehow caused a leak when he shut off the gas? Was she becoming asphyxiated?

Michelle couldn't tear her concentration away from the flickering reflection of the kerosene lamp. It seemed so far away. So very far away. Away. Away. Look away. Try to look away. Try . . . to . . . look . . . away . . .

But she couldn't. She was too heavy, and there was no communication between her mind and her extremities. She needed help, wanted to cry for Gaston, but she knew he could never hear her above the monotonous humming of the rain.

The humming of the rain . . .

No! Rain doesn't hum! She knew that. Rain does not hum.

My dear God, what's happening to me? Is this a heart attack? Am I having a heart attack? Am I having a stroke?

Her ears throbbed with the rain, the solid, sparkling crystals of glass rain that slid and scratched like diamonds against the windowpanes and tore viciously against the slate roof of the cottage.

None of this is right, she realized in a sudden, sickening terror.

She was perspiring now. Her solidifying muscles pushed sharp glassy beads of sweat from her soft pores. The delicate openings tore painfully. She wanted to scream.

With a tremendous effort of mind and body, she whirled from the window, crying, "Gaston!"

Her husband was sleeping in the chair.

Sleeping? How could he be sleeping?

Her muscles weren't working right. She was trembling violently, as if giant, invisible hands clutched her by the shoulders, shaking her mercilessly.

And she was cold, as if she were inhaling an arctic wind that froze her lungs and slowed the movement of her blood.

My dear God, I can't breathe!

The alcoholic liquid splashed from the trembling glass in her hand. It burned like acid as it coated her fingers, saturating her sweater and skirt. The glass rocketed from her grip and shattered on the floor. Diamonds. Crystal raindrops.

"Gaston! GASTON!"

He didn't move, and she couldn't. Michelle tried to go to her husband, realizing there was something wrong with him, too. Mercifully, in that moment of empathy, she forgot her own agony.

But when she tried to move, it was like trying to move in a nightmare. It was as if the air all around her had turned to sand.

Then the tremors returned. Violently. Like a million strong hands gripping her, trying to pull her in every direction at once.

She sank, as if her legs were melting into the cold pine floor. In her convulsions, she ground shards of broken glass into her palms and knees.

But now she didn't feel it.

4

Anthony and Ellie Capra had the car packed and were making the final rounds of their property before abandoning it to another island winter. Last year they had forgotten to cover the chimney. Snow had collected in the opening, melted, and created a sooty black liquid that ran down and stained the carpet in front of the fireplace.

Their plan was to skip dinner and have a light snack on the way home to Plattsburgh, maybe in Rouses Point, on the New York side of the toll bridge.

Mr. Capra placed a cardboard box into the trunk of the car. He shouted to his wife, "Is Bobby ready?"

"I'll get him." Ellie started toward Bobby's room. He had come back a little over an hour ago, looking exhausted and confused after a hard afternoon of playing. He was dirty from where he had fallen, and he was very, very tired. He had walked directly to his room in a somnolent fashion; within moments he was napping fretfully.

"Come on, Bobby. We have to be going." Ellie smiled at the sleeping boy from the door to his room.

He sat up in bed, rubbing his swollen eyes. He still looked very sleepy. Ellie was afraid he was getting sick with a cold or even the flu.

"Do you feel all right, dear?"

"Umm-hmm."

"Are you ready to start back?"

"Yup." He looked around. "I had a nightmare."

"A nightmare? What about?"

"I can't remember." Bobby yawned. Then he stood up.

"Do you have everything you want to bring back with you? Anything you forget stays here till next summer, you know."

"I got everything."

"Did you say good-bye to your friend Brigitte?"

"Yup. They left already."

Cappy picked up his sweater and struggled into it. He grabbed his BB gun and a pile of comic books, then stumbled groggily toward the door.

His mother laughed. "You look like you're walking in your sleep."

The boy went straight to the back seat of the car. He fell asleep again almost at once.

Within minutes the Capra family was in the car and on their way off the island. As they passed the Pelletier cottage, they noticed that the car was gone and the place seemed closed up tight.

They were almost to Alburg before their son began to stir.

The Witching Hour   8

I

All along, Nancy had known this would happen.

During some of their silences, she had even tried to prepare a tactful way to handle it. Now the time had come; she had to decide what she really thought. And felt.

When she and Harrison left the professor's house, it was dark. There was no wind. The night sky was clear as glass. For a while they pointed out constellations to each other, avoiding the question.

The subject of how hungry they were came up, but Nancy hesitated to ask Harrison to her house for something to eat. It was getting late, and there was school tomorrow.

A lone pickup truck passed them on the otherwise deserted street. It swerved a little too close, as if the driver either didn't see them or perhaps wanted to have a closer look. The noisy truck was strangely out of place in a night that seemed to belong to another era.

After passing the school, they turned on to Midway Road. No doubt Harrison intended to walk her home. She could see he was eager to accompany her.

"I felt like we were a couple of kids in a classroom," she said.

"Yeah, me too. He's a great old guy, though. I've got to talk to him some more about the monster."

"That monster really interests you, doesn't it?"

"It really does. I know this sounds stupid, but ever since I joined the American Cryptozoological Society, my main goal in life has been to see the thing. As a matter of fact, I can't recall a time when my life has had more purpose. Pretty sad, huh?"

"Not at all. It's . . . well, it's sort of romantic."

"And that's partly why I came here. Failing a face-to-face meeting with the monster, I want to at least research it. Maybe do an article, interview some of the people who *have* seen it."

"I'd never even heard of it before today. I'd love to see something like that!"

"Then why don't you come monster hunting with me sometime?"

"Well . . . sure. That would be fun!"

She felt Harrison cautiously take her hand. She took his without hesitation. They walked in silence for a long time. Dry leaves skittered invisibly about their feet.

His hand felt good to her. She was aware how soft it was, how warm in contrast to the chill evening air. It had been a long time since she had been with a man. Being close like this reminded her of how alone she often felt, how unattached. She thought of the months that had passed since she left Albany to come to Vermont, and of that last night with Eric, when they had made love like robots, before she had left him quickly and forever.

At first her nights alone had been difficult. She had found some relief in fantasy, but all too often only the languorous release of secret masturbation would permit her to sleep.

Was it simply the need for fantasy and relief that attracted her to this unfamiliar man at her side?

She tightened her grip on his hand and stopped walking, then turned to face him. She kissed him long and passionately.

When their ardent lips separated, she spoke before Harrison had a chance to. "Please don't ask me to spend the night with you, Harry. I will, I promise—but not tonight. Just say it's because I have to work tomorrow and I need my sleep."

He looked confused and a little hurt. Then, in the soft darkness his face spread into a beatific smile. His teeth were like small white stones in the pale moonlight. "I won't ask you anything at all," he whispered.

When he kissed her goodnight at the door to her cottage, he said, "Next weekend let's go monster hunting, okay? And maybe we'll even explore that old monastery. What do you say?"

"I was just going to suggest that," she whispered, and she kissed him again.

2

The only decision Cliff Ransom had made all day long was that he wasn't going to work on Monday. And that, by God, was for sure.

That night, as he drove back to Friar's Island from Swanton, drunk and more than a little pissed off, he figured he just might never go to work again. The days were getting real cold, and he knew he would get laid off pretty quick anyway. They shut down the quarry every winter, so what difference would a day or two make?

Cliff always looked forward to getting laid off. It was the same year after year: work during the summer months, vacation the rest of the year at the expense of the unemployment office. Fun-enjoyment, Cliff called it.

WLFE, 102.3 on the FM dial from St. Albans, blasted C&W from the radio. Cliff tapped the steering wheel, trying his best to sing along:

> Oh, I've had a lot of beer, a lot of women,
> Courted trouble nearly all of my life,
> But when that barroom clock strikes eleven,
> Head on home to the arms of my wife.

He thought about the bar he had just left in Swanton; half lit, smoke laden, filled with beer-woozy men in cowboy shirts and Levi's, and fat women with pointed tits and Dolly Parton hairstyles. That kind of shit wasn't for him. He knew a spot in Burlington that had a shitload more class. Maybe next weekend . . .

Too bad there wasn't a little action right here on the island.

The pickup bounced over the bridge from North Hero, and Cliff sped toward town, thinking how good his bed would feel.

As he neared the general store, now dark and empty, he was surprised to see the shadowy figures of a man and a woman walking close together along the roadside. The woman's height and long black hair alerted him that it was the schoolteacher. And who was that walking beside her? Cliff accelerated even more, steering much closer to the man than he should have.

That fuckin' flatlander from the captain's place. Sheee-ut, looks like some goddamn citified pansy to me! Like to take a fuckin' round out of him!

As soon as the couple had faded out of sight, Cliff began singing his song again. He pointed his truck toward home, the schoolteacher very much on his mind.

3

After he left Nancy at her cottage, it occurred to Harrison that the quickest route home would be to cut through the eastern end of Childe's Bog. However, he didn't feel familiar enough with the island's topography to attempt such a shortcut, especially in the dark. Instead, he opted to walk back across the island along Midway Road, then head south on West Shore Road to his house. A long way. West Shore Road led through the marsh, but it was a known route to him, so there would be no chance of getting lost or hurt.

With Nancy no longer at his side, he noticed for the first time how cold it was. He quickened his pace, arms folded tightly across his chest.

Now he was very much alone. The only sign of civilization was far behind him: the dim light from Nancy's cabin. It faded with each step and was quickly lost among a scattering of invisible bushes and thick-trunked trees.

Before him lay the indistinct image of the road, a cleared pathway through black underbrush and shadowy grasses.

No one around, no light, no traffic. The only sound was the high-pitched squeaking and bass rasping of the generations of frogs that lived in the marshland. The moonlight was bright enough to see where he was going, but he could make out no details of his surroundings. Ahead, the gray pathway of road was clear. If he followed it, he would be all right.

On both sides of him rounded clusters of brush looked like the dark, crouching shapes of huge animals waiting to spring. The outline of the marsh, although quite near, seemed like a vast range of black mountains far in the distance.

Beginning to feel the return of childhood fears of the dark— and now more than a little convinced of the existence of monsters —Harrison forced his mind back to Nancy Wells. Her hand had felt so warm in his, her lips so moist and eager. He knew he wanted to see her again. He wanted to be with her. He even permitted himself to hope they would someday make love, and that would be fine.

But there was something more, something important: He *liked* her. And for the first time in weeks, he felt a cautious optimism.

At that moment, much more than ever before, Harrison began to enjoy his life on this slow-moving anachronism called Friar's Island. The place was starting to feel very much like home.

He tried to recall the last time he had actually liked a woman. He couldn't count Andrea, of course; she was more a symbol than anything else. An ideal. And now she was nothing more than a painful part of his pre-island past.

Had it always been his inability to find satisfaction in female companionship that had made him feel like such a misfit? Sure, he had known a few women; he'd lived with one, had made love to several. But he had never felt—what was it? The electricity? The magic?

The love.

Of course, it was love that he'd never experienced. And its absence had long made him uncertain of himself. If he were unlovable, then he had no place, no roots, maybe no soul.

Sometimes he pictured himself maturing into a funny little old man, a lifelong bachelor tottering unsteadily in his tennis shoes, mumbling to himself, growing old all alone.

It was as he was passing through the marsh—walking down the middle of West Shore Road—that he heard the sound.

What was that?

His reverie vanished instantly. He stood like a statue, ears straining to detect vibrations in the night air. The sound had come from his right, from the depths of the bog. It had been perfectly distinct. He knew it wasn't frogs or wind or leaves; it was more like something solid, something that rustled the bushes deep within the oblivion of marshland.

His first thought was of Nancy. Could she be coming after him? Maybe she had changed her mind, wanted to call him back. But no, she would not be coming through the marsh. It could only be something wild, some kind of animal.

He stopped again. Listened.

And the rustling stopped.

An animal, most certainly. And, from the sound of it, a sizable one. He had heard that there were deer on the island, but he had yet to see one.

Would deer hide in the swamp?

Harrison began to walk faster. The soles of his shoes smacked on the packed dirt surface of the road. Their reports seemed strangely loud in the night air.

The rustling in the marsh started again.

There could be no doubt about it, no doubt at all. There was movement nearby. Something was hurriedly pushing branches aside. Something was crushing dry leaves, breaking twigs.

He stopped. And the sound stopped.

Lightning flashed along his spine. Suddenly he was wide awake, alert, nerves and reflexes tense and ready. His eyes felt unnaturally wide, straining against the trees and shadows, trying to drink in what little light there was.

Something was out there. Something motionless in the lightless bowels of the marsh, just beyond the range of his vision. Something hidden and wary. Something that was following him.

Frozen in position, his mind raced wildly. *Don't be silly,* he thought. *It's just some animal. A deer or a dog. Probably more afraid of me than I am of it.*

Harrison took a few cautious steps, then stopped abruptly. The sound did the same.

But wouldn't an animal run back into the trees? Why would it start and stop when he did? Why would it pace him like this?

Was it stalking him?

He peered again into the gloomy tangle of trees. His eyes, useless where there was no light, looked for movement, sought the red glow of animal eyes.

It was frightfully quiet. Even the frogs were silent now. Harrison's eyes and ears ached in their attempt to pick up some hint of what was near.

Frozen to the spot, Harrison felt the first wave of dread pass from some long-protected cavity at the center of his body. It flowed out to his motionless extremities, slashing from nerve to nerve, muscle to muscle, in a white-hot electric current.

Merciful Christ! Something's following me!

He began to move forward, trotting now, thinking only of getting inside, behind the locked door, with the old shotgun on the wall. He looked furtively over his shoulder as he moved, trying to watch in every direction at once, hoping to see. Hoping not to see.

Soon the marsh was well behind him. The protective silhouette of his house loomed not far ahead.

He turned his back on the house, walking awkwardly backward, looking at the shadowy passage of the road where it cut through the marsh.

Far off in the silvery glow of moonlight, he could just make out the nearly invisible shape of something moving out of the bushes and onto the road. It was like a dense shadow moving through the darkness. The moon didn't offer enough light to see it clearly, but there was one thing he could tell for sure: It was not a deer.

Whatever it was walked upright. It looked like a man. But who? The darkness and the distance made the figure impossible to identify.

Whoever it was just stood there, right in the middle of the road, watching Harrison run home.

A Change of Climate   9

I

Monday was unseasonably warm on the island. It was Indian summer, that deceitful time of the year when the weather takes a turn for the better before winter asserts itself with sprawling dunes of snow and brutal storms off the lake.

The temperature must have been in the fifties. The old men who gathered on the steps of the general store marveled that they could not see their breath.

"How would you know, anyways," said Cy Stoddard, "I don't see how you can tell if it's your damn cigar smoke or your own stinkin' exhaust."

Chief Lawrence Connelly blasted forth a giant cloud of gray-yellow smoke. "Don't make a bit of difference," said the chief. "At least you can tell I'm breathin'!"

"But *why* you are I couldn't tell ya," said Edwin Jakes, easing himself down to where his pancake-thin buttocks rested on the peeling porch steps. His palsied hands gripped a walking stick that stood between his legs like an erection.

At one time his family name had been "Jacques," but the phonetic subtleties of French pronunciation proved too taxing for the English-speaking islanders. So his family had become known as "Jakes." Ever since he was a boy his friends had called him simply Jake. So Jake he had become, Jake he called himself, and Jake he'd be when they laid him down to rest.

"Wha'd' ya mean, Jake?" Chief Connelly asked.

"The way you keep pumpin' them diesel fumes through yer lungs, sa wonder ya got any lungs left to breathe *with*."

"Never let the ol' fire die out, that's my motto," retorted the chief.

"Tell me somethin', Chief," said Cy Stoddard with a confidential squint of his rheumy eyes. "You got any idee what that fella's up to?"

"What fella's that, Cy?" The chief removed his brown Stetson and combed his fingernails over his bald pate as if he were running his fingers through a thick head of hair.

"You know," said the old man, "that fella—outa-stater looks like—who moved into the captain's place."

"I been wonderin' about him, too," said Jake, holding the cane by the top while running his other hand up and down the shaft.

"I'll tell you what he's up to, by God. Looks to me like that fella's up to mindin' his own damn business, that's what." The chief nodded with great finality, looking from Jake's eyes into Cy's.

Chief Lawrence Connelly wasn't really a chief at all. For nearly fifteen years he had been the island's only full-time police officer. Three years ago, when he began to talk about retirement, the town decided they no longer needed a police force, since there really wasn't any crime. Chief Connelly retired everything but his Stetson and his title. People still thought of him as the law, although now, officially, the town was under the jurisdiction of the Vermont State Police.

Nonetheless, Chief Connelly still kept his eyes and ears open, still made it his business to know just about everything that went on in Friar's Island. Yet he had to admit, if only to himself, he still hadn't gotten a handle on that new guy down there in the captain's house. The man didn't seem to work for a living, and word was out that he was asking a lot of questions about the Lake

Champlain Monster. Must be a reporter or something, the chief figured. He had resolved to get to the bottom of things, to find out for sure. Unlike his porch-sitting colleagues, the chief admitted to a definite tolerance for strangers, but no one could accuse him of liking them.

"Speaking of strangers . . ." said Jake, almost in a whisper.

The men fell into silence as the schoolteacher pulled up in her blue Honda. She got out and walked up the steps toward them.

"Good afternoon, gentlemen," she said, with no trace of affectation in her tone. The chief tipped his hat and said, "Nice day." The other two merely grunted, smiling toothlessly.

Nice girl, thought the chief, never once thinking of her as a stranger.

Jake vigorously massaged his cane, grinning in rude appreciation after Nancy passed and walked into the store. He and Cy giggled like teenagers while the chief, perhaps a bit embarrassed, walked off down the street.

2

Nancy was feeling on top of the world. Professor Hathaway's lecture had gone very well. The kids had left school with a satisfying excitement in their eyes.

And she was feeling excited, too. All day her thoughts had been about Harrison Allen. There was something intriguing about him, something a little mysterious. He had said so little about his past, about himself in general. Who was he? Where did he come from? He had a singular quality, a romantic air of mystery that made him different from any other man she had ever known. Most boasted, tried to build themselves up in her eyes, tried to impress her in grand and subtle ways. Instead, Harrison had a gentle humility, a quiet charm.

Though his pastime was perhaps a tad eccentric, the idea of his being a monster hunter was fun and exciting. She was eager for their lakeside outing when they'd look for signs of the mysterious creature. What a thrill it would be if they should actually see the monster!

To come face to face with the unknown . . .

It was scary, that was for sure, but exciting, too.

Maybe she should ask Harrison to be a guest lecturer at school. The students had loved Professor Hathaway; she was sure they'd also love to hear about the monster.

Yes, she'd ask him right away. He could talk about the monster and . . . What was the name of that association he belonged to? American Cryptozoologists, or Cryptobiologists, or something like that?

She was eager to invite him to school, but more—*come on, Nancy, fess up*—she was eager to see him again.

The warmth of the day and the school children's excitement left her feeling as if it were springtime. Her fears about memory loss and the possibility of another epileptic seizure had almost vanished from her mind. They just didn't seem so troublesome with Harrison nearby.

She recognized what she was thinking and quickly stopped. No, she wouldn't allow herself to become dependent on him. If they were to have any kind of relationship, it would have to be based on something stronger than dependency. She was confident that in time they'd discover all the right reasons to get together. For now, she knew that she liked him, and she was curious to get to know him better.

"And how are you today, Miss Nancy Wells?" said Abner Mott from his place behind the cash register.

"Just great, Mr. Mott. Came in to check my mail."

He took off his red hunting cap and replaced it with the green visor he always wore when he was in the mail room. After wiping his hands on his spotless butcher's apron, he walked back to the little booth labeled POST OFFICE, where he found a couple of magazines, some catalogs, and a bill for her.

As he brought them to her, a tall, uniformed Vermont State

Police officer entered the store. He wore dark sunglasses and a winter coat. He walked with a precision that clearly suggested a military background.

"Hi, Abner," he said.

"Ken Mitchell!" Abner beamed a smile that said long time, no see. "What brings you to the right side of the lake?"

Nancy waited patiently for Abner to give her the mail. Seeing that he was temporarily occupied, she remained politely silent. And curious.

"Just checking something out," said the policeman, his voice as precise as his gait. "We got a call from the New York State Police after *they* got a call from the RCMP. I guess the Mounties must think we're part of New York state."

"Don't that beat all," Abner mused. "Oughtta know better."

Nancy listened intently, trying not to appear interested. She noticed the policeman's use of "we" to imply that he, too, was an islander.

"They got a missing-persons report on the family of Mr. and Mrs. Gaston Pelletier and their daughter, Brigitte. Family's got a summer place up here on East Beach. You know them, Mr. Mott?"

"I believe I do."

"Well, apparently they were here on the weekend, closing down the place for the winter. They were supposed to drive back to Montreal on Sunday. The plan was to call Mrs. Pelletier's mother when they got home. But they never called. When they still hadn't showed up this morning, and when Mr. Pelletier didn't show up for work, the lady's mother got worried. Called the police."

"Mr. Pelletier was in here, guess it was Sat'day mornin'. Bought cigarettes and somethin' else, I forget what. Nice enough fella. 'Member him sayin' somethin' 'bout leavin'. Pretty sure that was the last I seen of him."

"Well, I'm pretty sure they made it off the island all right. I took a drive by their place; she's shut up tighter'n a drum. No sign of anyone. No car, nothin'. The thing is, there's been no report of an accident, no word from any of the hospitals along the route. Nothing. Funny thing, a whole family like that."

"Funny thing," agreed Abner.

"I mean you could see if it was just the guy or just the wife. But both of them, and the kid, too . . ."

"Prob'ly just decided to do a little more vacationin' 'fore winter sets in."

"Probably so," sighed the policeman.

"You oughtta talk to Chief Connelly about 'em. He was right outside a minute ago."

"That's my next stop. Well, thanks for your time, Abner. I don't need to tell you where to get in touch with me if you hear anything."

"Nope, you don't need to do that, Kenny."

The tall policeman started for the door. Then he stopped and turned. "Oh, by the way, I see someone's living in the old captain's house."

Nancy stiffened, alert to the new line of questioning.

"Yup," said Abner.

"You know who it is?"

"Friend of the owner, I guess. City fella."

"Know his name?

"Name's Allen. Harrison Allen. Least that's how his mail comes addressed to him."

"He okay?"

Abner smiled warmly, "Yup, for a city fella." He turned his smile to Nancy, and it broadened. "Ain't that right, Miss Nancy Wells?"

The policeman nodded to Abner, tipped his hat to Nancy, and left the store.

Abner, all at once remembering the mail in his hand, grinned sheepishly. "Oh, gosh, I'm sorry. Sometimes mail delivery's kinda slow in these islands."

3

The pickup bumped heavily over the worn and stony footpath. The up-down motion made Cliff belch. He hit the break and came to a full stop in order to take a pull from the bottle. This was one time he couldn't drink while driving.

After another belch, he resumed motion, inching along at fewer miles per hour than his speedometer could measure. The load of firewood was extremely heavy; there was over half a cord back there. Surely it weighed more than a ton. He was unusually cautious, not wanting to further damage his exhaust system or suspension.

Cliff never thought that he might be drunk. Drinking, he figured, was just a part of the routine of life. He was either feeling good, or he wasn't, and if he wasn't, a few beers would make him feel better. He wanted to be sure he was feeling very good for today's business.

Everyone knew about Cliff's drinking, and everyone at the quarry knew that he drank on the job. He wasn't the only one, either. Of course, all the guys had sense enough not to drink in front of the safety inspectors, and the safety inspectors knew better than to check covertly for workers drinking on the job. It was what Cliff called a balance of power. But all that didn't matter today because Cliff was skipping work.

As he stopped the truck for another swig, he thought of Abner Mott. The storekeeper often joked that Cliff's beer purchases kept the general store in business. And Cliff would surely put him out of business if he ever decided to cash in all his empties at the same time.

The bouncing pickup approached Abigail Snowdon's cottage. This time, Cliff calculated, about a year had passed since he'd been here. Yet the place never seemed to change between visits.

The ancient, weathered fence surrounding the yard had lost a few more pickets. Some sections leaned so far forward that it appeared the next heavy snowfall would drive them all the way to the ground. But year after year they never seemed to fall.

In the center of the fenced-in yard stood the tiny cottage. Like many buildings on the island, it was built partly of stone, partly of wood. Although constructed long before the days of energy conservation, an old-time sense of practical design demanded low ceilings, with small rooms that would heat easily, completely, and comfortably.

The porch was made from pine logs that had once stood as trees nearby. The tarpaper roof was patched with sheet metal. The chimney protruding through it was missing a few bricks and leaned dangerously to one side.

Chickens roamed freely in the yard. Pieces of ramshackle wood furniture leaned long unused against the weathered fence.

Jabez Snowdon, the woman's idiot son, stood alone beside the porch, watching the oncoming truck. More than anything else, he looked like a scarecrow standing motionless in a field. His long stringy hair was like yellow straw, and his dark, ill-fitting clothing made him look as if he were pieced together from cast-off garments, hay, and worthless pieces of junk.

Cliff backed the truck up against the fence. He adjusted his knitted toque and got out.

"'Lo, Jabe. Wanna help me take down this section of fence, so I can back the truck right up the shed?"

Jabez remained still as a scarecrow. He blinked a couple of times and looked bewildered.

The cottage door—made of three wide planks—opened, and Mrs. Snowdon came out on to the porch. She was a strikingly tall woman, slightly bent at the shoulders, with thick gray hair worn straight and long. She wore a dull red handkerchief—Cliff thought it was called a babushka—over her head and knotted below her square chin. The cloth framed a pale, wrinkled face. Her eyes were severe, her lips a tense, straight line. She was clothed in a faded denim barn jacket, with a long woolen skirt that fell well below her knees. Instead of stockings, she had cloth tied around her legs, apparently for warmth. The pieces extended from

above her hemline to the tops of her leather boots. She was wearing gloves.

Her eyes met Cliff's, but neither spoke; then her gaze swept
across the yard until it locked on her son. It seemed to animate him.

Jabez shuddered to life and walked over to the fence. The two
men removed an eight-foot section so that Cliff could back the
load of wood all the way to the shed for stacking. Without utter-
ing a word, Mrs. Snowdon returned to the house.

Cliff thought about the old woman as he and Jabez labored
silently, stacking the lengths of hardwood. Mrs. Snowdon must
have been quite a looker in her day. Her height, her bearing, the
thick head of hair all spoke of an elegant youth.

Cliff had no idea of how old Mrs. Snowdon might be. She had
been exactly as she was now for as long as Cliff could remember.
He recalled tales he had overheard as a child while he was supposed to be asleep. His father and his father's friends, warmed by
a snug wood fire and homemade applejack, had discussed how in
the old days a strange, wild woman ran naked among the pines.
The men of the village would abandon their hunting and trap lines
to follow the mystical sound of her song.

Could that woman have been Mrs. Snowdon?

Perhaps, but she was old now. Men didn't notice her in the way
they once had. She lived a lonely, modest life. Folks helped her
with the things she and Jabez couldn't manage on their own. No
one considered it a charity, for she was known to do favors for the
islanders as well—favors that were never discussed, even among
the closest of friends.

As they finished the last of the stacking, Cliff finished the last of
a six-pack. When he tossed the bottle into the back of the track, he
noticed that Mrs. Snowdon was standing beside him.

Cliff found himself looking into her strangely youthful eyes.
Suddenly the feeling was upon him, the feeling that he could be
nothing but honest with her. Even so, asking was difficult. He had
never asked for anything before. It was hard for him to put his
jumbled thoughts into words. How would he begin?

She looked at him patiently, her lake-clear eyes peering into his.

Like twin headlight beams, they seemed to penetrate the blackness inside his skull, searching around inside, trying to help him find the words he needed.

Then her eyes drew the words from him.

"It's that . . . it's that new schoolteacher, Mother Snowdon," he began. "If I could only—"

"I know," said the old woman. She removed her gloves and rested two scratchy forefingers against his trembling lips. "You must tell me in another way."

Cliff inhaled deeply when she took her hand away. His eyes never left hers. Tentatively, he leaned a bit forward, pressing his lips together as he moved.

"Yes," the old woman commanded, "kiss me."

He felt like a small boy bestowing an obligatory peck on the lips of an aging and unfamiliar aunt. Now Cliff understood completely. He took her in his arms, closing his eyes tightly as their faces moved closer together. He found the scent of wood fire in her clothing and hair; the smell of ginger was on her breath.

As they kissed, Cliff was aware of the rough feel of her dry lips, the coarse texture of her denim coat. He held his breath for the duration of the kiss, thinking of stacked wood, the last swallow of beer, the safety inspectors, anything but the feel of the old woman and the odd sensation of her bony hand on his prick.

He closed his eyes tightly, praying to God in heaven that he would in no way betray the surprise and the disgust he was experiencing as his member swelled and grew hard in her hand.

"You may do what you want," she said. "Now go home. Jabez will fix the fence."

"But the schoolteacher—?"

"I said go home."

4

Harrison Allen looked approvingly at the newly installed telephone. He couldn't believe it. Service was so quick up here. He'd

ordered it Monday morning, and today—Wednesday—he had a
phone!

Now he wanted to try it out. But who should he call?

Maybe Mark in Burlington? Maybe he should contact some
local folks about his monster hunting?

Or maybe Nancy. After all, it was because of Nancy that he'd
wanted a phone in the first place.

He picked up the black receiver and put it to his ear. The sooth-
ing hum of the dial tone was oddly comforting. It meant he was in
better contact with the rest of the world—he was safer.

But at the same time he resisted that nagging feeling that he
had sold out, that having a phone somehow complicated his life,
violating the pact he had made with himself to simplify everything.

He took Mark Chittenden's phone number from his wallet.
Slowly he dialed the first three digits, then, one—six—three—
four.

"Just remember the Battle of 1634," Mark had told him.

"Which battle was that?"

"See, you've forgotten already."

Bizzbit-bizzbit-bizzbit. Busy signal. Harrison hung up.

Was it too early to phone Nancy? Maybe he should wait until
eight o'clock, or at least seven-thirty.

He looked at his watch. Nine o'clock! My God, where had the
time gone?

He glanced at the dark glass of the window. Probably it was *too
late* to call her. She might be in bed. Tomorrow was a school day.
Surely it would be better to wait till then. He could drop by after
school just to say hello.

Automatically he reached for the bottle of bourbon that was on
the table near his easy chair. *No,* he thought, pushing the bottle
aside so he could reach a piece of paper instead.

Stretching comfortably, he began to compose a list of people
he wanted to interview about the monster:

1. Abner Mott
2. Oliver Ransom's son

3. Prof. Hathaway

4. Chief Connelly

He had never met Mr. Connelly, but the chief's name came up frequently in conversations.

Harrison thought for a long while, but couldn't summon another name. What about the old woman Professor Hathaway had mentioned—the one who lived on the other side of the marsh? What was her name?

He was surprised at how few people he knew on the island. He'd remember to ask for additional names whenever he interviewed someone.

And probably he could get more names from Mark, too. *By God, I will call him,* he decided, rising with great determination to return to the phone.

Then he heard a noise.

It was low and faint, almost like a scratching. Was it coming from overhead? As he slowly looked up, the sound's position changed, expanded until it seemed to come from all around him. He turned his head rapidly from side to side; his eyes explored frantically.

He felt hot and found that he was sweating.

The sound continued, growing in definition, now guttural and bass, but alternating with whines of a higher frequency. It was like some faraway miserable thing moaning, sobbing with anguish.

Frozen and tight-muscled, Harrison listened. An animal maybe? Some kind of owl?

Was it *in* the house, or outside?

It was impossible to tell.

He listened intently, trying to be sure.

God, it was upstairs!

Upstairs, where no sound should have been. He knew very well that nothing was up there. Rats or squirrels could get in, sure, but they couldn't make a sound like that.

The resonant bass, like a growl, and shrill keening tones in counterpoint wove in and out of his hearing. They gathered in volume, weaving a fabric of cacophonous discomfort, building to a horrific wail that was distant yet frighteningly near. The sound *was* in the house, yet reason told him that it couldn't be.

Was it an animal? Could it be human? What in God's name was it?

With the speculation, more icy sweat exploded from Harrison's forehead and underarms. The hair on the back of his neck stood up and prickled. Within his chest, his heart pounded like a caged and terrified animal trying to get free.

THERE'S SOMETHING IN THE HOUSE!

Slowly he turned his head before he dared to move his body. His eyes sought every corner of the room. He couldn't tell what he was going to do.

Would he investigate?

Or run?

As he took fearful step forward, the impact of his shoe on the wooden floor seemed impossibly loud.

And the sound was gone.

Again he listened, his ears straining against the stillness. If there really was something in the house, he had to find out what it was before he could hope to sleep.

Doubt returned. Had it really been in the house? Now, in the tense silence, he just couldn't tell. It might have been outside, and a long way off. Sounds carry strangely at night, he reminded himself. Sure, he was a long way from the lake, but on certain nights he could hear the waves as if they were in his dooryard.

Then again, maybe the sound had come from something on the roof. It could have been some small animal, the sounds of which were amplified by the attic and the empty rooms above.

He took his flashlight, then found a heavy stick from the woodpile near the stove. He hefted it. It was sturdy, potentially menacing, solid as stone.

With light and weapon Harrison began his slow climb up the stairs.

For some reason, he was sure there would be nothing there. Denial, maybe, but the thought gave him confidence. Some of his fear drained from him like liquid.

Harrison patrolled the second floor, looking around door frames, poking behind pieces of furniture, opening closets. There was nothing. Nothing.

He even climbed the stairs to the chill, empty attic, just to make his search complete. All the time, his heavy stick was raised and ready for attack.

There could be no doubt that Harrison was alone in the house.

All was silent now. His fear, like the sound, was entirely gone.

But he couldn't doubt himself for a moment. He *had* heard it, whatever it was. Those brooding low rumbles, the piercing wails, the ugly, sad cadence that sounded . . . he had it now! It had sounded almost like sobbing.

Yes, impossibly, it was the grotesquely distorted sound of a woman sobbing.

He hurried down the stairs. Before he had time to feel foolish about what he was about to say, he made the first call on his new telephone.

Professor Hathaway answered on the third ring.

"Tell me, Professor," Harrison asked, "does your knowledge of local legends include anything about my house being haunted?"

Visits

10

I

On Thursday, Cliff labored full-time just to keep busy; it was the only way he could keep his mind off things.

He'd gone to work and put in a full day at the quarry. At 4:30 he'd received his layoff notice, as he'd expected. It was just as well, too. Lately his attention was rarely on what he was doing.

He passed the evening reloading shotgun shells and, as always, drinking. Still, time seemed to move way too slowly. As the hour got later, it became increasingly difficult to concentrate on the tasks in front of him. He quit when he realized he'd loaded the last seven shells without putting in the powder.

His irritation peaked when he looked at the clock. The general store was already closed and he was down to his last six-pack of Bud. No chance of getting more till tomorrow.

His problem was that he couldn't get the schoolteacher out of his mind. Since the very first time he'd laid eyes on her, his attention had been riveted to her like sheet metal on the side of his pickup. She was a fixation. Not since he was a boy had he experienced such a disabling infatuation.

To Cliff, she was the equal of any of the girls whose

air-brushed forms decorated the collection of magazines he kept under his bed. Simply thinking of her produced the same reaction as did his stroke books.

He cupped his hands tightly over the ballooning mound at the front of his Levi's.

She was definitely the best thing he had ever seen on the island. He sighed at the thought of the explosive energy he could generate if she were writhing beneath him in his sleeping bag. By God, he'd give her something to remember, better than anything she ever got from any of those la-dee-da city fellas, with their stupid alligator shirts and pussy Perrier water.

Cliff bit his lower lip as he imagined her bare, erect nipples, hard but yielding, between his lips. Gently, he tugged his lower lip with his teeth, thinking of Nancy.

He pictured her round, tight ass, firm enough to crack an egg on.

His hand massaged the front of his pants, gathering and releasing his erect member beneath the tight, smooth denim.

"JESUS!" he cried, his voice harsh with frustration. His right hand tore away from his groin and smashed against the tabletop. Several dozen freshly loaded shells quivered and toppled. His last beer tumbled to its side and dribbled onto the floor, where it frothed like a puddle of semen.

He tried to recall exactly what Mrs. Snowdon had said to him. But what he remembered, he couldn't understand. He had confided his wish to her, and she had sent him home abruptly, without hearing him out. She had acted like some . . . some mother stopping her child from saying what she did not want to hear, trying to halt the discussion of an unsavory topic.

And she'd made him kiss her—that he remembered with embarrassing clarity. Her dry old lips had felt like sandpaper. And she had touched his pecker! Christ! Just a goddamn frustrated old whore, that's all she was!

Yet somehow—and this was very strange—ever since she took her hand away, his groin had tingled with fantastic electrical prickles of pleasure.

It was weird: Every time he thought of Mrs. Snowdon, his longing for the schoolteacher increased, and so did the throbbing in his pants.

Cliff had never before asked the old woman for a favor. In fact, he had pretty much avoided her, rarely offering anything more than a simple hello. Probably he should have held his tongue this time. Maybe it was not a proper topic to bring up with her. Christ, she hadn't even let him finish what he had to say!

"You may do what you want," she had said. Then she told him to go home.

What the fuck was that supposed to mean?

"God*damn* it!" he roared, slamming the table again. "Why the fuck should I do her any goddamn favors? Bring her goddamn wood year after year, patch her fuckin' roof. Why?"

He downed what was left of his beer and stood up.

"If I want somethin' bad enough, why, Christ, I gotta go right out and get it myself." Frenzied with purpose, he charged out the front door, slamming it behind him. He bolted toward his pickup truck. All his muscles were as tight as the steel cables on the quarry's cranes. Turning the ignition key, the engine sputtered, farted, then backfired like a rifle shot.

"FUCK!"

He tried the key again. Nothing.

"SHIT!" He roared, "SHIT, SHIT, SHIT!" He emphasized each expletive by pounding the dash. Tears of rage welled in his eyes. He swatted them away, embarrassed though completely alone.

He vaulted out, and threw open the hood.

Too dark to see a Christly thing. Maybe the rotor or a cracked coil. Back into the driver's seat again. He twisted the key, letting the starter work until the battery lost its charge. He listened helplessly as the starter motor groaned to a defeated silence.

Cliff abandoned the truck, leaving its door wide open, and stomped, tense and furious, into the night.

2

Professor Hathaway, dressed in a brown cardigan sweater and bow tie, brought out a bottle of Rémy Martin and poured a bit into two snifters. He had lost none of the animation that Harrison remembered from the previous visit. His eyes twinkled, his gestures were broad and theatrical. In fact, Harrison thought the professor's general enthusiasm seemed heightened by a kind of agitation. Repeatedly he ran his fingers through tufts of white hair, making them stand out eccentrically on the sides of his head.

"Oh, yes, I've heard many stories about your house, Harrison," he said, "but none suggesting that it might be haunted. There's the treasure-map story, of course. That one seems to have persisted a good long time. Frankly, I don't believe there's anything to it, but I must admit that it holds a certain fascination. The most seductive thing about such a tale, of course, is that it can never be proven false, at least not as long as there is one floorboard left undisturbed or one hearthstone left unturned.

"Historically, it does seem to be a fact that the place was built by a sea captain. And of course, among the fanciful, where there are men of the sea there must also be hidden treasure. So if we assume there's treasure, I suppose it isn't too ambitious a stretch of the imagination to think that the ghost of the old salt walks by night to guard his hidden loot."

The professor chuckled.

"But it really didn't sound like a sailor to me," said Harrison. "It sounded more than anything like a woman. A woman sobbing."

The old man lifted his eyebrows. "That *is* very interesting." For a moment he stared, transfixed, at the liquid in his glass. He moved the snifter in circular motions, the cognac rising to thinly coat the inside of the delicate globe. "Wonderful piece of engineering, the brandy snifter. Allows one to focus and savor the intoxicating fumes of the liquid before sampling its flavor. The hand warms the glass, you see, and the film of brandy evaporates—"

"But then, I really can't be sure I know just what I heard,"

Harrison persisted. "It *did* sound like a woman, but I can't be sure. At least you believe I heard something, don't you?"

"Oh, yes. Yes, I do. Of course." The professor looked up from his glass. "But let me tell you something, Harrison. When I was a much younger man, I became interested in magic. Not the occult ghosts-and-demons variety, but magic as a hobby, sleight-of-hand, parlor tricks with cards and coins, that kind of thing. What I learned then is still very much with me today: What we see and hear may not actually be what we see and hear."

Harrison blinked, confused. "What do you mean?"

"I mean you heard something that sounded like a woman sobbing. You heard it in what you proved — at least to your own satisfaction — to be an empty house. So the question is: What could there be in an old, creaky, long-deserted house that could make you think you heard a woman crying?"

"I've already thought about that," said Harrison. He knew he was beginning to sound defensive. "Boards groaning as the house settles, rats in the walls, wind in the attic, air in the pipes, stuff like that. I'm not an alarmist, Professor Hathaway. I tried to consider all possible rational explanations."

"And once you've eliminated the rational, what's left? It's like looking for that monster of yours, isn't it? If people are not seeing floating logs or a parade of beavers, the question becomes: What else can it be?"

"What do you think I should do, Professor?"

"Do? Nothing. Listen for it again. Take another crack at identifying it. You may hear it a second time, who knows."

Harrison felt a trifle diminished by the professor's skeptical, oddly unsympathetic demeanor. He stared sullenly into his glass, then took a sip, his eyes never leaving the surface of the brandy.

"Now look, my boy, don't be offended. I'm sorry I haven't any answers for you, but please be sure that I am very interested in your story. In fact, I'd willingly help you listen for a reoccurrence, if you like. But you'll have to agree that we must observe a bit more before we can make an identification. Maybe we should start by trying to learn more about the history of the house. Maybe there have been women there in the past, maybe women who died there. Such a woman would be a likely candidate for a haunting, don't you think?

"You see, in reality I don't know a great deal about that particular building. It's not your house so much as its position on the island that has interested me tremendously for a long time. Did you ever notice that it is the southernmost inhabitable structure on the island, while the old monastery is the northernmost?"

"Ah, I . . . never stopped to think about it," said Harrison with an involuntary chuckle. He didn't see the relevance of this observation.

"Well, I've thought about it," continued the professor, "But I must admit I'm not quite sure what to make of it . . ."

As the old man's voice trailed off, a sudden seriousness passed over him, transforming his sparkle-eyed congeniality into a hypnotic earnestness. "Look, Harrison, we both have an interest in this island. You are looking for—I don't know what—some kind of alternative, maybe? Or literary inspiration? Perhaps a book or article on an unknown species? Scientific recognition? Escape? Isolation? Whatever. I don't know for sure, and, frankly, it's none of my business.

"I, on the other hand, am looking for historical significance. That," he chuckled, "and a peaceful retirement."

Harrison nodded, trying to follow.

"But whether it's literary inspiration of historical documentation, there is an abundance of both buried in the folklore and legends of this place. Be that as it may, there's one thing you must always keep in mind: Friar's Island is by no means a typical Vermont town. It is enigmatic. A world unto itself.

"The people here are . . . different. They are not the rock-ribbed, able-bodied Yankees of a thousand clever anecdotes. They are standoffish couples, or they are loners like you and me and our friend Miss Wells. There is no real society on the island. People are content—possibly even trapped—within themselves. That is the one thing that has made historical research so damnably difficult."

"What are you trying to tell me, Professor? To mind my own business?"

The old man smiled amiably, looking Harrison in the eye. "Not so much that," he said. "More, I think, just to be careful of what you say, and to whom. Be careful what you ask. If you plan to live here and to fit in as comfortably as possible, don't give certain of these folks the impression that you're nosy or a meddler. Your sobbing woman, and your lake monster—these are things folks would just as soon not talk about."

"For Heaven's sake, why? They can't be that tight-lipped, can they?"

"Yes, indeed. I found that out the hard way." The professor sipped his brandy. "Ever since I retired and bought this place, I've been interested in the old monastery on the northern cliffs of the island. I am also interested in the spiritualists who were the last people to live there. But perhaps most of all, I'm curious about why no one at all has lived there since.

"You know, of course, that a few years ago some summer folks wanted to promote and capitalize on the island's tourist appeal. They wanted to restore the old place as kind of a resort hotel. The plans were forgotten, and no one will say just why."

"What do you think happened?"

"To be truthful, I have no idea. The point is, I'm sure the developers got the same kind of cold shoulder that I got when I started asking questions about it.

"People here just do not want to talk about some of the very things we outsiders find so fascinating. That monastery is a perfect example. And the spiritualists are an especially taboo topic with the natives. No one will admit to knowing anything at all about the colony. But I believe at least one person still living on this island not only knows about the spiritualists, but may actually have been an active member of the group."

Harrison leaned forward in his seat. He felt his eyes widen. His thoughts scanned the elderly people he knew for suspects: Abner Mott, the old men at the general store, the retired policeman . . .

Professor Hathaway's voice grew more excited. "Perhaps the

individual in question was born right there in the monastery, perhaps never having left the island in seventy or eighty years. Not once!"

"Do you know who that person is?"

"Well, let's say I have a suspicion. If it is who I think it is, it will be almost impossible to get any information." The professor lit a cigar; Harrison began to fill his corncob. Pungent-smelling smoke quickly filled the book-lined room and both men fell into a contemplative silence.

Harrison wanted to ask who the professor suspected, but he held his tongue. The older man's mind-your-own-business lecture had made him cautious. If he waited, perhaps the professor would volunteer the information on his own. Instead, Harrison finally asked, "Did you learn all this from those papers you found at the historical society?"

"Pretty much, yes."

"What else did you learn from them?"

"That they are incomplete. The missing papers—if they still exist—may very well be in the possession of the person I believe was a member of the spiritualist group."

"What do you suppose you might learn from those papers?"

Professor Hathaway raised both eyebrows noncommittally and exhaled cigar smoke.

Harrison decided to press a little. "I mean those spiritualists must have been up to something pretty appalling if the locals won't even discuss it after what?—eighty or more years!" Harrison held the professor's gaze.

"I think you're right in concluding they were up to something a little out of the ordinary. For one thing, they apparently were not allied with any of the major branches of the spiritualist movement that were so conspicuous at the time. They wanted nothing to do with anyone or anything that might gain them publicity. That's why they chose to isolate themselves in this remote area. It's as if they had a secret that they didn't want to share, so they hid out up here.

"Lord, can you imagine how desolate this island must have

been in the eighteen-eighties and nineties? Certainly it's bad
enough now, but *then*! Heavens, it must have been like another
world. Remember, the intent of many groups at the time was to
draw attention to themselves. They wanted to recruit new members, not drop completely out of sight, as these people did. Our
group apparently strove to gain further isolation through certain
studies and rituals."

"What kind of rituals? Devil worship?"

"I don't think so, not exactly devil worship. I don't believe
God and the devil were especially important to these folks. This is
just conjecture, you understand, but my theory is that they were
seeking a kind of harmony with nature, a primitive, elemental kind
of harmony that we modern folks have completely lost sight of.
It was closer to witchcraft— *Wicca*, as they call it—than Satanism,
I believe. But it wasn't identical."

Harrison puffed his pipe as the professor continued.

"If I may rather simplistically discuss good and evil as "forces,"
for want of better terms, I postulate that they were seeking a spe-
cialized environment in which to operate, an environment that was
somehow insulated against these forces. Good and evil were concepts of no importance whatsoever to them, concepts that would
only get in their way. They wanted nothing at all to do with them.

"This island was reputed to be conducive to that insulating
effort. Possibly the earlier monks—or "Black Catholics," as they
were called—settled here and built the monastery for the same
reason. And possibly the belief system goes even farther back. As
I told you and Miss Wells, there is reason to believe that even
Indian legend held that this was a special—if not exactly evil—
place. Remember I told you that Indians never settled here? There
must have been some reason for that. We'll probably never know
for sure.

"And we'll probably never learn much more about the first
group of monks, either. But the spiritualist community—that is a
different story. If that survivor I mentioned is still on the island,
well—"

"I can see why you're so eager to find out about them," said

Harrison, his curiosity now thoroughly piqued. But he was growing impatient. It was as if the professor were being evasive, as if he
were not disclosing something important.

"Why, of course! Aren't you eager, too? I'm sure we agree that
it's fascinating. And you never know, Harrison, all this may somehow relate to the noises you heard in your house. One way of
looking at what you heard is that it may not—I say, *may* not—
be an entirely natural phenomenon. But it may not be a haunting,
either. Maybe the best way to investigate is not through direct
question and answer."

More confused than ever, Harrison had become convinced the
professor's circumlocution was a deliberate evading technique.
The old man, once so open and congenial, now seemed to be hiding something. "Wait a minute, Professor," Harrison said. "You're
saying the sounds in my house may be related to the spiritualists
who were in the old monastery a hundred years ago?"

Harrison knew he looked incredulous—*so what?* He helped
himself to some more cognac.

The professor cleared his throat. "The two could be related,
I don't know. I have my suspicions. Remember, if I'm correct,
we're investigating a system of beliefs that promises to be remark-
ably different from anything else on record. If I'm right, what those
people practiced does not conform to any cult or religion recorded
in the history of Europe and the New World. Think of it! Something totally occult, hidden, undiscovered. Why, we even need to
borrow a vocabulary to discuss it."

"Borrow a vocabulary? I don't follow."

"I'm sure the people at the monastery didn't speak of 'spiritualism,' or 'good and evil,' or the devil, or God, or anything like
that. They had their own self-contained belief system, and perhaps
their own unique vocabulary to discuss it. But as different, eccentric, and nonconforming as they were, suppose"—he held up a
finger—"just suppose they were actually onto something."

"Like . . . ?"

"Well, they were a small group and never became a formal
movement. Their total historical impact was either wholly unob-

served or simply too insignificant to be remembered. Keep in mind they didn't even recruit new members. When people dropped out or died, no new people were brought in. Their order didn't grow or renew itself. If there *is* one survivor, as I believe, then that person is the last of a kind."

Privacy be damned, Harrison thought, his patience exhausted. Struggling to sound casual, he asked, "Will you tell me who you believe that person is?" His pipe was out but remained clenched in his teeth.

Professor Hathaway looked at him as if pondering a life-or-death decision. At last he nodded. "I believe it is Mrs. Abigail Snowdon, your nearest neighbor."

3

Nancy sat at the kitchen table, correcting social studies quizzes from the day before. The class had been studying a unit on Vermont history, and so far the test scores were good. The kids found Ethan Allen and the Green Mountain Boys' takeover of Fort Ticonderoga almost as exciting as an episode of *MacGyver.*

With Vermont Public Radio playing in the background, Nancy tapped her red pencil in time with Dvorak's *New World Symphony*. From time to time she'd hum along.

Sometimes her mind would wander and she'd think of Harrison. What would it be like to be with a man on the island? When she had come here, she had actually planned to be lonely. She'd wanted to take a stand as an independent, high-principled loner, to gradually earn the respect of a community that still held education and learning in high esteem, a community that still showed old-fashioned respect for the local schoolteacher.

Being caught in—or merely suspected of—an indiscretion could quickly get her ostracized, labeled as unfit to teach the island's young. Her predecessor, Miss Deborah Swain, had recently died an old maid. During her tenure of forty-five years, Miss Swain had given the whole community a definite impression of what a schoolteacher should be. It was a tough act to follow, a difficult role model to live up to.

And there was something else on her mind, a dark thought that intruded from time to time. It had to do with the state policeman she had overheard talking to Abner Mott. Hadn't he asked Abner for a character reference on Harrison? Did that mean he suspected Harrison of something? What could Harrison possibly have to do with the disappearance of the Pelletier family?

No, damn it, she was just being suspicious, almost paranoid. Harrison was new on the island. Locals are always suspicious of newcomers. She'd experienced it herself.

And yet, what did she really know about Harrison? What was the real reason he'd come to the island? He had no job, no apparent source of income. Could his entire purpose be exactly what he stated: learning all he could about the Lake Champlain Monster?

Oh, come on, Nancy, Harrison's okay. You're just getting tired.

That was it. Sure, she was tired.

She stood up and stretched, thinking it might be a good idea to go to bed now. She would get up bright and early to finish the papers.

As she turned off the light over the kitchen table, she thought she saw motion at the window by the door. The curtain moving in a draft? The reflection of the swinging kitchen light?

Maybe she'd better lock up, just to be sure. Humming along with the FM, she crossed to the kitchen door just in time to hear a faint tapping on the other side.

Her first thought was of Harrison. Then, for some reason she thought of Eric.

Could Eric have found her?

She took the cold knob in her hand and started to turn it. Then she hesitated.

"Who is it?" she asked.

The answer exploded in an avalanche of sound and motion. The heavy door burst inward, thrust open from outside. The impact sent her reeling backward against the kitchen table.

She cried out in surprise.

A large, swaying shape stood framed in the doorway. Nancy's

frantic mind fought to recognize the man. He wore a woolen shirt, blue jeans, and a yellow hat.

Now his heavy work boots thundered on the wooden floor as he crossed the kitchen toward her.

The back of her right hand jerked to her mouth as she leaned away from him, cowering.

"Wha . . . what do you want?" Her voice was abnormally shrill.

The man reached out, grabbed her biceps with strong, hairy hands. Squeezing her hard, he pulled her face close to his. The smell of beer was strong on his breath. It assaulted her in short nauseating blasts as he panted. When he began to kiss her, violently, his wet lips slid across the skin of her face, his whiskers scratching painfully.

Wrenching free with a strength born of panic, Nancy darted behind the table, crying, "Get out of here, leave me alone!"

She wanted to scream, but she refused to show him her terror. Besides, she knew there was no one close enough to hear.

Yet her shrill voice and defensive posture seemed to animate him more. With one forceful motion, he upended the table, sending papers and pencils into the air and around the room.

Her protective barrier gone, Nancy bolted for the bedroom. If she could slam the door and lock it . . . If she could find something to hit him with . . . If she could run . . .

The man grunted obscenely, then quick-stepped after her as she made for the bedroom.

She heard a grating sound as a pencil spun under his boot. He lost his footing.

"Fuck!" he growled.

She glanced back, saw him down on one knee as she slammed the bedroom door and groped frantically for the lock.

Another crash.

She knew what the sound meant: The man had leaped at the door, kicked his heavy boot against the spot directly below the doorknob. With a deafening *crack*, the door sprang open as if it were the lid of a jack-in-the-box.

The man almost fell into the bedroom. Staggering, he tried to recover his balance. His head rolled maniacally from side to side as he searched for his prey.

Nancy closed her eyes. *God no, this just can't be happening.*

Cliff breathed deeply, more steadily now, and something in him relaxed.

He saw her there on the bed, lying provocatively on her back, long black hair spread like a fine silken cloth on the white pillow. In her eyes there was a distant, lost look. Like a little girl.

As he watched, he saw her eyes—half closed and dreamy— shut all the way. The firm mounds beneath her sweater rose and fell rhythmically as she panted, out of breath. Her hips gyrated sensuously, making slow hypnotic circles with her pelvis.

Caressingly, her hands explored her body, cupped her ample breasts, pushed them together, then moved on to find the vee of fabric at her neckline. With almost superhuman strength, she tore away the sweater, exposing chalk-white flesh and her dark, hard nipples.

Cliff watched, not believing. He panted, too, out of breath and excited. He felt his manhood pushing hard against the inside of his jeans. His privates sparkled with electricity.

His mind reeled with anticipation; this was his dream, his fantasy!

He approached her bed, arms extended like those of a sleep-walker. His fingers spread as they descended to her breast. His lips found the secret, deliciously scented pocket between her shoulder and graceful neck, where he kissed her wildly. His passion mounted as her undulating hips beckoned him to the magic spot between her thighs.

Wantonly, she wriggled and squirmed beneath him, thrusting her wild pelvis at his, forcing her breasts against his greedy, sweat-slick hands.

She spoke to him softly, in a strange yet familiar voice. She said, "You may do what you want."

"Now go home . . ." she said when it was over.

Keeping Watch   11

I

The morning air was as chill as a mountain stream. Bolts of bright sunlight, working their way from behind dense gray clouds, offered no real warmth.

The ink-black lake rose and fell, shooting icy tentacles across the sand and between the rocks near where Harrison sat. Behind him on the snow-covered ground, peaked shadows of pine trees were huge arrows pointing west.

His bottom felt cold, its warmth drained into his stone chair.

With elbows resting on his knees, he tried to steady the binoculars. Slowly, very slowly, back and forth, he scanned the surface of the water. He could see south, past Grand Isle State Park, all the way down to South Hero. There were no boats to obstruct his vision. Their owners, even the diehards, had taken them in for the winter.

The only movement was the tossing of the water and the twirling snowflakes that danced in the wind.

How badly Harrison wanted to see that sleek black head break the surface and look around at the earth and sky. In his mind he had seen it clearly many times, but in reality the lake remained like an empty movie screen.

The play of the sun on the water, reflecting like millions of tiny mirrors, had a hypnotic effect. Harrison forgot about the cold, the hard rock, and his general discomfort.

Instead, he concentrated on the ever-changing patterns of light and dark revealed in the limited panorama of his binoculars.

"Whatcha lookin' at?" The gravelly voice, thick with mucus, came from behind him.

Harrison jumped. He jerked the glasses from his eyes and whirled around. The half-silhouetted face of an elderly man was interposed between Harrison's eyes and the bright morning sun.

"You scared me," Harrison said with a smile.

"Didn't mean to sneak up on ya. Kinda hard to hear, so close to the water."

The old man walked over and sat on a rock beside Harrison.

"Name's Connelly. Lawrence Connelly."

"Chief Connelly!" Harrison readily recognized the name if not the man. "I'm Harrison Allen. I've been hoping to meet you."

"Well, I'm happy to meet you, Mr. Allen. Always happy to meet a man who's brave enough to tackle a winter up here. Most people hightail it back where they came from 'fore November sets in. Summer folks. I hear you come to stay."

"For a while anyway. And please, call me Harry."

"And you can call me Chief; that is, if you've a mind to. Most people do around here. 'Course I gotta tell you, it ain't an official title no more. I'm retired. But most folks got used to it, and I sorta like the way it sounds."

The two men shook hands. Harrison noted the old man's firm grip.

"Mind tellin' me why you been hopin' to meet me, Harry?"

"Not at all. Mark Chittenden, the guy who owns the house I'm living in, suggested you as one of the people I should talk to. I'm a member of the American Cryptozoological Society. I'm here doing research on the Lake Champlain Monster. As a matter of fact, I'm on a monster watch right now."

"And what is this . . . cryptozoology?" Chief Connelly pronounced the word with great care, but Harrison didn't miss how skillfully he'd converted it from an adjective to a noun.

"Essentially, we investigate the zoology that's unknown to sci-ence. We look for mysterious animals that are often reported but never captured or cataloged: the yeti, the Loch Ness Monster, reports of a living dinosaur in Africa, that kind of thing. I consider myself lucky to have a monster right here in the neighborhood. Saves traveling to Scotland or Africa."

Without smiling, the chief stared silently out at the water, arms folded tightly across his chest. After a while he said, "You think there's somethin' out there, do you?"

"A lot of people do. There's a photograph —"

"You seen it yet?"

"The photograph?"

"Hell, no, the monster."

"No, I—"

"I figgered not." The chief took a breath. He coughed wetly. "Ever think you might be wastin' your time?"

"I've wasted a lot of time in my life."

"I s'pose you have." The old man looked Harrison full in the face. "So, what'd you want to meet me for?"

"To ask you if you've ever seen it. To see if you know anybody who has."

Chief Connelly took a bent Camel from a partially crushed pack. He lit it skillfully, shielding the flame of the match from the wind. After taking two or three long drags, he flicked a good half of it out into the water, where it disappeared.

"It's nothin' we like to talk about, Mr. Allen. It's fanciful talk. We're practical people up here. Down to earth. We got no time to chase no monsters. If there's somethin' out there, let it be, I say. If it ain't a threat to us, and if we can't catch it and eat it, I got no interest in it at all."

"You've never seen it?"

"I seen some mighty big eel. I seen a catfish the size of a dog. I'd say a fish that size is a monster."

"Do you know anyone who's seen it?"

"That ain't the sort of question I'd feel at liberty to ask, Mr. Allen."

Harrison felt a chill that was more than the cold in the air. He knew it would not be wise to press the old man for more information.

The chief took another Camel and lit it with the same practiced skill. This time he just took one deep drag before flicking it out to sea.

"I'm tryin' to quit," he said.

2

The children had been excited all day. It had a good deal to do with its being Friday, but more to do with the season's first snow-fall. Beginning that morning, big lazy snowflakes had drifted past the classroom windows like sailboats on the lake. At recess kids teamed up for snowball fights, and laughing boys washed the enraged faces of squealing girls. No one's mind was on lessons.

Nancy had felt unusually tired all day. She thought maybe she was coming down with something, a cold or the flu. Then, too, she was a little angry at herself; it had taken until this afternoon to return the quizzes to the kids. She was so late that she'd had to finish correcting them during afternoon break so she could pass them out before the kids went home. But there hadn't been that many quizzes to grade; there was no good reason why she hadn't done them.

She didn't want to be compulsive, but she had promised herself time and time again that she would be professionally responsible about her job. She had to discipline herself. This was her *career*, for Christ's sake! It wasn't like college, where she could cram all night for a test, or finish a paper thirty minutes before it was due.

Why hadn't she finished correcting them at home? That's what was really bothering her. She could clearly remember working on them . . . But then what? Had she dozed off? She couldn't recall getting into bed.

She remembered waking up this morning late, feeling exhausted and suffering from a headache she just couldn't believe. That's when she first suspected she might be coming down with something.

She was *sure* something was wrong the moment she had walked out of the bedroom to see the table overturned and papers all over the kitchen floor.

Had she been sleepwalking last night? She must have been; how else could she have gotten into bed? But God, she hadn't sleepwalked since she was a kid. Their old family doctor had assured Mom and Nancy that the sleepwalking would end because —finally—she had accepted her father's death. She no longer needed to search for him at night.

So now, according to the doctor, Nancy was supposed to rest easy and well.

But she didn't feel rested. She had been tired all day long. More than tired, actually; she felt sick, and that bothered her. The late test papers bothered her. And the mess in the kitchen, frankly, scared the hell out of her.

Maybe someone had broken in during the night and ransacked the place. No—she would have heard it. No one could have knocked the table over without waking her.

So what happened? And how did she get to bed?

She held back tears long enough to dismiss her young charges, feeling some minor relief as she watched them scramble out the door. Then, finally alone, she put her head in her hands and began to cry.

She knew what the trouble was. Really, she had known all along. But any explanation—sleepwalking, an intruder, *anything* —would have been preferable.

The epilepsy had come back.

After so many years, she'd had another seizure.

Why? Why now, when things were going so well?

Nancy sobbed a little harder, having admitted why she'd felt so terrible all day . . .

. . . and why the table was knocked over . . .

. . . and why she had black-and-blue marks all over her body.

She knew why.

She had known all along.

Visions of Nowhere   12

I

Every time there was a lull in the conversation, the two men looked up at the big front window of the general store. They watched the snowstorm. A profusion of downy white flakes danced magically beneath the store's exterior lamps.

It was already dark outside, and Abner was tired, eager to get home. He knew there would be no more customers on a stormy afternoon like this, but he didn't want to give the impression that he was in a hurry.

Abner picked up his black-handled knife and sliced about a quarter of a pound of Cabot cheddar from the partial wheel to his left.

He put the cheese on a piece of waxed paper and set it on the counter between himself and Chief Connelly. They broke off tiny chunks from time to time, and munched thoughtfully.

"Y'ever hear any more on them Pelletier folks?" asked Abner, using the nail of his little finger to remove a morsel of pasty cheese from his dentures.

"Nope," answered the chief, pushing his Stetson back on his head. "State boys figure they got off the island okay. Nobody knows what happened to 'em after that. I nosed around over to their place myself. Everything's A-okay."

"You talk to that fella from the captain's place? That Harrison Allen?"

"A-yuh. Just this mornin'. He's no problem."

"What's he *really* doin' here, he say?"

"Says he's lookin' for the Lake Champlain Monster."

"Shit. You believe him?"

"Sorta." Chief Connelly took another fragment of cheese. "I think he's a man's got a problem. I don't think it's got nothin' to do with us, though. Don't think it's got nothing to do with the monster, neither."

Abner sniffed, feeling a cold coming on. "Christ, we git all kinds up here, don't we?"

"Always did. Bad enough worryin' about the summer folks. Now it's monster hunters and schoolteachers."

"They're gettin' kinda lovey-dovey, ain't they?"

"Wouldn't surprise me. One comes here lookin' for the simple life, the other lookin' for God knows what."

"How long you s'pect it'll take 'em to realize life ain't so god-damn simple up here?"

"Couldn't say. I jes' hope he don't see nothin'."

"What d'ya mean?"

"Well, if he sees that eel, or whatever the hell it is, swimmin' around out there, he'll wanna tell everybody an' his brother."

"Yeah, right. And we'll have a whole gaggle of monster hunters nosin' around here." Abner wadded up the waxed paper and placed it in the trash bin under the counter. "Well, at least it'll be good for business."

"That kind of trade you don't need, Abner."

"None of us do, Chief. None of us do."

2

Nancy lifted her head off the desk and sat straight up. She bent her neck way back until she was looking at the ceiling. Stretching, arms extended to the sides, she took a deep breath, then wiped the few remaining tears away with her fingertips.

She would have to see a doctor. There was no way around it. And that would mean arranging for a substitute teacher, not an easy—

God, what if I have a seizure in front of the class? Or while driving?

There was no time to lose; she had to get a checkup right away.

Oh Lord, what am I going to do?

Maybe she should talk to Harrison. Head over there right now. She could ask him to drive her to see a neurologist in Burlington. True, she didn't know Harrison all that well, but he was the only person on the island she felt close to.

But suppose the epilepsy scares him off.

No. Not likely. It was her childhood fears again. Yet something made her hesitate. Something about Harrison troubled her. Uncertainty had been tugging at the back of her mind for some time now.

It had something to do with that state policeman. When she'd heard him ask Abner Mott about Harrison, she'd realized how little she knew of him.

Was that it? Was she suspicious of him? Had the policeman's interest made her doubt her new friend?

"He okay?" That's all the trooper had asked.

"He okay?" Not really enough to undermine her trust.

And Abner had replied, "Yup, for a city fella." Then—and this was the strange part—"Ain't that right, Miss Nancy Wells?"

Damn. That's it! Abner's remark had been a friendly one, sure, but how had he known? How had Abner known there was a connection between her and Harrison? There was no way for him to have known.

But he knew.

That's silly, she thought. It had been nothing more than an offhand remark, just a way of acknowledging her, including her in the conversation.

God, I'm tired. She sighed heavily. *Tired and getting paranoid. Must be I'm getting my period. That's all I need right now! Best thing to do is go home and take a nap.*

Nancy began gathering her papers and books. She piled them neatly on the corner of her desk, rested her elbows on its surface, and looked around the empty classroom. The place smelled of new desktop varnish and wet woolen clothing.

Thank God it was the weekend; she could use the rest. But what about their plans? She was supposed to meet Harrison tomorrow to explore the old monastery. That would be fun and adventurous, yet now there was a certain dread in the anticipation.

Come on, Nancy, get to the point.

Was she going to get *involved* with him? That was the big question.

Nancy knew herself well enough to realize what she was avoiding. She *liked* Harrison; that much was easy. He was interesting and kind and humorous, just like a big kid.

So why avoid him? A day together would certainly decide if they were going to get any more involved. Such a day would probably be the best thing in the world for her; it would get her mind off less pleasant topics. It would be fun.

Involved—what a stupid word. Was she going to sleep with him? That was really the question. She had practically promised him that she would. Somehow, on a gut level, she knew just what the answer would be.

When the door started to open slowly, it startled her, reminded her that she was still at school. Who could be coming in when it was time to go home?

Nancy looked up, smiling, expecting to see that Harrison had dropped by to pick her up. Instead, she saw an unfamiliar man standing in the doorway, looking around the room. His long yellow hair was wet with snow. He shook his head like a dog, as if trying to dry it by throwing off the moisture.

His old gray overcoat hung almost to the floor. It must have been a very long coat, because he was a very tall man.

There was a vacant, fixed look on his ruddy face as he gawked around. Nancy felt cold air rushing past him from the open door. It carried an odd, earthy smell to her nostrils.

She knew better than to show that she was alarmed. But fear

seized her when she realized who he was. She had always heard he was harmless. Profoundly retarded, yes, but not dangerous.

"Why don't you close the door," she asked, with as good-natured a voice as she could muster. This was her turf; she felt that she should be in control.

He stared blankly at her, blinked once, and slowly pulled the door closed behind him. He moved awkwardly, almost stumbling, as he began to pace around the room. His head moved up and down as if on a string, as he looked not only at the pictures on the walls but, seemingly, at the walls themselves.

"May I help you?" Nancy asked. Right away she felt it was a stupid thing to say.

His attention turned slowly from the wall until he was staring directly at her. He blinked again.

"I'm Miss Wells," Nancy said. "I'm the schoolteacher. Can you tell me your name?"

The answer seemed to start with a crackle way down in his chest. It scraped its way up his throat, until finally it burst forth as a poorly articulated growl, "I yust ta go ta school here."

Looking around again, he surveyed the circle of desks in apparent bewilderment. He walked around them, examining each one closely.

Finally he settled on one, and he pushed it nearly to the center of the room, facing front. Then he sat in it. Nancy had to suppress a laugh as he tried to fold more than six feet of himself into the child's desk.

"This here's whar I set," he informed her.

Nancy stepped in front of him, standing beside her own desk. Her fingertips rested on her desktop. "Can you tell me your name?" she asked again with a practiced professional patience.

"Jay-biz," he answered.

"Jabez what?"

"I don' loik school."

Nancy smiled. "Sometimes I can't blame you. Nobody likes it all the time. Not even the teacher. Especially when it's snowing out and it's Friday." She felt as if she were talking to a child.

"I never loik it."

"If you don't like it, why did you come back?"

They looked at each other for a long while. This time he didn't blink at all. His strange, fixed stare began to frighten her; she feared what his answer might be.

Nancy wasn't sure what to say to him. Her mind raced to find conversation. Thinking only prolonged the silence. She moved behind her desk, where she felt at least somewhat protected, and sat down.

Jabez stood up and walked over to her. His blank, staring eyes never left hers. As the distance between them diminished, she became acutely aware that it was only the wooden barrier of her desk that separated them.

Suddenly he was like a big, clumsy schoolboy standing penitently before the teacher. She looked up at him, trying to find some hint in his vacant eyes of what he had on his mind.

Nancy had no idea how long they stayed like that. It was as if they were both frozen. When he finally spoke, it was a simple statement that surprised her very much.

"You be careful a my sister," he said.

"Your sister?" asked Nancy. "Who is your sister? Do I know her?"

Jabez only stared at her. Somewhere behind his vapid expression she thought she could see something like worry or concern.

His sister? Who is his sister? As far as she knew, he didn't even have a sister.

"Who's that, Jabez? Is your sister in my class?"

He didn't seem to understand a word she was saying. "Does she have the same last name as you?" Jabez turned and began to walk away.

"Have I *not* been careful of her, Jabez? You can tell me. Have I done something to hurt her?"

She tried to recall a little girl that she had reprimanded or inadvertently offended.

"Jabez!" she called after him, desperate with questions and confusion.

When he paused by the door, turned, and spoke, the question he asked surprised her a second time.

"Are you all right?"

3

At six o'clock, after a beer and a salami sandwich, Cliff tried to decide whether he should phone Nancy or just go right over to her place. Either way it would be a pain in the ass, because he'd have to drive to a phone or drive to her house.

He had been thinking about her all week. Now that he wasn't working, he could think of little else; her eager, greedy hips, her large firm breasts, the exciting scent that had lingered on his fingers long after he'd left her alone and exhausted on the bed.

He bet she had never been fucked like that before, not by no long-haired faggot college kid or prickless preppy. And especially not by that pansy Jew flatlander, Harrison Allen.

Cliff remembered exploding inside her like a blast from his shotgun, and how she whimpered and moaned and tore at him like a crazy woman.

He thought of her at night when he was alone in his bed. Sometimes he woke up with the sweet taste of her on his tongue. He rubbed his hand over his pants, massaging his groin, and swigged from a fresh bottle of Bud.

A moment later he was pulling on his deerskin gloves.

Yes, sir, by God, he'd drive right on over there! He'd never been comfortable using a telephone, anyway.

4

The relentlessly falling snow hadn't accumulated enough to make the road slippery, but Cliff knew it would need plowing before morning. His wipers fought the onslaught as he drove a little slower than usual, because visibility was piss poor.

When he arrived at Nancy's cottage, he saw that she was in the process of leaving. He'd caught her plodding from the front door toward her Honda. How great she looked, bundled up in her winter coat and knitted hat, moving with difficulty as she kicked her way through the new-fallen snow.

"Hi!" he said as he jumped out of his truck. He tried to smile, but it didn't come naturally for him.

"Hi?" she replied, her voice tentative, quizzical.

Cliff's confidence drained from him. "I thought I'd give you a visit. Friday night. You know . . . ?"

"Is there something you want?"

"No . . . ah . . . just to say hello. I . . ."

A look of impatience flashed across the schoolteacher's face. "Look, what do you want anyway? Are you selling something or what?"

"No, I—"

"What is it, then?"

"I . . . I . . ." Cliff's face knotted up painfully, tight as a clenched fist. His stomach hurt, his legs turned to Jell-O.

"Look, mister, I don't know what you have on your mind, but you can be sure of one thing: I'm not in the habit of accepting unannounced visitors, especially people I don't even know. Now if you'll excuse me, I was just on my way out."

She marched off to her car, got in, and drove away.

Cliff stood, collecting snowflakes on his face and clothing. He removed his yellow toque and slapped it against his hand to remove the snow. Then he put it on again, watching the red taillights of Nancy's Honda disappear into the distance and the snowy night.

She had caught him off guard; that's all. And it pissed him off. But what pissed him off more was the total, chilling lack of recognition in her face and voice. She didn't know him. She was not playing some feminine game; she really didn't fucking know him. It was just as if the other night had never happened.

He wandered through the snow, down to the old ferry landing near her house. Sitting on a cold stone wall, he watched the water, like liquid night, churning at his feet.

She really didn't know him.

He cursed Mrs. Snowdon, but not too loudly, and figured he'd sit in the pickup and finish the six-pack before he followed the schoolteacher. The trail of her tires would be real clear in the fresh snow.

5

When Nancy made up her mind to spend the night, she began to feel better. Although in many ways it was against her better judgment, she had finally made the choice. And by God, she'd stick with it.

Still, she questioned her motives. On the surface of her mind she knew she liked Harrison, but was that simply due to a process of elimination? After all, he was the only normal single man on the island who had expressed any real interest in her.

She readily admitted that she was lonely, and as she prodded at her motives she realized that she had good reason to fear returning home alone.

She'd stay here. And sometime before morning she'd find the opportunity, and the courage, to talk to Harrison about her . . . situation.

Lord, it's been a strange day! Her odd assortment of visitors had left her unnerved. That, on top of being anxious, lonely, and worried about her health. *Wow! I'm a total basket case!*

But underneath it all—below the self-exploration, the rationalization, and the mental rhetoric—she knew perfectly well that she had decided to spend the night a long time ago, and to hell with the consequences. There should be no problem, though; the islanders were not gossipy types. And even if they were, how could they possibly know where she was and what she was doing? Certainly she could not be spotted, since no traffic passed Harrison's house at night. And there were no neighbors at all on Harrison's side of the marsh.

Now, in the captain's house way down on the southernmost tip

of Friar's Island, she and Harrison were very much alone, far removed from the rest of the community and the rest of the world.

Alone.

The thought pleased Nancy; she took comfort in their isolation, their solitude. She was feeling better. Now she felt safe,
almost relaxed.

Sitting cross-legged on the rug in front of the fireplace, they
watched orange and blue flames dancing atop the black logs. They
sipped whiskey, and before long Nancy was laughing at the events
of the day.

"I don't think you should find it very flattering that all your
rivals are, literally, idiots." She laughed. "I wonder what it is about
me that attracts them?"

"Well, you *are* a schoolteacher," said Harrison. "They must be
attracted to your mind."

"I hate the way men are only interested in me for my mind,"
she said, a bit drunkenly. She giggled mischievously.

Harrison leaned over and kissed her. They settled back against
sofa pillows. The fire bathed them in its warm, soft light as they
surrounded each other with tentative embraces.

Finally Harrison rolled away, stretching languorously. He
reached for his drink and sipped lazily.

"You have a wonderful mind," he said, pulling her to him again.
"I've been thinking about it all week."

Face to face, she whispered to his lips, "You'd never give a
thought to a girl's body, I guess?"

They kissed again. Shifting slightly, they positioned themselves
to watch the fire. Harrison's arm encircled Nancy; Nancy's head
rested on Harrison's shoulder.

"Harry, can I ask you something?"

"Mmm-hmm."

"Tell me the truth, okay? Are you really here to find the
monster?"

"Yeah, mostly."

"And what else?"

Harrison looked directly at her. The reflection of the fire sparkled in his eyes. He smiled sadly and turned away. "To find myself, I guess. Does that sound trite?"

"No. Not when *you* say it . . ."

"It should. I've led a trite and an unremarkable life. No hassles, no commitments. I even got to thinking of myself as 'Mr. Electric' because I always took the course of least resistance."

He chuckled dryly, facing her. She held his gaze, interested but not smiling, unwilling to let him get sidetracked with humor.

Apparently encouraged by her attention, he looked back into the flames and went on. "When I was working in Boston, I didn't think about it much; I kept too busy. I reacted to things, ran away from things, and every time I reacted or ran, I lied to myself and called it progress. Sometimes I'd get fancy and call it growth."

She rested a hand on his shoulder and squeezed it reassuringly.

Harrison put his hand on hers. "You know, I often think I've never really known anyone. Not *really*. Oh, I've had buddies, sure, but never friends; I've had girlfriends but never lovers, never a wife. I've never even taken the time to get to know myself. Here I am, approaching middle age, and I still don't know what kind of person I am. Can I accomplish something important? Can I love? Be loved? Can I create?"

He shook his head. "I've never dared to measure myself against anything that really challenged me. Christ, I don't even know whether I'm brave or a coward. Pretty pathetic, eh?"

"I don't think so. Not to me. But I still don't understand: Where does the monster fit in?"

He was silent, seeming to collect his thoughts. Then he turned so that they were lying face to face on the pillow. Nancy's eyes explored the lines and contours of his face. His forehead was wide and high, his hairline receding just a bit. He would probably never be bald, but his hair would never grow thick and coarse. An aristocratic touch of gray lightened his temples. His nose was regal, thin, perhaps a bit too long. His eyes were deep and brown, gentle but confused.

"I don't know exactly. I ask myself that all the time. For one thing, looking for the monster is an adventure, a quest. But also, I'm looking for it because I *want* it to be there. Do you know what I mean?"

She smiled at him, silently encouraging him to continue.

"I don't mean this to sound as though I'm hopelessly jaded and world-weary, but I guess I want there to be something more than what science and the day-to-day working world have to offer. I want magic and mystery. I want there to be little men in flying saucers and ghosts and fortune-tellers. I *want* there to be a monster in that lake. Do you understand what I mean?"

"I think so. But if you *do* find him, then he'll be just another page in some zoology text, along with mountain gorillas and leather-backed turtles."

"You're right, of course. He'll be like a magic trick after the secret is known." Harrison paused, reflected. "But while you're thinking, 'Gee, how was that done? How did he make that girl disappear?' it's still magic, you see. It's the search that's important."

"And if you find him? Then what?"

"Then I'll look for something else, I guess."

She kissed his cheek. "I think you're kind of a romantic, you know that?"

"You're right," he whispered emphatically, rolling over onto her, kissing her tenderly, burying his face in her hair.

Her body jerked involuntarily.

OH GOD! OH!

Nancy felt her spine heave and stiffen. She became rigid in Harrison's arms. With her eyes locked on the nearest window, she pulled away from him in rapid little spasms. A series of terrified gasps grew, stopping just short of a scream.

"Wha . . . what is it?" he stammered, drawing back. Fear filled his voice.

"There . . ." She pointed. "The window. Look!"

Perhaps it was the ripples in the ancient glass. Perhaps a reflection in its mirrorlike surface. But she saw—or thought she saw— a gray grotesque face, monstrous and dark, topped by a mane of yellow hair. She thought she saw a hideous nose flattened against the windowpane and beside it a huge leathery hand. And the eyes, God, the black staring eyes . . .

Nancy's outstretched arm seemed to hang in the air; her index finger pointed. "S-s-something at the window. A face . . . horrible . . . watching us!"

She fought not to sob as Harrison leapt to his feet and ran to the door.

"NO!" she cried. "Don't go out there. Don't! It was horrible!"

But he had opened the door and was standing outside, his head snapping from side to side, his eyes squinting into the snowy darkness. "The flashlight on the mantel, bring it."

She obeyed without hesitation.

Harrison selected a stick from the pile of kindling beside the door. It was the thickness of a broom handle. Nancy felt safer when he had picked it up.

With light in hand, they walked huddled together along the side of the house.

"Was this the window?" he asked, pointing with the bright beam.

She nodded. Harrison shone the light around, exploring the bushes near the house, illuminating the snow-covered pathway leading to his front door.

The light diffused, became ineffective as he directed it away from the building. It swept the long black fields surrounding the house, then rippled over motionless, naked trees in the marshland. They seemed to wait, just beyond her vision, like silent, sinister creatures of the night.

Then the beam collected and focused as Harrison brought it back from his surveillance of the empty marsh. He shone it directly downward, where it created a three-foot luminous circle beneath the window.

"My God, look at this!" he said.

Nancy stepped closer. She clutched his arm as they looked down into the pool of light at their feet.

There, in front of the window, were tracks in the snow. They were matted and confusing near the house where someone had obviously been standing, packing the snow and peering inside at Harrison and Nancy.

Moving the light away from the house, the prints became distinct and wide-spaced where someone had sprinted away, bounding across the snow-covered meadows towards Childe's Bog.

"They're footprints," said Nancy, not believing.

And that's exactly what they were; not the marks of heavy winter boots, but the clearly defined prints of naked feet in the cold snow.

She bent down and examined them more closely. They almost looked human but— Maybe it was because the snow had melted at their perimeter, slightly increasing their size. Or maybe whoever made them had not been perfectly sure-footed, so their shape was distorted a little. But there was something about them that was not quite right. Something that didn't look exactly . . . human.

6

At eleven o'clock Professor Hathaway put down his book and rubbed his eyes. He carefully placed the notes he had made into the manila folder, then locked it in his desk drawer. He went over to check the fire in his stove, a part of his evening ritual before going to bed.

He sensed that something was finally happening; he knew the answer was very close.

Small discoveries in old volumes, offhand remarks from the islanders, bits and pieces of information from thousands of different, easily overlooked sources were all beginning to come together, fitting snugly like well-designed fragments of an intricate jigsaw puzzle. Soon he would find the most important piece, the piece that would clarify the placement of all the remaining sections. From there, he was confident, the final solution would come rapidly.

It would be just a matter of days now. Days. He would remain patient. His greatest strength was that he had always been patient.

Research was slow, painstaking work, full of false starts, wrong turns, and dead ends. It required endurance and determination. And he had been at it for so long, so very long.

Until finally this time the end was in sight!

Yes, he would be patient. There was no way to hurry things now.

As he walked up the unlit stairs to his bed, he felt excited, almost . . . aroused, for the first time in years.

He knew that sleep would not come easily this night.

Night Thoughts 13

I

Harrison wasn't sure what time it was. He knew it was very late. As yet there was not the slightest suggestion of dawn. Everything was tunnel-black in the old house. The walls of his bedroom were a dark, invisible barrier.

Some time ago he had been awakened by a scratching sound overhead. Something in the attic?

He had listened in great suspense long after the noise had stopped. Now he couldn't get back to sleep. Night thoughts kept him awake.

He knew he was groggy; maybe he was also confused. The scratching he'd heard might have been something else. Part of a dream, perhaps? As he rose higher from the well of unconsciousness, he suspected that the noise was in reality the sound of Nancy snoring at his side.

Experiencing momentary pleasure at the unfamiliar warmth in his bed, he rested his hand on the smooth round softness of her hip. He smiled a bit, thinking that this lovely woman, invisible in his cold bedroom, was snoring like a truck driver!

So what had really awakened him, snoring or scratching?

If he had dreamed the scratching, it was probably because his unconscious mind dreaded the return of the fearful sobbing that had frightened him the other night.

This time there had been no weeping, no sobs, just the memory of a sound, and no more. A squirrel? A chipmunk? Maybe a field mouse taking refuge from the cold night between the boards overhead.

He'd been aware of his animal visitors for some time, so why hadn't he set a trap? He had planned to long ago, but had done nothing.

Harrison couldn't shut off his compulsive internal monologue. He quickly grew impatient with himself. God, he wasn't acting sensibly.

Now, in the perfect darkness of his room, he had begun to question his own behavior. It was all quite clear. Undeniable. Lately he had been acting inappropriately in several ways. Odd and mysterious things were happening all around him, yet in the daylight hours the strange events seemed commonplace, even mundane.

But *now* there was no denying it. Weird things *were* happening. Had he not been followed through Childe's Bog by some unidentifiable shape stealing silently through the darkness and mist? Had he not discovered an odd assortment of objects on his stone stoop? Had he not heard the sound of a woman sobbing somewhere, everywhere, right here in his own house? Heard it with such clarity that he'd phoned Professor Hathaway to ask if his place could be haunted?

And perhaps most frightening of all, had he not seen—or rather, had Nancy not seen—a horrible face at the window? Without a doubt Harrison himself had seen the naked footprints in the snow.

Naked footprints.

But the profoundly unsettling fact was that this group of odd occurrences had not upset him at all!

Why hadn't he phoned the police the night he was followed? Or immediately after he and Nancy had discovered they were being watched in their intimacy?

How could he be so indifferent?

Somehow, none of his actions, or inaction, made any sense when viewed objectively.

And what about his research project? Hadn't he come here to investigate the monster and to contemplate a new direction for his life? So far he had made little progress toward either goal. As usual, he felt at the mercy of the wind, waiting for some chance breeze that would decide his fate for him.

Yes, by God! He was too passive. He was permitting something other than Harrison Allen to control his actions, his life, his destiny.

Sure, he had made a token stab at research, but the islanders he'd approached were uniformly reticent about discussing the monster. It was a subject they conspicuously, sometimes rudely, avoided. Even Professor Hathaway had seemed curiously evasive the last time they'd talked.

Christ, what the hell is going on?

Tomorrow, he vowed, he would lay the whole thing out for Nancy: the noises in the house, the figure on the road, the strange offerings. Then they'd discuss the face at the window and the tracks in the snow. He'd hold back nothing. She could tell him if he had lost his sense of perspective. Maybe together they could make sense of things.

In the unyielding darkness Harrison's mind reeled and drifted. He knew for certain things were not right.

For the first time in his life, Harrison Allen feared the approach of madness.

2

In the morning when Harrison awoke, he had no recollection of how long he had lain there, staring wide-eyed and unseeing at all the disturbing images cascading above him in the lightless bedroom. But when his eyes met the new and welcome dawn, he had maintained his renewed sense of resolve.

Today he would straighten things out. He would take things by the horns. Seize control. By God, he'd be in charge!

He planned to begin by disclosing everything to Nancy. Together they'd sort through all the mysterious happenings, search for a pattern. If they got hung up, they could seek guidance from Professor Hathaway.

Mysterious happenings. How melodramatic that sounded as he performed the everyday tasks of slipping out of bed and deep breathing the chill morning air.

Nancy was still asleep, lying on her side, curled into a tight ball. Only her long black hair was visible outside the covers.

Harrison smiled down at her, then crossed the room to where he stood naked in front of the mirror over the antique dresser. He felt pleased with the sight of his body. For a long time he had not been so aware of his maleness. He was desirable, attractive. He had felt his power combust and he'd loved with an excitement he'd long feared he was doomed only to remember. His sexuality was like a recovered youth, vigorous and strong in the arms of this handsome young woman.

Maybe it really is possible to start over.

His reflected image looked fine to him. Not too flabby around the waist, arms and legs firm and powerful, shoulders broad and poised. At thirty-five his hair was thinning only slightly. As he looked deeply into the eyes of his reflection, he saw a sensual, sensitive man, a man full of mystery and fascination, love and commitment.

Yes—he nodded at his reflection—he was pleased with himself.

The threat of madness had vanished with the night; in his new-found confidence he felt fresh and young.

Today was the day his new life would begin.

He smiled once again at the mirror, then—with great satisfaction—at Nancy, still sleeping in his bed. He pulled on his robe and went downstairs to make their breakfast.

Odd Jobs

"Jesus Christ, Cliff, will ya jes' try a little?"

Stubby Baron held the smoking marijuana cigarette across the littered tabletop, waving it in front of Cliff's face.

Stubby was a stocky little man with a round florid face and a military crew cut. What appeared to be excess flesh was in reality rock-solid muscle. The only flab on his body was the collection of chins above his collar button. He laughed quickly—and always a little too loudly—while flapping his arms at his sides, giving the impression of a penguin. In the past, some guys at the quarry had taken to calling him "Penguin," but it never caught on; he wouldn't stand for it. So what if he was only five-four? He was barrel-solid, brawny as a bull, and could kick the b'jesus out of anyone on the island. In this particular case, he kicked the shit out of the guys who called him Penguin.

The name "Stubby" was okay, though. It was the name his father had given him when he was a child, and anything his father did was A-okay. Besides, it was a better name than Enoch; that was the name his mother had given him. Now, anyone calling him Enoch was likely to be treated exactly as if they had called him Penguin.

After a silent supper with his wife, Stubby had gone out for a drive, testing his four-wheel-drive Scout on the island's snow-slick roads. He'd decided to drop in on his friend Cliff to see if he was agreeable to taking a ride over to the interstate. The idea was to find flatlanders who had skidded off the road and to pull them back on, an activity that was always great fun and usually profitable. Between Swanton and Burlington they could probably find five or six stranded cars at twenty-five dollars apiece. Hell, they could have a few laughs, and make some money to boot.

Instead, Stubby had found his friend off the road not far from Eastern Way. The fender of Cliff's pickup was crinkled like a chewing-gum wrapper.

When Stubby arrived, Cliff was in the pickup, rocking it back and forth, angrily racing the engine. The back wheels were spewing snow, dead grass, and dirt.

"Whatsa matter, stuck?" asked Stubby, walking up to the door of the vehicle and scratching his head.

Cliff glared at him, teeth clenched, face red and pinched in anger. "Naw, doin' an early plowin'. What the hell's it look like, ya fuckhead!"

"Need a tow?"

"I'll give you a toe, right up your ass. You got a fuckin' chain with ya?"

Stubby patted his jacket pockets as if he were looking for something. "A chain, you say? Think I got one in the Scout. Usually do in this weather, case I run into some damn fool don't know how to drive in the snow."

Stubby's Scout easily pulled the pickup back onto the road. The two men convoyed the short distance to Cliff's house, where they had a cold beer to warm up.

"Thought we might take the four-wheeler over to 89 and do a little fishin'. The flatlanders oughtta be runnin' pretty good this season."

Cliff thought about that. "Might not be a bad idea," he said, then spat into the wood stove. "Good way to earn a little Christmas money."

"No shit," said Stubby, wide-eyed in mock amazement. "Who you gonna be buyin' a Christmas present for?"

"Same as always. Myself."

The two men laughed, Stubby a little louder than necessary, and chugged their beers.

Then Stubby pulled out the joint, lit it, and offered some to Cliff.

Cliff just shook his head.

"Jes' try a little, it won't hurt ya." Stubby waved the joint insistently.

"Naw, fucks up yer head."

Stubby knew when to back off and change the subject. "Thought I might raise my price a bit this year," he said. "Cost a livin' an' all. Thirty-five bucks a tow for out-a-staters. Whatta ya think?"

"Why not? Best service in town, oughtta be worth somethin', right?"

"Damn straight. Course, I don't take none a them, whatcha call, credit cards. 'You don't pay, here you stay,' that's my motto. Course, for the ladies maybe we can extend a little credit . . ."

"Extend a little somethin'."

"Fuck you. Naw, we'll let the ladies pay on time."

" 'Bout ten seconds, the way I hears it." Cliff roared with laughter at his own joke and slid another beer across the table to Stubby. The little man scooped it up and popped the top absently. Then he looked around, a critical expression darkening his face. "Jesus Christ, Cliff, when you gonna clean up this pigsty?"

"What's the matter with it?"

"Looks like the inside of a trash can."

"Well, when I get around to doin' my spring cleanin', I gotta have somethin' to clean, right?"

"Looks just the same's it did when ya finished your spring cleanin' last year." He tossed his empty beer can into the corner, where it joined its twins beside an overflowing shopping bag. "Come on, let's take a drive."

"Shit, I don't think we'll get much business. Nobody's gonna be on the roads at this hour."

"That's what I'm countin' on," said Stubby as he stood up.

Cliff got up, too. Each man grabbed his coat and a six-pack. Then they set our to seek their fortunes on the dark, snowy highways.

The Monastery   15

I

The sun was up, bright and sharp, and the air was comfortably cold. Snow melted fast; it would probably be gone by the end of the day, leaving the ground damp and the boggy perimeter of the marsh greatly enlarged.

Because the monastery was on the far end of the island, Harrison and Nancy decided to take the car. It was too cold to enjoy the long walk, and the hike back would be torture.

"I have some things I'd like to tell you," began Harrison, hesitantly. "I don't want to put it off any longer. It's . . . well, there are things I'm trying to put out of my mind. I've been trying not to think about them, you know?"

Nancy looked at him, then away. Her body seemed to visibly stiffen, as if bracing herself for something uncomfortable. Her eyes remained riveted to the road straight ahead as they passed the marsh and headed north toward the school.

Harrison struggled to continue, his hands too forcefully grasping the wheel. "There's a series of things I want to tell you, really. Some about myself, and some are things that have happened to me since I've come to the island."

Nancy laughed nervously. "You're not going to tell me you're wanted by the police or something like that, are you?"

Harrison smiled, somewhat relieved. "No. Nothing like that."

"You're married, then?"

"No. In fact, I've never been married." He took a breath. "But I haven't been completely honest with you just the same, and I want to be, even about little things. As I was saying last night, I really did come here to look for the monster; that much is true. However, I may have intentionally implied more than that. You see, I am not actually *employed* by the American Cryptozoological Society. As a matter of fact, I'm not employed anywhere. The only grant that is funding my research is Unemployment Insurance."

She didn't look at him.

"And . . . well, I've . . . I've been kind of worried about some things lately." Harrison felt his temperature rising in the car's cool interior. He feared he might be blushing. Still, he was determined to go on. He forced himself.

"Look, Nancy, I'm thirty-five years old, and already my life has reached sort of a cul-de-sac. I've been in marketing for years, a fittingly unexciting and nondemanding occupation for a person with no real goals. But now I've started to look back on my life somewhat critically for the first time, and all I see is years of waiting, putting things off, avoiding challenges and commitments." He chuckled dryly, without humor. "It's like I've lived my life in the waiting room of a dentist's office, and now I've got nothing at all to show for it; no job, no skill, no home, no future. God, most of the people I knew ten or fifteen years ago have careers by now and are working on their second set of kids. But me . . . well, after thirty-five years of waiting, I realize what a . . . a misfit I've let myself become. Christ, I've never even had a steady girlfriend or a long-term relationship, or whatever you call it nowadays."

He had only begun to say what he wanted to say. But at least he had started. He knew he was repeating things he had already told her, but they were necessary groundwork for today's disclosures. Now he wasn't sure quite how to continue.

When Nancy didn't reply at all, Harrison felt himself grow tense and uncomfortable. She just kept looking at the road as they passed Professor Hathaway's house.

More words were welling up inside him; he wanted to pour them out, tell her everything he was thinking and feeling. He wanted to tell her what he feared. And he would, too, even at the risk of saying the wrong thing.

But he would say nothing more until she made some response, acknowledged him in some way.

They drove a short distance in silence. When Nancy finally began to speak, it was almost a whisper. "I'm happy you want to tell me things, Harry. But you don't need to. You don't owe me any explanations. We get along fine with things just as they are. Please don't feel that you have to explain yourself. You don't have to say anything until you're ready. You don't have to say anything at all."

Tension passed from Harrison like smoke through a screen door. He smiled and reached for her hand. He found it halfway, reaching for his.

"That's just it," he said, "I'm ready. Finally, at thirty-five, I'm ready. I *want* to talk to you. I've avoided it like I've avoided a lot of things. I . . . what I'm trying to say is, well . . . I've worked real hard never to feel about anyone as I'm beginning to feel about you. Now that it's started, I don't want to say or do anything to ruin it."

He felt her hand tighten around his. "But there is something more I want to say. Something I want to discuss with you."

Nancy turned to look at him. He could see the fear in her eyes, fear of what might be coming. "What is it?" she said. "Please feel you can tell me."

"It's difficult to explain. Some . . . very odd things have been happening to me lately—"

As they were about to turn right onto the road that led to the monastery, a fast-moving Scout with two men in it cut them off, nearly smashing into their car.

"Jesus!" cried Harrison, swerving to the right to avoid a collision. In his rearview mirror he watched the Scout accelerating, its tires spitting gravel as it pulled away.

Harrison and Nancy waited for their pulses to slow down. As they drove toward the monastery, they shared their personal fears, and chronicled all the odd and frightening things that had happened to each of them.

Now, more than ever, Harrison felt he had found an ally in what had always been an alien world.

2

The dangerously pitted dirt road ended far short of the monastery. A narrow footpath, overgrown and muddy, cut through the pines, curving upward toward the ancient stone structure. Where the pinewood divided, the building came clearly into view. It was simple in design, nowhere near as large as Harrison had expected. Yet it had a certain grandeur about it. It stood stately and proud, overlooking the lake and the island from atop its steep granite cliff. Though very old, it was not a ruin; it seemed solid and dignified, rising like a sculpted extension of the rock itself. At first glance, it seemed like a fortress, maybe even a castle.

Castle is a better word, thought Harrison. For a moment he envisioned the two of them as children in a fairy tale. Holding hands, unable to feel each other's warmth through their gloves, they looked up at the building in a kind of awe. They moved closer, tentatively approaching, as if it were the domain of some mysterious and unknown lord.

It was a two-story structure, long and narrow, a perfect rectangle. There were no anachronistic additions or abutments. The roof, made of slates—many of which were broken or missing— sloped downward from the building's peak toward its long, flat sides.

The granite blocks in the walls were dark-stained and weathered, but perfectly fitted, solid as the ages. All the windows were boarded up, apparently having been so for many years. Their rough plank coverings had turned gray from the elements.

The security measures suggested by the boarded-up windows

turned the image of a castle into one of a prison. Harrison shuddered at the maverick suspicion that the planks had been put up, not to keep prowlers out, but to keep something in. He decided not to share his unsettling fantasy with Nancy.

The door on the near end of the building was made of two massive planks that still looked sturdy enough to repel any intruder, ancient or modern. If the door proved to be locked, it occurred to Harrison, it might be impossible to get in.

"This place was really made to last," Harrison mumbled.

After staring in silence for a few minutes, they began to walk around the building, looking up at it, surveying the grounds that had once been cleared. Nancy remarked how, over the years, the brush, the grass, and the forest had crept slowly back, reclaiming all but the building itself.

When they had walked all around the monastery, they realized that the only entrance was the one they had seen at the beginning. "Must not have had very strict fire codes in those days," Nancy said.

On the grounds, amid brambles and small trees, were the tumbled ruins of various outbuildings. They must have been barns or sheds that had surrendered long ago to the ravages of time.

No structure in the area was more worthy of exploration than the monastery itself. The outbuildings could wait.

Harrison tried the door. Just as he'd expected, it would not open.

He tugged on the rusty iron crossbar, hinged on one side of the frame and padlocked on the other. It didn't budge. The ancient lock was irreparably corroded. The whereabouts of the key was a mystery, but even if they'd had it, the lock was surely rusted closed forever.

Nancy said, "It's hard to believe this place has been locked up since the twenties. I got the impression Professor Hathaway had been in here, didn't you?"

"I thought that's what he said."

"I wonder how he got in?"

"Beats me." Harrison shrugged. "Let's try the windows."

Together they pulled at the heavy boards covering one of the windows. "Forget it," said Harrison, quickly frustrated by the tenacity of the big spikes that fixed the boards to thick wooden window frames. "We'll need tools to get these off."

"Did you bring any?"

"No. We could go back home and get some. Or . . . wait a minute! Maybe we could use the jack handle as a crowbar."

"I don't know. I feel like we're breaking and entering. Who owns this place, anyway?"

"I've got no idea. We could check with the town clerk."

"She's only open on Wednesday afternoons. It's not a full-time job, you know."

"What do you say we do, then?" asked Harrison.

Nancy squinted at the door, her lips pursed in thought. Then she grinned mischievously, "Let's get the jack handle."

They turned from the building to start back down the hill. Harrison stopped short; there was a man watching them.

The stranger stood motionless upon the path between them and the car, making no attempt to conceal himself.

"That's one of the men I told you about," Nancy whispered. "That's the one who came to school. Jabez."

Jabez's gaze was fixed on them. He acted as if he were uncertain whether to approach. His pale eyes were glassy and unblinking.

"Hello, Jabez," Nancy called in a friendly tone, waving to him. "He's harmless," she whispered to Harrison. "He's kind of simple."

Jabez started toward them in his stumbling sort of way, lurching forward for a few quick steps, then proceeding slowly for the next few, as if he were occasionally shoved from behind by an invisible hand.

When all three stood facing each other in the shadow of the monastery, Nancy said, "Jabez, this is my friend Harry. Harry, this is Jabez; he visited me at school yesterday."

"Hello, Jabez," said Harrison, extending his right hand.

Jabez ignored it, never lowering his eyes from Nancy's. "My sister . . ." said Jabez in a hollow tone.

They studied him, then looked at each other. Both waited for Jabez to say more.

"What about your sister?" Nancy coaxed.

"I'm worried," he replied. "Maybe she needs help."

"Where is she?" asked Harrison.

Jabez didn't reply. He just walked past them and around to the front of the building, all the time gazing at the water. The wind whipped his strawlike hair, twisting it grotesquely, and tugged at the frayed tails of his long black coat. He looked like a stranded sailor watching for a rescue ship on an empty sea.

Harrison and Nancy moved to his side. Nancy asked, "Is your sister in some kind of trouble?"

"I'm . . . worried about her," he replied to the lake and to the wind. Then he turned to them and asked, "You want to go in here?" He motioned toward the monastery with a flick of his head.

"We wanted to explore it, but it's locked."

"Come on," he said, lurching past them. They followed Jabez as he hobbled over some rocks and quick-stepped down a little incline to a jagged, snow-covered path on the face of the steep cliff. The cliff descended straight down to the lake. A fall would be fatal.

When they were about a hundred feet below the foundation of the building, they came to a hollowed-out area in the face of the granite ledge. It looked like a cave, but it was the opening of a tunnel. Mortared stonework framed a rusted iron door. In spite of the corrosion, the heavy door swung freely—if noisily—on its hinges.

Jabez pointed at it. Harrison pulled it open all the way so he and Nancy could see the dark passageway beyond.

"Does it lead into the cellar?" asked Harrison, turning to Jabez. But when he turned around, Jabez was gone.

A Conspiracy of Shadows 16

I

Cliff and Stubby bounced along in the Scout, drunk and seventy-five dollars richer. They were shouting and singing country-and-western songs along with the radio. Most of the night had been spent on the interstate. They had driven all the way to Burlington, where they had bought gas before heading for home, giddy with fatigue.

Stubby was at the wheel when they got back to the island. He cursed savagely as he nearly ran into a silver Saab with Massachusetts plates.

"Fuckin' flatlanders, think they own the fuckin' road."

"Yeah," Cliff agreed. "Let's go back to my place and get my fuckin' shotgun."

"Let's go back to your place and get some more beer."

"You get beer, I want my gun."

"You serious? What you want it for?"

"Oh, I thought I might shoot me some cans."

"Cans?"

"Afri-cans, Puerto Ri-cans, Mexi-cans."

The men laughed raucously. Beer splattered down the front of Stubby's filthy parka.

"You don't really want your gun, do you?" Stubby asked, tears in his eyes, chest heaving from laughing too hard.

"Damn straight I do."

"You tell me why."

"They scared us, didn't they? Let's scare 'em back."

"Who?"

"Them flatlanders."

"Wha' for?"

"For fun."

"With a gun?"

"That'll scare 'em, won't it?"

"I dunno."

"Pussy."

2

Harrison's right hand fumbled in the deep pocket of his coat, groping for his flashlight. Holding Nancy's hand in his left, guiding her, he eased his way along the damp, cold passageway toward the interior of the building. He could hear water dripping somewhere deep within the bowels of the tunnel. The noise bounced around, amplified and unpleasant in the lightless depths.

Harrison flicked on the light.

Ahead of them, the beam swept past gray-green moss on the walls and rippled along the earthen floor. Harrison sought barriers, holes, and obstructions that might prove dangerous to them. Occasionally a partially rotted board on the ground—more mud now then wood—provided a crude bridge over some swampy depression where feculent brown water had collected. The whole place smelled like foul earth and decay.

Nancy gripped his hand tighter as they proceeded deeper and deeper into the tomblike cavern, inching their way toward the monastery itself. Now and then a dangling hairy root would tickle Harrison's face. He'd swat at it irritably or spit if it touched his mouth.

Away from all sunlight now, the chill air seemed like a moist and living thing. It penetrated fabric and flesh, seeking its way to their bones. There was no warmth among the stark shadows; the cold white flashlight beam provided illumination without heat.

Eventually the passage opened into a vast stone dungeon. There two sets of slab rock stairways led upward in different directions. Four wooden doors in the piled granite walls promised other areas to explore. Harrison tried the doors one at a time; they were all locked.

"Wow," said Harrison, "all these locked doors really get my curiosity going."

"What could be in there?" Nancy asked.

"Treasure. Priceless bottles of old wine. Maybe the devil himself is a prisoner here."

"Cut it out!" Nancy laughed nervously, the sound small and hollow in the stone cellar.

"Let's go check upstairs." Harrison led her toward the stairway to the right.

They climbed cautiously, studying each step in the pale flashlight beam. The wooden door at the top opened freely, and they found themselves in another long corridor. It ran the entire length of the first floor.

"This must be the center of the building," Harrison whispered.

On the far end, very faintly, Harrison could detect what must have been the barred door to the outside. No light came in through any cracks around it. Except for the flashlight, no light at all found its way inside the ancient walls.

Perpetual night, he thought.

Along both sides of the corridor Harrison saw a series of doors, some open, some closed, according to no discernible pattern. Trying the nearest door, he found that it opened into a tiny room.

"These must have been the monks' bedrooms," said Nancy, peering over his shoulder.

"Really basic," agreed Harrison. "Not even a window in this one. It's more like a closet."

"Or a cell. Brrrrr. This is worse than my college dorm."

They walked along the corridor, shining the light into the small, barren cubicles. From time to time Harrison would lean into a room and sweep it with the light while Nancy held his upper arm, gazing around him.

"This is really something," said Harrison. "Imagine living like this."

"No, thank you." Nancy shuddered. "I was hoping we'd find some things to poke through, books or old junk or something. The place is really empty."

Double doors at the opposite end of the passage led to what, by comparison, seemed a massive room. It contained solid wooden tables in an area that might have been a kitchen. The huge stone fireplace was boarded up.

"Look at the ovens built into the fireplace," said Harrison.

"I wonder how the little rooms were heated. Did you notice there weren't any fireplaces in any of them?" Her voice was full of compassion for people long gone.

"Maybe warmth was not among their worldly comforts," said Harrison.

"Maybe they froze to death." She looked around and whispered, "God, it's really quiet in here."

3

Cliff and Stubby got out of the Scout and surveyed the grounds of the monastery.

"Wonder what they're doing here?" mused Stubby, tugging on his earlobe.

"Prob'ly lookin' for local color." Cliff pulled his shotgun from the rear seat of the Scout.

"What you got against them, anyways, Cliff?"

"I jes' wanna make friends with 'em, that's all."

"You ain't got no shells in that thing, do ya?"

"They're in my pocket."

"Well, you see to it you keep 'em there. What are we gonna do to 'em anyways?"

"Nothin' they wouldn't get done to 'em if they was back in the city."

"Well, Jesus, let's make a plan or somethin'. I feel like I'm jes' taggin' along."

"Okay. Let's plan to show that little squack that her boyfriend ain't too much of a man."

"That shouldn't be hard to do," said Stubby, and then he laughed a little too loudly.

Cliff walked quickly in the direction of the secret entrance, with Stubby right behind him, scampering to keep up.

4

Nearly half of the monastery's top floor was devoted to an expansive room with a high, peaked ceiling and exposed beams. At the room's far end, a huge stone fireplace atop an elevated platform covered the entire wall.

This must have been their chapel, Nancy thought. She looked at the gabled windows. If they had not been boarded up, they would have provided magnificent views of the island and the lake. The remainder of the top floor, like the floor below, was comprised of a series of smaller rooms, each containing a heavy wooden table. These must have been writing or study rooms.

Harrison looked puzzled. "This is really odd," he whispered. "It's as if the living area was downstairs and the work area up here."

"The chapel is closer to heaven," Nancy said, smiling, "So they must have been Christian monks after all. But if Professor Hathaway was right about them, you'd think the chapel would be in the cellar!"

The whole place had an unshakable feeling of isolation about it. Nancy shivered, realizing they were cut off from the warmth of daylight by the tightly sealed windows, and from the elements by the thick stone walls which seemed to radiate a damp chill. It wasn't so much like viewing a relic from the past as it was like actually being a part of another era. As she stood in the chapel room, she felt as if she could be in any century. The only reference to modern times was the flashlight in Harrison's hand.

It was spooky, but it was wonderful.

"I have to find out more about this place," she said. "It's so fantastic, I've never seen anything like it. They ought to turn it into a museum or something."

Harrison's eyes were wide, following the light beam around the room. "Imagine spending your whole life in this place, sleeping in those tiny cold rooms, working the land, worshipping *whoever* at night by firelight in this drafty hall."

"You sound like a gothic novel."

"I feel like I'm in one."

Harrison swept the flashlight beam around the chapel one last time. The bright circle rippled along the masonry and across the massive hand-hewn beams that supported the walls and ceiling.

"Listen," Nancy whispered.

"Wh . . . what?"

"It's so quiet."

She giggled, then strained her ears to hear sounds from the outside: the wind, birds, the splashing of the lake.

Nothing.

The place was impervious to sound. She couldn't even detect the predictable noises of an ancient building—no floorboards creaking, no groans of the structure settling, no wind whistling through the cracks in the walls. They were all alone in the tomblike darkness, engulfed in a silence undisturbed for more than half a century.

Moving hand in hand through the chapel, she let Harrison lead her along the white pathway of their light.

"Listen," Nancy said again. Then with more alarm, "LISTEN!"

Now there really was a sound—a low moaning, a shattered, suffering sound from somewhere beyond the shadows and the darkness.

Harrison's light darted wildly across the stone walls, trying to locate the source of the eerie keening. Nancy squeezed his arm.

The moan continued, rising in tone and volume until it was joined by a second moan, louder and more shrill.

Both sounds stopped abruptly.

Before the silence became complete, Nancy heard a slow, deliberate knocking. It grew louder and louder until it sounded like someone pounding rhythmically on one of the wooden doors.

BAM! — BAM! — BAM!

"Holy shit," said Harrison.

The pounding echoed in the empty halls.

"The door!" he whispered as his light locked on the door from which the knocking seemed to come.

"Oh God . . ." Nancy knew her voice was trembling as much as her hands.

Slowly, ever so slowly, the heavy wooden door began to open inward. Toward them. Screeching in agony on its rusty hinges.

As the crack widened, they saw nothing but cavernous blackness beyond.

Then the low, painful moaning resumed, tremulant, rising in volume and fervor until it exploded into wild laughter. Nancy watched a dull metal cylinder slide through the door's opening.

A masculine voice that sounded almost familiar commanded, "Point that fuckin' light at yer feet or I'll blow yer fuckin' hand off."

Two men stepped into the room, their dark forms barely visible in the stray light that bounced around inside. The taller, thinner shadow held the shotgun. The shorter, fatter one flapped his arms at his sides. Neither man was laughing now.

"Now you jes' leave that fuckin' light pointin' at the floor," said the gunman as he began to pace in a wide circle around them, talking as he moved. "You two hadn't ought to be pokin' aroun' these ol' buildin's like this. They ain't safe. People come in here, get theirselves hurt or lost, maybe never come out again. Ain't that right, Stub?"

"Yes, sir, Cliff, you can't get no righter'n that."

"Damn straight. An' I don't know if you folks heard the stories about this ol' place, have ya?"

Nancy felt Harrison clinging to her. It was as if her right side were cemented to him. Neither answered.

"Well, have ya?" Cliff demanded, louder.

"You better answer him," encouraged Stubby.

"We haven't heard any stories," Harrison said flatly.

"Well, I guess that means you don't come from this island, 'cause if you came from this island you'd a heard lots of stories. You from outa state, are you?"

"You better answer him," said Stubby.

"Yes, we're from out of state."

"And you fuckin' march right in here as if you own the god-damn place! Shit—nobody from the island comes in here, no! But *you*, Mr. La-dee-dah Flatlander, you fuckin' march right in like you own the Christly premises. Now that jes' ain't right. An' it ain't polite, I'll tell ya that. Fact is, it's damn *im*polite, you ask me. Ain't it, Stub?"

"It surely is."

"Don't you think so, mister? Don't you think you're bein' just a damn bit impolite?"

"You better answer him, mister."

"Well, we didn't know the place was off limits—"

"Off limits! Son of a bitch! I didn't ask you if it was off limits. I asked you if you wasn't bein' impolite!"

Nancy dug her fingertips into Harrison's arm. She could feel him trembling. She could sense his indecision.

"Look," he finally said, "just what is it you guys want?"

"We want to know if you're fuckin' impolite or not. And you ain't answerin' my question. An' I'd say that's pretty fuckin' impolite, too. Wouldn't you, Stub?"

"Damn rude, I'd say. Damn rude."

"Tell ya somethin', if I'da ever been as rude as you, mister, my daddy woulda whopped me within an inch a my life."

Cliff continued to pace in a wide circle around them. Harrison squinted, as if trying to make out the features of the boisterous man and his little fat companion. In the semidarkness they were nothing more than black forms gliding through the shadows.

Maybe if he'd just flash the light in their eyes, Nancy thought, it would blind them long enough so she and Harrison could make a run for it.

But there was the shotgun. Oh, God . . .

"You know, mister, when I was a kid I come up here once, me an' another kid. An' I'll tell you, when my daddy found out, he slapped me aroun' somethin' fierce. He give me a wicked welpin'. 'Course he done it for my own good, you understand. I shouldn't a been up here in the first place; it weren't my property. So now I'm gonna do somethin' for your own good, mister, 'cause you shouldn't be up here neither. An' worse yet, you went right ahead and drug this pretty little city girl right up here with you. Don't know what you had in mind, but whatever it was, I'll jes' bet her daddy wouldn't be too goddamn happy about it."

Nancy knew what was coming. She sensed the muscles tensing as Harrison tightened his grip on the flashlight, his only weapon.

"Here, Stub, you hold on to my shotgun while I talk business with my friend here. Now, Miss Schoolteacher, you jes' better step out of the way."

Nancy didn't move. "Why don't you quit showing off," she said. "You're acting like one of my first-graders."

"Now, honey, why don't you jes' leave the talking to the men. You jes' step back out of the way like a good girl."

"Step back, Nancy," said Harrison. He gave her a forceful shove as Cliff lunged at him.

The rest happened so quickly that Nancy couldn't make sense of it.

Harrison lifted the beam of light, shining it directly into Cliff's oncoming face. Cliff's features appeared like a flashing white mask in the darkness. In reflex, he squinted against the brightness, lifting his hands to shield his eyes.

Exactly then, Harrison slammed the butt of the flashlight against Cliff's forehead. There were two dull thuds: one as the flashlight connected with flesh, the other as the light, knocked from Harrison's hand, struck the floor. It rolled away, magically unbroken.

Cliff screamed in rage and pain, slapping his hands against his wounded forehead. Harrison lifted a rapid kick to his groin. Cliff fell howling, doubled up like a fist, his hands buried between his legs.

Nancy watched a fury take hold of Harrison. It zapped like electricity through his body. "Son of a bitch," he cried, falling upon the writhing Cliff, pummeling him with unfeeling fists.

"The gun," begged Cliff almost crying. "Get him off me, Stub. Get the friggin' gun!"

Stubby took the shotgun by the barrel. Holding it like a baseball bat, he moved menacingly toward the struggling men.

"Stop it!" screamed Nancy.

In the dull glow from the fallen light, she witnessed the bizarre outcome of the drama.

The door through which the men had entered burst open with a resounding crash.

A third shape entered the room. It seemed much larger than the other two, and somehow darker. It gave the impression of an oversized man dressed in a wetsuit and wearing a shaggy yellow fright wig.

An unpleasant odor polluted the moist air.

Breathing in raspy gasps, the newcomer moved with incredible speed and animal agility. Long, twisted arms dangled at its sides. Its feet made odd scratching sounds on the stone floor as it sped toward the small, fat man with the shotgun.

Someone shrieked. Nancy couldn't tell who.

Stubby dropped to the floor, bawling. The thing picked him up as if he were an obese child. His screams changed abruptly to a hysterical wail as the dreadful shape hurled him with terrible force against the boarded window. On impact the rotting timbers split as if they were paper. Stubby's body disappeared from sight. Nancy heard his diminishing cry, as he plunged toward the rocks below.

Instantly, through the frightful hole, a painful brilliance flooded the room. Nancy's eyes were paralyzed with horror. Her blind gaze was glued to the sunny spot where Stubby had vanished.

Surely no one got a good look at his killer, who fled quickly, silently from the room.

Nancy thought she had caught a quick glimpse, but what she saw was like nothing she had ever seen before.

A Collection of Darkness 17

I

When Mrs. Snowdon entered the general store, Chief Lawrence Connelly politely tipped his hat and quickly left.

Abner Mott smiled tentatively; briefly, his eyes met the dark, deep-set eyes of the old woman. She didn't speak, but Abner knew she was here for her week's groceries.

"Anything I can help you with, Mrs. Snowdon?" he asked with a deference that transcended salesmanship and courteous customer relations.

"I'll find what I need, Abner. You can cut me some cheese and a bit of beef for a stew."

"Right away, ma'am."

She walked with a conspicuous dignity through the narrow aisles, paying little attention to Abner's scrawled signs, automatically stopping for rice, dried beans, and an assortment of canned goods. She never paused to compare brands and prices.

When she presented herself at the counter with an armload of supplies, Abner was waiting for her. He was ready with wrapped packages of cheese, stew beef, and a third parcel.

"Threw in a couple of nice pork chops for you and Jabe—real nice cut."

"There's no call for givin' what we don't require, Abner," she said. The refusal was neither impolite nor gracious.

As Abner placed the food in a brown bag, Mrs. Snowdon visibly stiffened. She looked up and over Abner's head, through and beyond the parcel-covered wall behind the storekeeper, and out into the invisible distance. Abner watched her facial expression change slightly; the frozen look of her stern refusal softened into an aspect of concern.

She said, "Jabez'll be here lookin' for me in a few minutes. You tell him I've gone to the monastery."

"The monastery?" said Abner with surprise.

"I'll be back for these," she said.

Before Abner could formulate another question, Mrs. Snowdon had abandoned her groceries and was out the door and gone.

2

In the empty house the newly installed telephone rang and rang.

In Burlington, Mark Chittenden placed the receiver back onto its cradle. He looked thoughtful as he returned to the couch to sit beside his wife.

"Still not home?" Judy asked.

"Naw. Wonder what he's doing up there? You'd think he'd check in once in a while. At least let us know if our house is still standing."

"He wouldn't leave the island without telling us, would he?"

"I don't think so, but who can say? Knowing Harry, he's probably found himself some rustic little country wench to keep house with. Right now I'll bet he's lazing around in front of some fireplace somewhere, sipping California burgundy and fantasizing that he's some sort of cold-weather Gauguin."

"Why don't you take a ride up there if you want to see him. It's not that far."

"I don't know . . ."

"What else is there to do on a Saturday afternoon? You might as well. It might make you feel better."

"I guess so. Sure. You want to come?"

"No, thanks. I think I'd like to stay right here and read. Bring him back for dinner, if you want to."

"Good idea. Sure you don't want to come, babe?"

"You go ahead, Mark. It'll do the two of you good to spend some time together."

3

"Oh, Jesus, oh, Jesus, oh Jesus!" Cliff was crying frantically, mindlessly. He crawled on hands and knees toward the gun. But it was out of reach, lying on the floor under the exploded window.

Nancy saw the motion jolt Harrison from his immobility. Apparently realizing what Cliff was after, Harrison dove for the weapon.

Both men grabbed it at exactly the same instant. A violent tug-of-war ensued. Nancy watched helplessly as Harrison held firmly to the barrel and Cliff held the stock. Whipping the metal back and forth, Harrison fought to wrench the gun from Cliff's hands. Why didn't Cliff pull the trigger? Harry was directly in the line of fire.

But before Cliff could shoot, Harrison pulled the weapon sharply toward himself, then with a massive display of strength, pushed the barrel up and, with both hands, shoved it away.

The metal slammed into Cliff's wounded forehead, smashing his nose. Flattened tissue erupted in a crimson fountain. The speed of the assault caused the smooth barrel to slip from Harrison's hands. Cliff staggered backward, clutching the gun while groping for something in his jacket pocket.

Suddenly Nancy realized what was going on. "It's not loaded!" she cried to Harrison.

On that signal, she and Harrison lunged at the bleeding man, but too late. With practiced smoothness, Cliff broke open the weapon and slid in the shells with amazing speed.

The couple stopped in their tracks.

"Bastard!" said Cliff. Again he had complete control of the situation. "Now let's all jes' take a little rest. Jes' take it real easy." His voice was falsely calm.

Cliff's eyes, like the twin barrels of the shotgun, never wavered as he circled around them. When he stopped, he was in front of the window. He peered through the dreadful opening, looking down. Breathing heavily, blood and mucus bubbled in his nose. His barrel chest rose and fell in spasms. His eyes darted wildly. Perspiration poured from his bloody forehead. Absently, he wiped the fluids from his nose onto the sleeve of his woolen jacket.

He was pale as a gull. A low moan began to rise from his heaving chest, "Ohhh . . . Ooohhh . . . OOOOOOHHHHHHHH!"

Nancy thought the man was about to become hysterical.

Clutching the shotgun, Cliff continued to moan. He looked first into Harrison's eyes, then Nancy's, plaintively, as if he were begging for some kind of help.

Then his expression changed; apparently he had remembered they were his enemy.

"Oh, Jesus . . . Oh, God . . . We're in trouble now. Oh, Christ, we gotta get the hell out of here. Quick! We gotta get movin'." Becoming more agitated, he motioned to the flashlight with the gun, then flicked the barrel toward the door. Harrison picked the light up off the floor.

"Git movin'," Cliff commanded. He had regained some of his composure. "Quick! We gotta go. NOW!"

Nancy clutched Harrison's arm as they began their walk from the sunlit chamber into the deepening darkness of the monastery's interior. The rippling white flashlight beam led the way. Cliff followed, muttering and panicky, weapon in hand.

At this point there could be no doubt. Nancy knew they were in the hands of a madman.

4

The sky was aglow. The dark mountains to the west looked as if they were on fire. From where Professor Hathaway parked his car

—hidden in the bushes not far from the abandoned quarry—he had a clear view of the crimson sunset. *It is very much like fire,* he thought—the intense reds and the billowing black cloud formations that offset them. He had to pause for a moment to admire the beauty.

This was going to be a very special moment, one that had been years in the making. He felt momentarily self-conscious that his plans had briefly taken a backseat to something as mundane as a sunset. Anyone who showed that much interest in nature, he chided himself, displays a decided lack of imagination. Now where had he heard that? Well, no matter . . .

Perhaps he was just putting off what had to be done, deferring gratification, savoring the moment that he had devoted all his retirement years to bringing about.

He turned his back on the sunset and walked away from his carefully concealed car, approaching the house. A blue Honda was in the yard—the schoolteacher's car—but Harrison's Saab was gone.

Good. All was going according to plan! The young couple was away somewhere. But for how long? The safest thing would be to act fast. Of course, what he had to do wouldn't take long.

He'd known from the beginning that there was no treasure map in that old house: It was just a local legend. But there was a treasure, and now he would possess it.

At long last, all the bits of his research—the discovery of each new and elegant piece of the puzzle—were finally falling together, forming a map of their own. It was a map that led inexorably to the captain's house.

And to the treasure: Hidden somewhere in those ancient rooms were the collected papers of Cortney Dare.

According to Professor Hathaway's studies, Dare had been the leader of the spiritualist colony on Friar's Island until it faded into oblivion sometime before 1930.

Dare, the philanthropist. Dare, the humanitarian. Dare, the deceiver. He had lived a double life, posing as a retired New York City industrialist who had retreated to Friar's Island for reasons of health. His ready smile, his generosity, and his keen attention to civic matters had quickly endeared him to the local population in the early 1900s.

He had been a founder of, and trustee in, the limited island library, aiding in the selection of books, often paying for them out of his own pocket. He had declined a nomination to the Vermont legislature in 1904, and in 1907 he donated most of the land on The Jaw to the town. This land was then developed into a profitable quarry, a source of wealth and livelihood for the community. Dare had been the kind of man that mothers insisted their sons should grow up to emulate.

And Cortney Dare had lived so far from the old monastery—all the way on the opposite side of the island—that folks just knew he had nothing to do with the peculiar goings-on at that accursed old place.

Apparently, in all the years Dare had lived on Friar's Island, no one had ever suspected that he was involved with—indeed, was the leader of—those godless heathens that lived in the north end.

Professor Hathaway chuckled silently.

When Dare died in 1919, he was given a Christian burial. Most of the local women cried at his funeral; husbands stood with their eyes cast down, never suspecting that he was not a Christian at all, never realizing that he had come to their island for reasons far removed from retirement, health, and municipal participation.

And no one on the island ever learned of the woman Cortney Dare had abandoned many years before . . .

Were it not for Professor Hathaway's research—more than sixty years after Dare's death—the suspicion linking him with the spiritualists would never have arisen. Dare's arrival on the island had only slightly predated the formation of the spiritualist community. Its death, and his, were similarly synchronous. Only the passage of time, and the perseverance of a diligent researcher, could ever have connected the two.

Still, the bottom line was that it was only a suspicion, a theory, and it would remain that way until proof could be found. Professor Hathaway was confident that an insightful perusal of the old house's attic—or cellar, or anywhere that old papers might have been hidden—just might disclose the unknown factor in the equation he had labored so long to balance.

As he neared the house, a chill of anticipation permeated his body. The place was perfect, so out of the way that any activities within could never be scrutinized by the curious townspeople. The place's privacy, its isolation, would guarantee the occupant total freedom of motion. Professor Hathaway planned to take advantage of that freedom now by searching the interior.

The windows of the house in the last light of day looked black, as if the building were filled with nighttime. For him, the dark windows articulated a long-sought invitation. They beckoned like the eyes of a sensuous lover: This is it. This is what you've been looking for. Come to me . . .

It was as if a sixth sense were assuring him that he was in exactly the right place. He trusted that sense would lead him directly to the object of his search.

After opening the unlocked door, he stepped into the hallway and looked around. He saw pillows on the floor of the living room, empty glasses by the fireplace.

Harrison had been entertaining. That was good. The empty house and the Honda in the yard confirmed that Harrison and Nancy were exploring the old monastery, just as Harrison said they would—just as Professor Hathaway had planned. How suggestible they were!

But to work! The professor guessed he would have a minimum of one hour of safe, uninterrupted searching.

He thought—with some amusement and no less satisfaction—about Harrison's notion that the house was haunted. Professor Hathaway had been truthful when he'd said he'd never heard that it was. But he had long *suspected* that it might be. If the spectral occupant was not the disincarnate spirit of the house's sailor builder, then more likely it was the spirit of Cortney Dare himself. The fact that Harrison claimed he had heard what sounded like a woman in tears meant very little. It could as well have sounded like a moan or a rattling chain or slamming door, or anything at all—anything the spirit wanted to sound like.

And Harrison had said the noise seemed to come from upstairs: as good a place as any for Professor Hathaway to begin the search.

With little difficulty, he found his way up the creaking stairs to the second floor, then to the narrow passageway leading to the attic. As he climbed the long-unpainted steps, the smell of the attic became more and more pronounced. There was the odor of wood and creosote, of things left long ago to dry: old clothes in storage, once important, now decades forgotten. The smell of age and years wafting past his nose provided a pleasant sensual link with the past.

He paused at the top of the stairs, looking around at the long-accumulated array of memorabilia. It was like stepping into a time capsule prepared a half century ago. At his feet he saw a box of antique mason jars, nearby a wooden crate of hardbound books. There were storage trunks and wooden file cabinets. Across the attic, in the shadow of the brick chimney, there was what looked like an old strongbox.

Where to start?

If this were to have been a random search, he would have gone directly to the strongbox. But he'd never planned to be random. His years of devotion to the arcane disciplines—starting with an innocent hobby of parlor tricks and magic—had taught him much more about communication than he had ever learned studying or teaching at the university.

He knew exactly what to do. He sat cross-legged on the wide pine planks of the floor, close to the top of the stairs. His old legs moved with a youthful agility. Facing his palms, he crossed his hands, knuckles to palms, touching his closed eyes with the opposite index fingers, resting thumbs on his temples. In position now, he exhaled, slowly voiding his lungs of all air. He waited, not breathing, until the beating of his heart reverberated throughout his body, pounding like the clapper of a bell. His mind, empty but for the words *Cortney Dare*, called silently to the outer and inner voids. He spoke the name soundlessly; he wrote it in his mind, as if with stark white paint on the limitless blackboard behind his closed eyes.

Then, after nearly three minutes, he began to inhale slowly. The ritual, practiced and automatic, occurred without effort and with great concentration. As he inhaled, he took in more than the musty air. With it came the pulsations of life and spirit that had lingered for untold years in the atmosphere of the ancient house. The stark white letters—*Cortney Dare*—gradually turned to smoke before his closed eyes; his ears detected faint syllables, like a distant station on a poorly tuned radio.

He had made contact! There could be no doubt. But there would be no dialogue, no conversation—his powers were not yet that highly developed—just the communication of a single thought, a single image across time and space.

And then the picture was there behind his eyes, sculpted from the churning smoke that had once spelled *Cortney Dare*.

It was the final piece of the puzzle.

At last, for the first time in a long life of study and frustration, Professor Sheldon Hathaway would experience power.

5

"Get in that fuckin' Scout." Cliff waved the shotgun. "You drive, fella. Christ, I gotta get the fuck outa here!"

Cliff crawled into the back seat. Obediently, Harrison followed Nancy into the front. Harrison took the wheel.

"Now don't go losin' your head, lover boy, or the little lady is gonna lose hers—an' I ain't shittin'." Cliff rested the barrel of the shotgun on the back of Nancy's seat, its muzzle in firm contact with her spine. To prove he wasn't shittin', he pushed the metal hard against her vertebrae. She lurched forward, crying out in pain and surprise.

Harrison was convinced of the helplessness of their situation. Any false move, any show of noncooperation would trigger aggression toward Nancy. Even if their captor was truly insane, there was no reason to believe he was a liar.

Looking out of the corner of his eye, without turning his head, Harrison saw Nancy cowering in the passenger's seat, her shoulder and head pressed firmly against the window. Her hands were locked tightly together, knuckles white, the tip of her right thumb clenched in her teeth.

He could not recall ever feeling so frightened and powerless. But he was surprised to feel something else: Somewhere below his trembling limbs and chattering teeth there was a calm spot in his mind, a spot where thought processes were going on very clearly. He couldn't take time to think about it; he couldn't analyze it or debate whether he might ultimately prove to be a coward. He just continued, rationally, to assess their situation, knowing that he was nowhere near as terrified as the man in the back seat.

Harrison knew the next move could be his. It would have to be a careful move, well timed, planned and perfect. Maybe he could regain control.

"I'll do whatever you say," he told his captor.

"Get this fuckin' thing movin'."

"Where to?"

"Drive to . . . drive to my house. No! Shit! She'll look for me there. Gotta hide. Gotta git off the friggin' island."

Harrison backed up the Scout, turned around, and headed down the road toward the bridge to North Hero.

"NO!" shouted Cliff. "They could be waiting for me at the bridge. A boat! I'll have to get a boat."

"What are you so scared of, man?"

"Scared? Christ, you don't know what she can do!"

"What *who* can do?"

"She can git inside your head. Make you do things. Anything."

With those words a dreadful realization seized Harrison. It removed forever any possibility of doubt: The man *was* insane, completely out of touch with reality. Harrison thought of the gun on the wall at home, the fireplace poker, the knives in the kitchen, the hatchet he used to shave wood for kindling.

"Let's go to my house," he said. "It's on the other end of the island. No one would look for you there."

"Yeah. Yeah, okay," Cliff said emphatically. "Drive."

6

The hidden drawer in the bottom of the wooden file cabinet contained about thirty pages of handwritten manuscript. The ink was faded and brown. The tiny, cramped, and crablike script, scratched onto each yellowing page with a fountain pen, caused the professor to squint uncomfortably. He would have to get it home, where he could study it under direct light and with a magnifying glass.

As he rose and started down the stairs, he heard the poorly muffled roar of an engine. Stopping on the landing on the second floor, he peeked out between the shutters and saw three people pull up in a decrepit-looking Scout. It was a familiar vehicle, one he had often seen around the island.

Visitors, no doubt. They would not find Harrison at home and they would quickly leave.

To be sure that the house appeared empty, he stepped back, closed the door at the bottom of the attic stairs and returned to the safety of the loft. He would hide until he heard the growling engine again as the visitors left.

Although he waited in suspense for many long minutes, he felt completely safe and protected.

But too much time passed.

Apparently the guests had decided to wait a while for Harrison to return. They might be waiting in the Scout, but probably not. More likely they had exercised the age-old island custom of walking right in and making themselves "to home." It would be easy to enter; the professor knew the door was unlocked. Better stay right here, he thought. May as well do a little reading.

Huddled below a dusty attic window, he brought out the manuscript and began to examine it in the failing light.

. . . and above all, the ancestry is most interesting. There is evidence of an unbroken record of psychic power extending over several generations. The grandmother four times removed was sentenced, if not hanged as a witch, in the infamous Salem trials of 1692. My own research corroborates at least the former after a careful study of trial records and the genealogical linkage.

There are as many living now who would design to take a similar position with the mediums, and so the mother, who was herself strongly psychic and perhaps equally as shrewd, masked those powers over which she could exercise control so successfully that she was married to a simple rustic who had no idea of his spouse's well-concealed talents.

There was to be no similar refuge for the less fortunate Abby. The psychic phenomena used to follow her everywhere and repeatedly manifested themselves involuntarily. In the schoolroom she would excite the reviling of the ignorant little barbarians around her.

At home, when young Abby fell into a trance, her father, an unjust and religious brute, would pour boiling water over her legs and once placed a red-hot coal upon her hand, leaving an indelible scar. The girl fortunately slept on.

The same ignorant zealot who turned the girl's home into a hell upon earth later tried to make some money out of the very powers which he had once so brutally discouraged, and hired the girl out as a medium. It was under these wretched circumstances that I first made her acquaintance.

No one has to this date made public or adequately described the tortures which public mediums occasionally undergo at the hands of idiotic investigators and cruel skeptics. I myself have witnessed the girl's arms and hands grooved with marks of ligatures and scarred with burning oil or wax. I have seen where pieces of flesh were pinched out by handcuffs. And, although I have not witnessed the atrocity, I have no doubt that her claim of blood oozing out from below her fingernails from the compression of arteries is absolutely true.

It required little additional provocation for me to relieve the opportunistic brute of the burden of fatherhood. Our escape to Vermont was without event and, I believe, went completely unobserved by anyone in authority.

She proves a far more satisfactory subject than anyone else to date, and in the accepting atmosphere of the colony she has rapidly learned not to be afraid of her talents and, upon occasion, to display them with pride.

At first, upon the initial introduction to several members of the colony, I observed her unconscious effect upon them. With no effort of will she is able to cause confusion among those who surround her. Perhaps it is a psychic projection of the confusion she herself experienced in unfamiliar surroundings amid a group of doting though hitherto unknown individuals. Perhaps the consequences that befell Peveral Holmes are the most illustrative. Upon making the acquaintance of the girl, he began to become muddled in his normally eloquent speech. Apparently believing himself to be back at university, he commenced chanting the conjugation of certain Latin verbs. The reaction of the others, though less dramatic, was illustrated by their indifference to Holmes's condition. I might add that the condition vanished when Holmes was led from the room.

It should be noted here that her influence upon many was much less marked and upon a few was not at all. I myself find that I am immune to her intentional and unintentional persuasion. There seems to be no explanation that will account for who is affected and who is not. It is my intention to investigate this further.

As I have said at great length on previous pages, I abhor the neo-Christian cults that are asserting themselves to become the religion of the future.

The term "spiritualism" and even Doyle's patronizing term "psychic religion" are destined to do the science a great disservice.

The church and its many tentacles, like the body and legs

of the black widow, will surely poison the science and suck out
its essence before it grows to benefit mankind as a new—

Here Professor Hathaway flipped a few pages, looking for
something more interesting. He heard sounds from downstairs:
doors slamming, feet pounding on floorboards, the drone of
muffled conversation. Ignoring the noise, he continued reading:

> . . . to aid the girl in her training. My research supports the
> following conclusion. I postulate thusly: If human evolution
> were in fact initiated by the perverse coupling of higher with
> lower primitive "humans," then a subsequent rung of the evo-
> lutionary ladder may be attained with the union of a suitably
> adept human female and a superior being of another plane.
> Since communication with these beings is impossible for all
> but a select few, it must be one of these who encourages the
> union. This will be my task for Abby.

Ah! This was exactly what he wanted.

But Professor Hathaway's eyes were beginning to hurt as they
strained in the faded light. The cramped handwriting became
blurred and impossible to read. He had been so engrossed in the
manuscript that he'd failed to notice how uncomfortable he had
become in his awkward position below the window. The circula-
tion in his right leg had been cut off; a numb, prickling sensation
threatened to become painful.

He stretched his legs out in front of him, trying hard not to
make any noise that might betray his presence to the unknown
guests waiting below.

His heavy right leg scraped across the wooden floor.

The impact of what he had just read was staggering. Was the
seemingly idiotic Jabez Snowdon the product of an experiment in
the bizarre union of a gifted psychic and—what was the term?—
a cryptosentient being? Was Jabez in fact an experiment that
failed? An earthbound body with a mind trapped uselessly on another plane? Or did the boy in some way contribute to the strange

hold that Abigail Snowdon—surely the "Abby" of the manuscript—had over the islanders?

What, exactly, was the nature of this mysterious hold she exercised over them? What was the true source of her enigmatic
power? Professor Hathaway had always known better than to ask
the islanders any of these questions. But his patience had paid off;
now he knew the answer was at hand.

He was eager to return to his house to read the rest of the papers in a more comfortable environment.

If only the people downstairs would leave!

But then again, he had waited this long, a bit longer would do
no harm. It would not even be unreasonable to spend the night in
the dusty attic, if that was what he had to do.

He settled back, a bit more comfortably now, his legs stretched
out before him. With the diversion of reading no longer possible,
he began to wait again as the attic's darkness became complete.

7

Even in the cool living room, Harrison could see that the man was
sweating profusely. His eyes darted back and forth, and all too frequently he jumped up, weapon in hand, and paced from window
to window, looking out over the fields or at the road that ended in
front of Harrison's house.

The man's nervousness was infectious.

Harrison knew he'd have to be extremely careful not to alarm
or provoke him. He noticed that Nancy was looking at the man
strangely, almost with a kind of recognition. But the time had not
yet been right to question her about it.

"Listen," said Harrison, "can I offer you a drink, some coffee
or something?"

"Got any beer? I could use a beer."

"No beer. I have some bourbon."

"Yeah, great. I'll have a shot."

With glass in hand, and calmed somewhat by the humane

exchange, the man seemed to relax a bit. He sat down in the easy chair by the fireplace, the shotgun across his knees. Harrison and Nancy sat close together on the couch nearby.

Secretly, Harrison stole a glance at the antique shotgun mounted on the wall above the mantel.

"Look," said Harrison, trying to sound as reasonable as possible, "I really don't know what this is all about, but I want to help you if I can. The thing that happened back there in the monastery, you had nothing to do with it. We both saw that it wasn't you. Maybe we couldn't see who it was that killed your friend, but we saw it wasn't you."

"Listen, you don't know what you're talkin' about. And the only fuckin' thing you can do for me is to get me off this friggin' island. None of us can do nothin' about what happened back there. Nothin'."

"But what are you so afraid of? Do you think whoever it was will come back for you?"

"Look, mister, you don't know nothin' about it. An' you don't wanna know, believe me you don't."

"But you're not in any trouble. We saw that you didn't hurt your friend. It can't be the police you're afraid of—"

"I AIN'T AFRAID!" Cliff wiped the back of a trembling hand across his mouth. "I ain't afraid. I'm jest bein' careful, that's all."

"But if you level with me, maybe I can help you. Look, we were attacked by a maniac, all of us. But it was your friend who got hurt. The cops'll take our word for it. Think about it: If there's a crazy man on the island, they ought to be out looking for him. Nancy and I can clear you. We can all tell the same story about what happened."

"It's got nothin' to do with the friggin' cops," Cliff shouted. He stood up, like a soldier snapping to attention. Then he walked over to where the couple sat, towering over them, weapon across his chest. "Look, I don't know why the fuck that happened to Stubby, and I don't know who done it, okay? But I got a pretty good idea where they come from. An' I'll tell you somethin' more; ain't *none* of us here is safe—not you, not me, not the schoolteacher here. An' they's nothing' you can do to help me. An' nothin' I can do to help you. So I want you—I want both of you—to jes' fuckin' set there an' shut up an' let me think."

At that moment, as if on cue, there was a noise from upstairs, the grating squeak of a board as if under the weight of a man's foot.

Instantly Cliff went white, his eyes widened with a fear approaching panic. He backed up against the wall, his weapon ready for action.

"She's here," he muttered. "She's here. Oh, Christ, she's found me. Oh, shit, oh, shit, she knows I'm here, she—"

"*Who?*" Harrison pressed, holding Nancy's hand tightly. "Who are you talking about?"

"The ol' woman—who the fuck do you think? The ol' witch woman. The one who—" Cliff turned abruptly, his frightened eyes met Nancy's. "You two ain't from aroun' here. You don't know what she is, what she can do. You don't even know what she done to you already, an' what she's gonna do when she gets here. Christ, I think she's here already. I think she's upstairs!"

"That was just a noise. This old house is full of them. Go on up and look."

"Fuck you, 'go up an' look.' "

Still, the man seemed to calm down a little. Chancing a careful walk to the foot of the stairs, he looked up. "Maybe you're right. Maybe I am gettin' awful goddamn jumpy. I gotta think this thing through. If she don't know I'm here, then she, or maybe Jabe, is prob'ly waitin' for me at my house or on the bridge or—"

Cliff walked back to the chair and sat down. His posture was stiff, erect, and the weapon was always ready. His gaze darted between the window and the front door, then toward the stairs.

"If I don't show up at neither place, then they're gonna come lookin' for me, that's for sure. Now, how'll they find me? How? Is there any way they can know I'm here?"

"Your car," said Nancy meekly, her tiny voice cracking with the effort of speech.

"Fuck, yes! Stub's goddamn Scout! We gotta get the fuckin'

thing outa sight." He jumped up and charged to the window. "Christ, I might as well have my fuckin' name on the mailbox."

"I can move it," Harrison offered.

"Yup. Yup, you can. That'll be your job. You jes' drive it down south an' hide it in the bushes all the way down on The Jaw. An' do it quiet. Don't turn on the lights or nothin'. An' if you're back within ten minutes, I won't do nothin' to your girlfriend here, you unnerstan'?"

Harrison nodded.

The message was absolutely clear.

Harrison left the house, Cliff at the front window watching every move. He jumped into the Scout. When he turned the ignition key, the engine roared to life.

8

When he heard the car pull away, Professor Hathaway thought he was again alone in the old house. He hurried down the stairs, giving no heed to the clatter of his leather boots on the wooden steps.

When he reached the landing on the second floor, it occurred to him that maybe he was being careless, perhaps taking too much for granted. He slowed down. Stopped. Listened.

Strange.

Could one of the visitors have stayed? Maybe he wasn't alone after all.

No. Surely he was. There was no noise downstairs, no sound from the outside, none from the wide, dry flooring nor from the ancient timbers settling and breathing.

Still, it wouldn't hurt to be careful.

In the weakening half-light of the disposable flashlight in his hand, and with Cortney Dare's papers clutched tightly to his chest, Professor Hathaway began his final descent. He placed his feet gingerly on the outside of each step, close to the wall, trying to prevent more telltale noises.

Below him the rooms of the house were dark and ominous.

9

Harrison drove to the end of the dirt road and parked the Scout where it was thoroughly hidden by The Jaw's proliferation of brush and brambles. His only thoughts were of Nancy and the vulnerable position in which he had left her.

He had to hurry back. Speed was the most important thing in the world right now. If he could not help her, at least he could be with her, watch over her, make a move to protect her if he got the chance.

If only he had a weapon. There were stones and heavy sticks all around him, but these were too bulky, difficult to conceal. He would have to leave them where they were.

Perhaps he could find something in the Scout. Frantically, he rummaged through the glove box, amid the empty beer cans and bottles on the floor, in the rear compartment, searching for a screwdriver, a jack handle, anything that might be used against the lunatic wielding the shotgun.

There was no time to spare; every minute he looked around would cause their captor to become more agitated.

Finding nothing, he abandoned his search.

A thick, damp fog rolled in slowly from the lake. Now, in the deep twilight, the lights of Grand Isle were barely visible.

Turning away from the water, Harrison studied the dark bulk of his house. With no interior lights burning, it seemed little more than a concentrated knot of shadows, offering no aid and no inspiration.

A ways off to his right, close to the shore of the lake, he saw a towering, leafless oak whose dark trunk and jagged branches gave it the appearance of frozen black lightning against sky.

Wait! Near the trunk of the tree—he was sure of it—a lone figure stood watching him. A primitive fear seized Harrison. He couldn't tell who or what was observing him, but somehow he knew it was no one who'd offer any help. Instinct cautioned that it might even be dangerous to summon the stranger. When Harrison blinked, the figure was gone.

Harrison began to run toward the house, knowing he had to get back before any harm was done to the woman he loved.

10

Cliff froze at the sound of footfalls. There was no question about it, someone—someone who had never entered the house—was coming down the stairs!

He cowered against the wall, his face bone-white. He shook so violently that Nancy could see the motion from way across the room. A whimpering, pathetic and frightened, escaped at regular intervals from his throat.

"Oh, God . . . oh, God . . . oh, God," he said while inhaling, his voice a hoarse whisper.

His gun was ready to meet the intruder, but Cliff obviously was not. Nancy saw him look over his shoulder at her, his expression imploring, as if begging her for help.

Her own terror mounted as the footsteps came closer and closer. She wanted Harrison to come back. She wanted to run. In her mind the horrible face that she'd seen at the window returned, attaching itself to whatever was coming down those stairs.

Could it be Harrison, returned by some back entrance, sneaking in to save her, thinking he was being silent? Of course, it must be Harrison. Who else could be in the house?

From where she sat, she saw a tall, shadowy form becoming visible on the stairs. The form was definitely human, and somehow familiar. She watched Cliff become tense and ready, his shotgun like the head of a cobra poised for a lethal strike. When the shape on the stairs turned from the darkness to face them, she acted without plan or thought. Jumping up, she screamed, "Harry, RUN!"

Jolted by the sudden cry, Cliff's finger reflexed on the trigger. The shotgun exploded with the impact of a bomb.

The dark form jerked off its feet. In midair it doubled up like a jackknife, then collapsed lifeless amid a snowfall of papers that had flown from its hand.

In the violence and confusion—though it lasted only a moment —Nancy sped through the front door and into the misty evening.

11

The explosion stopped Harrison as if he had slammed into an invisible wall. He stood paralyzed, holding his breath. He saw a shape, indistinct but definitely Nancy, bolt from the house.

"NANCY!" he cried against the muffling fog. But she neither heard nor heeded as she ran north along the road toward the marsh.

He shouted again, louder, as the gunman stumbled out the front door.

"NANCY!"

Harrison heard the gun explode again. The bushes rustled on his left as if pushed by a sudden wind.

He's shooting at me!

He about-faced, diving back for the Scout. Regaining his place in the driver's seat, he fired the engine, pointing the vehicle toward the fleeing woman. As he roared past the man standing in the front yard, he heard another explosion. The glass on the passenger's side of the front window imploded, scattering shards like deadly hail throughout the Scout's interior.

Harrison cried out in surprise, veering the nose of the vehicle toward the man.

Groping in his pocket, apparently for more shells, the man began to run. Foolishly, he didn't run toward the house but along the open road. He looked repeatedly over his shoulder at the oncoming Scout, his eyes wide, terror-stricken in the headlights.

I've got you now!

Harrison accelerated, easily gaining ground. Cliff hurled the useless weapon; it clattered against the passenger's door and vanished out of sight.

Cliff dashed away from the road, running to the right, moving across the field toward the bog.

Harrison veered right, following him. The Scout was designed for just such terrain.

The impact was abrupt and satisfying. The front bumper lifted Cliff's legs out from under him, rolled his body across the hood, and pitched him headfirst through the shattered passenger-side window. For a horrible second Harrison and Cliff were face to face before Cliff's body slid to the side and off the moving Scout. The soft flesh under his chin impaled on the jagged window glass. The Scout dragged the flailing man until his heavy boots caught on a sapling. His jaw and much of the side of his face tore away in a crimson spray.

Without slowing down, Harrison redirected the vehicle back toward the road. He had to find Nancy. He could see her solitary form still running for her life. When she neared the bridge that crossed the marsh she must have been nearly two hundred yards away.

But Christ, what's that?

Not far behind her was a second figure, much bigger, seemingly darker, running with long loping strides. Elongated arms dangled motionless at its sides.

Harrison floored the accelerator, speeding wildly down the dirt road, blasting the horn, trying to alert Nancy that he was coming, warning her pursuer that help was on the way.

When the horn blew and the engine surged, the dark, loping figure put on a burst of speed. It easily overtook Nancy and effortlessly scooped her up into its long arms. Then it dashed into the dark protection of the marsh.

Even above the noise of the roaring engine, Harrison could swear he heard Nancy's screams.

12

Mark Chittenden was puzzled to see the abandoned Scout at the roadside. Normally there wouldn't be anything unusual about a vehicle parked near the bog during hunting season, but not after dark, not at this awkward angle, not with the driver's door wide open and the engine running. Mark knew that something was not quite as it should be.

His suspicion was quickly confirmed when he pulled up to the house. There was an unfamiliar Honda in the yard, and Harrison's Saab was nowhere in sight. Also, without leaving his car, Mark could see that the door to the house was open.

What's going on?

The uneasy feeling—far worse than he had experienced when he couldn't reach Harrison by phone—escalated now. Cautiously Mark eased himself out of the car, looking around for signs or motion.

"Harry!" he called from the yard. He waited for an answer that never came. He slowly approached the front door, pushed it open all the way, and looked into the dark interior.

As he stepped across the threshold, it somehow felt colder inside, colder than the bitter evening mists. Mark tried to sort out the tangle of shadows that met his eyes. Though it was his house, he forgot momentarily that there was no electricity; he groped at the wall beside the door, trying to find a light switch, never moving his eyes from the dim interior.

Unconsciously remembering the layout of the building, Mark easily found his way into the living room. On the table in front of the southern window he found a kerosene lamp. He lighted it with nearby matches.

An orange glow filled the room with warm illumination, pushing the confusing shadows closer to the walls. A quick inspection didn't speak well of Harrison's house-cleaning skills, but revealed nothing amiss.

After backtracking into the hall, kerosene lamp in hand, Mark walked deeper into the house. In the dull back border just beyond the circle of lamplight, he saw what appeared to be a pile of equipment, or possibly a bundle of clothing, near the foot of the stairs. He approached it slowly, the perimeter of his light washing over it like water over rocks on the shoreline.

His mind wrestled to perceive something other than a body.

"Har . . ." He cleared his throat. "Harry?"

But it wasn't Harrison.

Mark tore his eyes away from the unfamiliar face of an elderly man. Nearly crippled with revulsion, Mark forced himself to look at the man's body. The stomach was ripped apart. Through a gaping, meaty hole, blue and black intestines, like the coils of a bloody snake, tried to escape.

Mark vomited violently on the gory paper-strewn floor.

Fighting white-hot waves of nausea, he forced himself to think about Harry. He recalled his friend's brief visit to Burlington, his distraught appearance, his strangely erratic conversational patterns.

His preoccupation with monster hunting.

Could those have been the first signs of developing mania? Could Harry have done this thing?

He felt no inclination to further examine the old man's body. Still, there was a mild curiosity about the papers that were scattered all around it. Mark gave no thought to responsibility or civic duty. It was simply automatic that he sought the location of the newly installed telephone and placed a call to the state police.

13

Bushes slapped at Harrison's face; twigs, like animal claws, dug at his flesh. All around, the confusing tangle of trees and brush slowed his progress, made it nearly impossible to maintain a chosen direction.

Long ago Nancy's screams had faded away to nothing. Now the only noises in the foggy marsh were the obscene sucking sounds of his boots in the mud and his own cries of rage and frustration.

And it was so dark! The twisted shapes of bent trees and tangled brush made every direction look the same. No more than one hundred yards into the marsh and he was hopelessly lost.

Harrison had no time to contemplate the nagging realization that he had never been in a situation like this before. Christ, he had just caused the death of one man—mowed him down like roadkill—and was now pursuing another.

But he couldn't think about it now. And he couldn't take time to remedy his discomfort. He was cold, lost, and his feet were wet and numb, but he was driven by a single thought: to push forward, to pick up the trail of the abductor, and to fight, to die if he must, risking everything to save his beloved Nancy.

He paused, gasping for breath, looking around.

Above him the three-quarter moon was a pale and ghostly light, veiled in mist and woven into the fabric of crisscrossing tree limbs. The silhouetted branches, like a loathsome web, seemed to trap the white moon against the black sky. Harrison felt that he, too, was the captive of some monstrous spider. It was waiting for him to reach the point of exhaustion, waiting silently, just out of sight, for the moment to strike and kill.

Still he squinted into the darkness, knowing that something was waiting in the shadows or hidden among the contorted trees. It was something that was much more at home in the inhospitable environment of the swamp than he could ever be. As he stood alone, fearful and still, Harrison realized for the first time that he was not armed. He had entered the swamp with no weapon and no experience in the inevitable task he would soon face.

God! He didn't know how to fight!

He gave brief thought to his efforts, many years ago, to avoid military service. If he had done time in the jungles of Vietnam, perhaps now he would not feel so out of place, so helpless.

But there was no time for such thoughts.

Near his foot he found a thick thirty-inch stick that was heavy enough to serve as a club. Close by, he picked up a rock the size of his fist. With these firmly in his grip, he plunged deeper into the mud and shadows of Childe's Bog.

To his right an owl called, "Wh-whoooo, wh-whoooo." Harrison ran in the other direction, thinking the owl would not have called if someone were near.

The fog was so thick it felt like rain against his face. He was hot and cold at the same time, brave and terrified.

"NANCY!" he called into the darkness. "Nancy, where are you?"

Stumbling blindly through the rocks and bushes, unable to balance himself with the hands that held his weapons, Harrison's foot found an exposed root. He pitched forward, landing full-front in the muck. He gasped, inhaling in a noseful of putrid swamp water.

Spitting and choking, he rose to his knees. He looked around, feeling as if he had been pushed.

Soaked and sore, fear and desperation brought tears to his eyes. The salty drops slid down his cheeks, warm and irritating.

"NAAAANCYYYYYYYYY!" he screamed. There was no answer; not even an echo.

Blundering half blindly ahead, he soon found himself on firmer ground. His footing was more definite now; the thick undergrowth began to thin out.

Had he crossed the marsh? There was no way to be sure. He continued in a straight line until the ground stopped sucking at his feet and the branches stopped slashing at him.

Through layers of fog to his right, and far in the distance, he could see the hazy glow of an orange lamp. Walking toward it, he found he was on a footpath that ran parallel to the bog. For the first time he began to trust his sense of direction. This was the path he'd seen branching off West Shore Road. He knew it would either lead him directly to the ghostly glow at his right—or, if he went left, to the road home.

What could that light be? He recalled seeing no house so near the marsh. But he did remember planning one day to explore the very path that was now underfoot.

And he remembered something Professor Hathaway had said, something about "Mrs. Abigail Snowdon, your nearest neighbor."

So that was her house!

And the house of her son, Jabez, the idiot man who had visited Nancy at school, and who had appeared so suddenly at the monastery, showing them the way in.

Of course! It had to be Jabez Snowdon. He'd fixated on her, followed her, and grabbed her before running into what he considered the safety of the marsh.

It all made sense to Harrison. He had better approach the lighted cabin with a high degree of caution.

Gripping the stick firmly, he walked toward the indistinct glow. He remained within the protection of the shadows, keeping low to the ground, stalking like a wild animal.

14

The door to Cliff Ransom's house burst open as if it had been shoved by invisible hands.

The old woman, her arms beneath her shawl, stepped across the threshold into the foul-smelling kitchen. With an air of command and dignity, she crossed the room to the table in its center. There was an open jar of French's mustard on the tabletop, its glass mouth black and crusted. Crumbs and papers and many empty Budweiser cans cluttered the table. More empties covered the floor and every other available surface in the room.

She looked back at the door and motioned quickly with her head. Timidly the awkward man lurched forward into the room. The vapid expression on his flat white face showed no more than a hint of discomfort.

The old woman looked at him sternly, her eyes full of meaning. His hands flew to his ears as if he were trying to shut out a painful nose. "I can't do it no more, Ma. Jes' talk to me. Please. My head hurts."

"He ain't here, Jabe. I can't tell nothin' from him. I can't tell where he is." Her voice was a patient whisper. "Maybe he's asleep someplace."

"Wha'd ya wanna find him for, Ma?"

"I told you Jabe, I wanna fix him so he don't remember nothin', that's all."

"But them other two, what about them?"

"They're from away, Jabe. They don't know what they seen. We'll fix them, too, but I ain't so worried about them."

"I'm scairt, Mom."

The old woman walked over to him, unfolding her arms, wrapping them and her shawl around him like brown wings. "I know you are, Jabe. But I'll take care of you, jes' like I always done. You know how important the fam'ly is to me. You know Ma's never let nothin' happen to you."

"I know," he said in a small, cracking voice, his huge shoulders heaving with muffled sobs.

"There," she said. "There, there." She patted his hair until the sobbing subsided. "Now you wait for me on the porch. I'm goin' to try to hear him again."

Jabez stepped obediently out into the night as the old woman sat down at the kitchen table. She closed her eyes and took several deep, slow breaths in an effort to relax. A calm seemed to pass over her, relaxing muscles softened the deep wrinkles in her face. Then the wrinkles seemed to fade, smoothing magically, until her aspect was almost youthful.

Then, as if she had received a sudden jolt, her eyes opened abruptly, like car headlights turning on.

As if he had been called, Jabez rushed back into the house.

"Wha'sa matter, Ma?"

"There's trouble to home, Jabe. We gotta get over there."

They left hurriedly, cutting across mid-island paths and secret, unmarked routes they both knew better than they knew the island's roads.

15

Chief Lawrence Connelly sat by himself on the cold concrete frame of the bridge to North Hero, the one bridge off the island. His Stetson and light wool jacket offered little protection against the chill night and bone-numbing mist. He gave no thought to moving or pacing to keep warm. Somewhere, way in the back of his mind, he might have known he was cold. But it didn't matter. He wasn't able to concentrate on anything. His eyes were locked unblinking on the entrance to the bridge. He was not able to turn them away.

Each attempted thought faded quickly, like a dream, the moment it began to form.

He was not able to think at all.

Except for one thing.

He had to watch for Cliff Ransom. He had to stop Cliff Ransom from leaving the island.

Moments ago, when the police car had driven over the bridge to the island, he hadn't even seen it. He wasn't watching for that. He was watching for Cliff Ransom.

And that's what he would continue to do. He had to. He'd been given a command.

16

The place was empty—Harrison was confident of that.

Twice he had circled the tiny cottage; the third time around he had stopped at each window to peer inside. Although a kerosene lamp had been left burning, the house was deserted.

He had briefly considered forcing his way in for a more thorough search, but there was something oddly tranquil about the place, something undisturbed. It convinced him that no one was hiding inside.

So he turned away, again facing the shadow-black marshland. *A wild-goose chase,* he thought. *Whoever grabbed Nancy has never left the swamp.*

What should he do now? Where should he go? His mind recoiled from the reality of the situation. If only this were a game, he thought, if only a good-natured cry of "Okay, I give up" would put an end to it.

Paralyzed with indecision, he didn't know whether to continue his one-man search of the marsh or race back to his house and call the police.

But the thought of Nancy in the hands of that half-wit rekindled his drive. Jabez was dangerous, unpredictable. Who could guess what distorted thoughts were going through his limited mind? What variety of perversion might he inflict on the terrified woman?

Gathering what remained of his strength, Harrison again set out into the bog. A new assault of icy water penetrated the seams of his boots as he fought sucking mud and groping branches, plunging ever deeper into the swampland.

Thickly tangled bushes loomed before him like a wall. He carefully parted them. Stepping through, he faced more of the same— a twisted, knotted nightmare of wiry vegetation.

Slowly he began to realize just how eerie his surroundings were. There was no sound but that of the obscene slurping mud. The smells of rich earth, rotting wood, and decaying organic matter mingled in a nauseating bouquet. He felt as if he were going to vomit, but he feared the sound it would make and the vulnerable position it would leave him in.

And there was another feeling—the feeling of being watched. It was as if he were suddenly surrounded by unseen eyes that peered at him from every tree, stone, and fallen log.

On his left a scampering squirrel made him jump. His heart beat faster. Yet he forged ahead. If something was going to get him, why make it easy by standing still?

Wandering blindly, he had no sense of progress or direction. There were no sounds to follow, no distinct visible landmarks for orientation.

Something grabbed his shoulder!

His heart stopped as if squeezed by an icy fist. But he saw only the gnarled branch of a dying tree, its wet leaves heavy as flesh.

Visibility seemed to improve when he wandered into a small, raised clearing. It was like an island in the middle of the marsh. Its surface, lighter and drier than its surroundings, made walking easier.

There he saw—

Even with his improved vision, his eyes might still be playing tricks on him. There *appeared* to be something straight ahead. Something sheet-white and motionless. It loomed in the distance on the far side of the clearing. In the pale moonlight the thing seemed to emit an unearthly glow. It moved and throbbed like an unformed mass of ghostly ectoplasm. His curiosity to approach wrestled with a primal urge to run away.

With great care, Harrison moved toward the thing, peering at it through swirls of mist. His eyes left it only long enough to assure himself that there was nothing more menacing lurking just beyond the edge of the clearing.

He held his breath.

His club was raised and ready.

As he got closer, the lines of the thing became more distinct. What he saw was far worse than he had feared. The grotesque white mass became the shape of—

Dear God, it's Nancy!

She lay stark naked, curled tightly into a fetal ball on the muddy earth.

As he ran to her, he saw the thick rope, one end tied around the trunk of the nearest tree, the other around her neck.

Harrison could not stop to question what he saw. Only one thought drove him: the woman he had sought for so long was there, helpless in front of him.

He ran to her.

In some hidden corner of his mind he wondered why she might be tethered, naked and alone, in that dark clearing. Some part of him knew this surely was a trap. But an overriding urgency thrust him onward: pure instinct. Like a hungry wolf discovering a white lamb tied to a stake—he could act no differently.

Kneeling beside her motionless form, he hesitated to touch her. "Nancy," he whispered. "Nancy?"

The awkward position of her body troubled him. Even in this dim light he could see where the rope had burned ugly welts on her throat. Mud, dried and crusty, coated her limbs. Her long black hair was matted and foul.

"Nancy," he whispered, louder now, more urgently. Harrison

faltered as he reached out to touch her face. He dreaded what his touch might reveal. What if . . .

. . . he had lost her?

When her eyes flickered, he dared hope. Placing his ear close to her mouth, Harrison experienced untold relief at weak but steady breathing.

As if waking from a long, restful sleep, she slowly opened her eyes.

"Harry," the whispered word, distant, hollow. She reached out to embrace him, but froze mid-motion. Her eyes widened. A soul-shattering gasp seemed to flatten her against the ground.

Harrison turned his head, his eyes following her terror-filled gaze. Not fifty feet in front of them, someone stood just outside the clearing. The tall figure at the edge of the forest was so painted by shadows that it appeared to be nothing more than a broken tree trunk. It stood perfectly still, perfectly camouflaged. Harrison hoped his eyes were playing tricks on him. He blinked. Blinked again, hoping it wasn't really there.

But it was.

At that moment the hours of desperation, anger, and wild fury erupted in Harrison Allen. The bizarre events of the day, the mindless, hopeless trek through the marsh, the sight of his loved one bound and naked, all exploded in a terrible rage.

With the heavy length of log in his hand, he ran screaming at the lurker in the shadows. Eyes wide, weapon raised, his cry of fury filled the night as he fell upon the motionless figure.

Harrison brought the heavy piece of wood down in a deadly arc, but it was stopped in mid-descent, arrested by the quick motion of a leathery hand.

It felt as if his wrist was locked in a rough leather glove. Fighting body to body now, he was too close to see the face of his enemy.

He screamed maniacally, wrestling with the stronger foe. The club tumbled uselessly from his hand. A strength far greater than his own forced his raised arm downward until both struggling limbs were pinned ineffectually at his sides. He knew the muscular arms surrounding him could easily squeeze his life away.

The side of his face flattened against his opponent's shoulder. It felt like a coarse leather jacket on his cheek.

Harrison sensed a sharp, fetid odor. It was the smell of sweat, an earthy stench of rot and corruption. Pinned tightly to its source, he felt an overpowering nausea. To escape the rankness he folded backward as far as his spine would permit.

He struggled not to pass out when he found himself looking into the face of the thing that held him.

I'm crazy, he thought. *Good God, I must be dreaming.*

The face, only inches away, was something from a madman's nightmare. Black as a snake, wrinkled as the bark of an ancient tree, the skin had the appearance of old, neglected leather. Wisps of yellow hair grew like weeds from the knobby ebony scalp.

Thick lips, blacker than the skin surrounding them, resembled the jowls of a dog.

Pulled closer, he smelled the breath again, renewing his impulse to vomit. The muscles of his abdomen tightened as the strong arms found a tighter hold. Locked in this foul embrace, Harrison resisted the disgusting smell and the abhorrent feel of the leathery hide.

And then he saw the eyes. Black, like stones under water. Lifeless, like a doll's eyes. There was no white, no iris, no emotion.

When the hideous mouth began to open, Harrison knew he was going to die. Smooth black lips retracted, revealing long, pointed teeth.

My Jesus, it's going to bite me, he thought, resigned that now he could do nothing to save himself or Nancy.

But when the loathsome lips touched his face, there was no sensation of pain, just a wet, ugly sucking as a dry tongue flicked like a serpent's against his cheek. Then the leathery lips, like hideous worms, wriggled against his mouth.

Harrison couldn't move; his limbs would not obey the panic messages from his brain.

The persistent probing tongue battered against his lips and teeth, working its way into his mouth. He gagged, fought to turn away, but an iron hand capped the back of his head, holding it immobile.

The other hand made frenzied trips up and down his spine. Harrison heaved and bucked, growling in terror and disgust. He could not break away, could not purge the writhing tongue from his mouth. He bit down on it. Hard. But his teeth had no effect on the leathery hide.

Suddenly he felt the two oversized hands slipping underneath his jacket, touching his flesh.

He tried to scream but the intrusive tongue muffled it. Then it retracted, slithered along his neck like a serpent.

"Oh, my God, my God," he moaned when he realized what the thing was doing to him. As the strength of the bear hug increased, he could feel twin, muscular mounds pressing hard against his chest. The thing's ghastly hand moved from behind him and began to grope for his belt.

Somewhere in the distance Nancy screamed his name.

The force of her cries broke the thing's concentration. It turned on her viciously, fangs bared, snarling like a demon.

Buckling at the knees, Harrison slid down through the creature's loosening grip. On all fours he scrambled away out of reach.

The thing stood immobile between Harrison and Nancy, looking from one to the other. In mechanical jerks, its head moved this way and that. Apparently it was trying to decide who to attack next.

Its gaze locked on Nancy.

I've got to act now, Harrison thought.

As the distorted body turned on her, Harrison moved with lightning speed. He picked up a large rock and hurled it. The creature howled as stone slammed against the side of its head. Its hands jumped to the wound. Harrison heard nearly human pain in its anguished wail.

And it turned to face Harrison.

He picked up another rock, larger this time. With both hands he lifted it above his head. When he was about to hurl it, a voice cried, "NO, PLEASE!"

Harrison and the creature froze like statues in a waxworks. Nancy continued screaming.

Somehow Harrison became aware that the unearthly tableau of screaming woman, terrified man, and loathsome beast was being scrutinized by another couple who had silently entered the clearing.

He recognized Jabez and immediately realized that the old woman he was following had to be Mrs. Snowdon. She stepped forward, her dark shawl pulled tightly to her neck.

Seeing her, the creature recoiled as if confused. In its halting mechanical way, it shifted its gaze from the old woman to Nancy, to Harrison. A sound started to rumble within its chest, a sound that rose like steam through a pipe until a ferocious cry, pregnant with anger and despair, burst from its lips.

It lunged at Nancy, murderous in its intent, arms flailing and mouth wide.

"Jenny, STOP IT!" Mrs. Snowdon commanded.

And the thing stopped, frozen in mid-attack. It pitched forward, landed on its knees, straddling Nancy's body.

"Jenny . . ."

The act of raising its head seemed difficult; it looked entreatingly at the old woman. Without rising, it moved closer to her, walking on its knees, arms extended. A dry scratching noise hissed from its throat.

The old woman remained immobile, firm of posture, severe of face. She showed no fear of the reptilian deformity that crept toward her. Softly, almost in a whisper, she spoke. "I said no, Jenny."

That simple phrase, so quietly uttered, seemed to have a powerful impact on the creature. Its ink-black eyes held on the old woman for a while, then turned timidly toward Harrison.

He tried to look away, but could not as he watched the being collapse to the ground. It cried out, high-pitched, joyless, uncontrollable.

Harrison recognized the sound of that anguished weeping. He had heard it before in his own house, heard it just as clearly as he heard it now. It was the sound that triggered his suspicion that the captain's house was haunted—the sound of a woman weeping.

But the specters he'd imagined then could not be as horrible as the cringing thing on the ground before him.

He looked at Mrs. Snowdon, hoping for an explanation. She looked back; her expression revealed nothing.

As the creature wept, Harrison moved quickly to Nancy. When he reached out to touch her, she cried out, recoiled in terror. It was as if she didn't recognize him.

"Jabez," the old woman said, "see to Jenny."

Mrs. Snowdon walked over to Harrison and Nancy, removed her shawl, and placed it over Nancy's trembling shoulders.

"There now," she said soothingly, "there, there. There's nothing to be afraid of."

The old woman looked deeply into Nancy's red-rimmed eyes. As if responding to a silent command, Nancy eased herself to the ground and fell asleep.

"It might be easier for her if she don't remember none of this tomorrow," Mrs. Snowdon said to Harrison. "You pick her up now. We'll take her to my house. We'll get her warmed up and I'll see to her scratches. Jabez, you take your sister on home."

17

Nancy slept soundlessly on the cot by the woodstove. Thick layers of heavy quilts concealed the contours of her body. If it weren't for her face and her long black hair, the cot would have appeared empty.

Jabez stood by the door. His eyes, unblinking, were fixed on some mysterious spot on the ceiling.

Dazed and shaken, Harrison sat on a wooden chair at the round kitchen table. He sipped a cup of steaming herb tea that Mrs. Snowdon had prepared. She looked at him impassively from her seat across the table.

"I let it go on for way too long," she was saying. "And I covered up for her way too many times. Now that I look back on it, I 'spect the very first time was one time too many.

"But you know, Mr. Allen, nothin' like this ever happened with her before. That is, not before you come to this island."

She sipped her tea, looking very, very old. The confidence and majesty had vanished from her posture; her voice was tired, far away. "It ain't that I blame you, you understand, not any more than I can blame the schoolteacher over there for Jenny's feelin's of . . . well, I gotta say it . . . jealousy."

Harrison shuddered.

"I know how that must sound to you, Mr. Allen, 'specially now that you got a good look at her. But so help me it's the truth—Jenny loved you. It's jes' that pure an' simple."

Harrison felt himself trembling, more from Mrs. Snowdon's disclosure than from the deep-rooted cold that felt as if it would never leave his body. The thought of that misshapen gargoyle ac-tually *loving* him, the memory of those tight membranous lips pulling at, kissing his cheek, his mouth . . .

He tried to remain calm, giving the old woman his full atten-tion. He didn't want to anger her or say anything that might up-set her, at least not until he could decide whether she was as insane as this situation that had brought them all together.

"No," Mrs. Snowdon continued, "I don't blame no one but myself." She sniffed, massaged her eyes with her fingertips, and looked at Harrison. "I guess you got a right to know the whole story, Mr. Allen, 'specially after all that's happened. You see, I done some things when I was a young 'un that I'll need a whole lot more livin' to set right. And havin' Jenny around every day to remind me . . . well, that don't make none of it too easy to forget. You believe in God, Mr. Allen?"

Startled by the incongruity of the question, Harrison wasn't sure of the least dangerous answer. In his confusion he blurted out the truth. "No, I don't think I do. It's never been an easy thing for me to believe in."

She looked at him intently. "Ain't it any easier now that you've seen the devil?"

"Why, I . . . uh . . . I'm sorry, I don't know what you mean."

"Lookit, I got no idea how much you know about this island,

Mr. Allen. I know you seen that old monastery up there on the north end. Well, fact is, the story starts there. That old place used to be the meetin' hall for a group of spiritists. They was tryin' to build some kinda bridge connectin' this world to the next. Turned out they was fixin' to use me as that bridge. I was s'pose to learn how to do it—how to be the connection. I got tutored by a man name a Cortney Dare. Ever hear of him?"

Harrison shook his head.

"He used to live right in your house. 'Course, he pretended he didn't know nothin' about the spiritists, when all the time he was the ringleader of the whole thing! He believed there was another world, jes' like this one pretty much, but invisible to us, even though it's all around us. The folks over there, on the other side, are a whole lot stronger an' more powerful than we are. Some people call 'em angels and devils, I guess, but Cortney Dare, he didn't go in for none of that religious stuff. He looked at the whole thing kinda scientific-like.

"Now these folks from the other side, they can make us work for them without us even knowin' it. Turns out they got an awful lot more to do with our lives than any of us could ever realize.

"Anyways, Cortney Dare thought if he could turn the tables— get *them* to work for *him*—why then, he'd be the most powerful man in this world. More'n any king or president or pope or whatever. See, Mr. Dare, he wanted to control more than jest the colony a spiritists, he wanted to control . . . well, he wanted to control anything he *wanted* to control. An' he *did* control a lot a folks, me included.

"But don't get him wrong, now. He was a special man, Mr. Allen, a grand an' shinin' man. There weren't an ounce of bad in his makeup; that's the important thing to remember. He didn't want to do nobody no harm. Jest wanted to make things better all around. Why, thinkin' of him now, I believe that man had more charm than anyone should ever be allowed to have. That's how he got me to do what I done.

"Him an' the others at the monastery trained me. See, I always had a touch a the second sight. So did my mother, an' some of my other ancestors, too. Guess I had a pretty strong dose of it, from what they told me. Anyways, they trained me. Got me so I could talk to folks without even movin' my mouth—I'd jest think a what I wanted to say to 'em, an' they'd hear it, even if they was a long ways off. I kep' gettin' better at it, too. Pretty quick I could tell folks what to do, an' they'd jest do it without ever givin' it a thought. I can put thoughts in folks' heads that was never there before, an' I can make folks ferget things, too. I'm ashamed to say it, Mr. Allen, but sometimes I can do harm to folks without so much as even layin' a finger on 'em."

Harrison shivered.

"So I kep' workin' and practicin', an' when I got my powers up to where Cortney Dare figgered they was strong enough, he got me to talkin' with them folks nobody can see, them invisible folks that's all around us an' all over ever'where.

"Oh, I guess I ain't the first to talk to 'em, or even the first to see 'em, but I might jest be the first one who ever tried to entice one of 'em with the idea of havin' his baby.

"First time things didn't go too good. Some kinda connection got made, all right, but nothin' much happened.

"But that Cortney Dare, he wasn't never one to give up on somethin'. Like I said, he was a charmer, an' pretty quick he got me to try again. This time he had me fix my attention on another daddy—one a the real strong ones.

"An' that's what you see in them two kids of mine. 'Specially Jenny. She's my daughter, all right, but her daddy's one a them outside ones. Jabez, too, for that matter, but he jest don't look so strange.

"So you see what happened? After all was said and done, Cortney Dare's idea jest didn't work, 'cause Jenny, she got her daddy's looks okay, but her insides is jest as human as can be. Jest as human as your schoolteacher friend, I guess. Must be, 'cause they both of 'em feel the same way about you.

"Jenny can't hear thinkin' the way me an' Jabe can. But she don't need to in order to tell how people'd feel if they seen her. She knows she's as ugly as sin. An' that breaks my heart, Mr.

Allen. 'Cause by the time I got around to birthin' her an' Jabez, I knew that Cortney Dare was jest leadin' me on. Why, I wasn't no bridge, I wasn't no experiment, I was jest the mother a two kids, plain and simple.

"Oh, I know how that sounds to you. An' I know it's somethin' you'll never understand, not even if you was a woman. But you gotta believe me, them two kids is real special to me. I want what's right for 'em, an' I'd do jest about anything to make 'em happy, 'specially when I think about all the stuff they got goin' against 'em.

"Sure, I knew what was happenin' when Jenny started gettin' sweet on you. I seen how she brung you things an' followed you around, an' how she protected you. Broke my heart when I found out she kilt a little girl who snuck into your house. Jenny thought the little one meant to hurt you, I s'pose, or maybe figgered she had designs on you herself. Jenny, she don't really think too clear, ya see. I gotta say she's kinda simple. But after she done what she done, there was no way of bringin' that little gal back again, not after Jenny finished with her. 'Course I knew how her parents woulda felt, same as I would losin' one a my kids like that—why, I'd wanna die. So I helped 'em with that, you know. Dyin', I mean. I felt terrible doin' it to 'em, but I thought it was the best thing all around . . ."

Harrison's hands tightened on his mug of tea. He couldn't think of anything to say, but he didn't have to. The old woman continued, " 'Course it was Jenny saved you from them boys with the shotgun, ya know. That was her doin', not mine. And maybe it was good what she done, I can't say for sure.

"But I'm sure about this: She got all crazy with love an' jealousy an' things went from bad to worse. It's my belief, Mr. Allen, that she meant to hurt your lady friend, too. I'm afraid she was gonna do more'n jes' use her to lure you into the swamp."

Harrison watched as the old woman wiped a tear from the corner of her eye. Then she said, "That's when I knew things had gone too far. Things had finally got outa hand. See, I been hidin' her here on the island for a lotta years. An' in all that time she never before started actin' the way she has since you come here. You must have somethin' pretty powerful workin' for you mister, that's all I can say. You waked up somethin' in that girl that ain't stirred for sixty or more years.

"Y'see, Jenny grows old real slow. A lot slower than other people. Same as Jabez. That's another thing they get from their father, I guess. But now, after all this time, Jenny's come of age, an'—no different than any of the rest of us—once she comes of age, she ain't never gonna be the same again.

"I tried to help her out a little. Tried to use young Ransom to get the schoolteacher out of the picture. Thinkin' about it now, though, I guess that was pretty stupid of me. I shoulda known a fancy city girl like that would never take a shine to none of the island boys. Too bad, too. Prob'ly woulda worked out better in the long run, though who can say."

As she poured some more herb tea into Harrison's cup, he noticed her hand. The palm was wrinkled and brown with an ancient scar that looked like a burn mark. Harrison took the cup gratefully, relieved to have something tangible to hold on to in this atmosphere of unreality.

"We've had a pretty good life here on the island," the old woman continued. "Folks leave us to ourselves pretty much. They do little favors to help us, and I do what I can in return. It works out. They don't ask no questions, an' I don't give 'em nothin' to ask questions about. 'Cept maybe now. I'm afraid it's gonna be a little hard to get things quieted down again."

"Quieted down? I . . . I don't understand."

"No? Well, think about it. Right now Cliff Ransom's lyin' dead outside of your place, an' some friend of yours from Burl'ton jest called in the police from Grand Isle. They're gonna find what happened to Cliff pretty quick, ya know, an' they ain't never gonna realize how much he had it comin'. They're gonna find another dead body in your hall, too—that old snoop of a college perfesser."

Harrison couldn't believe it. "Professor Hathaway's dead?"

"Yes, he is, sir. Gunned down by young Ransom."

He heard horror and wonder combining in his voice. "My

God," he asked slowly, "how do you know all those things happened?"

"I can see things, that's what I'm tryin' to tell you. I can shine my mind over this island like the beam from a lighthouse. I can always tell what's goin' on. Everyone around here knows that."

"S . . . so what do you intend to do?"

The old woman shook her head slowly, sadly. "That I don't rightly know. Not exactly." She tapped her fingertips on the tabletop. "Maybe I *do* know everything that's goin' on in town, but so does most any other ol' lady. Trouble is, I don't always know the best thing to *do* about it. One thing I'll tell you for sure: Things don't look very good for you right now, Mr. Allen."

"For me? What do you mean?"

"I mean you could have an awful lot of explainin' to do."

"Explaining?"

"You don't get it, do you, son? It's like I said. There's them two bodies on your property, an' you ain't anywheres around. Now how do you s'pose that looks? Jabe an' me, we took care of that other fella's body, the one over to the monastery, Stubby Baron. But sooner or later somebody's gonna notice he's missin', jes' like folks already noticed that little girl an' her parents ain't around. We took care of their bodies, too, an' Jabe sunk their car in the marsh. But we can't go on like this, Mr. Allen. The bodies jest keep pilin' up. Now these things gotta stop. They ain't right."

Harrison didn't know what to say.

" 'Course, now with young Ransom dead, nobody can connect us, or you, with any of it. Trouble is, we didn't have no time for hidin' them dead folks at your place . . ." She took a deep breath. "Like I say, it's gonna be a little hard to get things quieted down again."

Harrison began to feel uncomfortably warm. His heart pounded as if it were trying to break free of the bone and muscle enclosing it. Beads of sweat burst from his forehead and formed under his arms. They ran down his sides in icy rivulets. He braced himself; he had a strong sense of what was coming.

"What about Nancy?" he asked.

"Looks to me like she slept right through the worst of it. I got a feelin' when she wakes up she won't remember much of anything that happened. Jabez can fix things so she can wake up right to home, right in her own bed. Be a shame to have her miss a day of school tomorrow."

Harrison had only one question to ask. It was difficult for him, and it came slowly. After what seemed a very long silence, he finally spoke. He could manage nothing more than a whisper.

"And . . . what about me?" he asked.

Awakenings

18

I

It was as if a great weight suddenly had been lifted. For the first time in more than three hours, Chief Lawrence Connelly shifted his position on the cold concrete bridge. Suddenly he realized how chilly it had become; he figured he'd better be getting along home.

He glanced groggily at his watch. It was one of those digital affairs, the kind with just numbers and no face. He still wasn't sure that he liked it. But it had a little built-in light that blinked on so he could tell what time it was, even when it was pitch-black outside.

It was 8:02. He could still make it home in time for a late supper.

No point staying here any longer. If that Cliff Ransom had been going to show up, he would have done it by now.

The chief got up and walked away. His legs ached from sitting too long in one position. His arthritic knees were stiff from prolonged contact with the cold stone. They hurt something wicked when he flexed them, as if the joints were lubricated with ground glass. Still, he had a feeling of satisfaction, accomplishment. He had done his job well.

He knew his stakeout had been successful. He had not seen Cliff, which meant Cliff had not crossed the bridge.

2

It was painful to look at the body. For a long while after he'd called the state police, Mark Chittenden had ignored the dead man in the hallway. He found it easy to avert his eyes; averting his mind was another thing altogether.

He tried walking around outside, not wanting to be in the same house as a dead man. But he quickly found the cold and the dampness less hospitable than the slaughterhouse atmosphere within.

As time passed, his curiosity began to heighten. He walked from the living room into the hall, where he examined the body from a safe distance. Any closer and the smell of the wound would have been overpowering.

The man looked familiar. Surely he was an islander, somebody Mark had seen before. Holding his breath, he walked a little closer, his steps tentative. If it became necessary he was prepared to make a rapid retreat.

The body, slouched against the wall, was an elderly, moderately distinguished looking man. The cadaver's thick white hair was obvious as his head jutted forward, chin pressed tightly against his chest. Mark intentionally avoided the sight of the ruined abdomen where torn strands of clothing were woven tightly with shreds of flesh, all matted together in a paste of thick red-black blood.

He backed away. Turned. Redirected his thoughts.

So where was Harrison? His Saab was nowhere around. Had he done this and run away? Was Mark's old college pal capable of such a violent act? Why would he do it? What could possibly have been the motive? Mark searched his memories of Harrison for signs of violence. Or insanity.

Though his mind continued to reject thinking about the corpse, Mark's attention was again caught by the papers that littered the floor. Mystery novels and cop shows had taught him that he wasn't supposed to touch anything at the scene of a murder. But picking up just one paper . . .

After reading one, he picked up another. And another. He had finished reading long before the police came. Prior to today—

before this very moment, in fact—Mark never would have imagined himself as one capable of concealing evidence from a police investigation. But these papers were different. They were written in his grandfather's own handwriting.

And they hinted at a terrible secret.

3

When Nancy Wells awoke, she found herself in her own bed. She felt tense, irritable, as if she had just awakened from a bad dream. Yet try as she might, she could not remember what she had been dreaming.

When she attempted to sit up, it was like a mallet blow against the interior of her skull. Flinching, she painfully, slowly, settled back into the warmth of her bed. She gently eased her throbbing head into the still-warm indentation in her pillow.

Where did this headache come from?

Closing her eyes, she waited for the painful drumbeat to slow down. At first it felt like a hangover, but she had no recollection of drinking anything the night before.

In fact, she had no recollection of the night before at all! With this realization, she became frightened. Her eyes opened wide, in spite of the painful daylight.

A total lapse of memory!

Dear God, it IS happening again!

Her senses sharply tuned now, she began to experience a tingling of sensation in the rest of her body. It was like blood returning to a numbed limb.

How her arms and legs ached! Had she banged and bruised them while thrashing around on the floor, caught helplessly in the violent throes of a seizure?

Deep inside, Nancy finally knew she could no longer deny that the seizures had returned. She had always known there was a possibility that they might. Now they had. God, how much more indication did she need?

Then and there she resolved to put it off no longer. She would make an appointment with a neurologist today. At once. She'd even go to the emergency room at a hospital if she had to. It would be best if she got someone to drive her. Maybe she'd call Professor Hathaway or . . .

Or . . .

Who else was there?

No one.

She began to sob, not knowing exactly why. As if to comfort her, a soft, caring voice whispered from somewhere in the back of her mind, "There, there, now. Call Eric, honey. Eric loves you."

Yes, thought Nancy, all at once feeling better. *Yes. Eric loves me.* She could easily remember his phone number in Albany.

4

Somehow Harrison seemed to sense where he was long before he opened his eyes. There was an overwhelming feeling of familiarity about his surroundings; he just couldn't name the place.

He inventoried the various sensations. He was cold. Damp. The musty smell of earth was all around him. Yet it was a familiar smell, one he had experienced just recently.

He was not on a bed; he knew that. He was on a hard surface. He could feel it underneath the blanket he was lying on. Through the fabric tiny lumps like pebbles pushed against his sensitive flesh.

For a long time he couldn't move at all. It was as if his mind were commanding his body to remain motionless. But his mind had issued no such command.

At least he could think. But all he could think about was how cold he was, and how uncomfortable he felt, and that he could do nothing to change either.

He took a deep breath. The cellarlike odor was almost tactile. It burrowed deep into his lungs, where it seemed to take root and chill him from within. It smelled so familiar, like the odor of returning home after a long time away, or the lingering scent of a lover's perfume. But he had a poorly developed olfactory memory; he just couldn't place the scent.

If he could only open his eyes! It was like waking from a sound sleep, knowing he should get up but not having quite enough willpower to lift his eyelids and face the new day.

Willpower! Yes. That's what he needed!

He concentrated on a single thought: to open his eyes.

And they opened!

From his position on the floor—lying flat on his back wrapped in a scratchy woolen blanket—he looked around the dim, candle-lit room.

In the orange flicker of the single flame, he could make out the stone formation of walls and dark outlines of thick timbers far above his head.

Scanning the walls, he saw no windows, but his eyes stopped somewhere to his right where he saw a heavy wooden door.

Closed.

At first he was sure he was in a cellar. But no. That wasn't right.

Again he tried searching his memory.

There! He almost had it.

The remembered odor of the place with its familiar-looking stonework finally told him where he was. He was in the old monastery.

He fought the paralysis, trying—trying so hard—to move. With a monumental effort of will he was able to pry himself into a sitting position, slowly peeling his aching back away from the sweat-drenched blanket on the floor.

He was naked! God! Why was he naked?

His right hand lifted the blanket to cover his shoulders. He held it closed at the neck.

Oh! The motion reminded him that his muscles ached. Rolling his head around on his neck, he felt little cracks and snaps as tendons, joints, and muscles flexed and relaxed. He stretched his shoulders, his arms, his back, feeling similar relief before he dared to try standing up.

Woodenly, unsteadily, he found his way to his feet. His head reeled as if it were floating unattached in some tropical mist. Struggling for clarity of mind, he stumbled to the door, fully expecting to find it locked.

With what little strength he had, he pushed against the door. It would not budge. He pushed again, feeling the beginnings of panic coursing like electricity through his numbed limbs. Then in momentary relief, half smiling to himself, he pulled on the door. It opened easily.

He peered out into the darkness; it was utter and complete. With an effortless motion he picked up the stub of a candle—the sole light within the room—and held it up in the doorway against the profound gloom.

He saw the central passageway that he had seen . . . seen when? Not so very long ago.

Was he *back* in the monastery? Or was he *still* in the monastery? Could it be that he had never left?

A sudden confusion seized him then, a confusion that memory could not relieve. Had he fallen here? Hit his head, maybe? Had he been here all this time, dreaming strange dreams that now were impossible to remember?

Well, no matter. If he couldn't remember how long he had been here, at least he could remember the way out.

Holding the candle high, his hand protecting its flame from the draft created by his rapid stride, Harrison made his way toward the far end of the corridor. There, he clearly remembered, was a stairway to the basement. And from the basement a tunnel led to the outside.

After passing doorways all along the passage, he arrived at the place where the stairs should have been. Instead, he found a heavy wooden door—closed. He put his weight against the thick planks, somehow knowing it was pointless. Neither pushing nor pulling would move it a bit.

After pounding on it a dozen times, he turned away, leaned his back against it, and tried to catch his breath. He knew he had the right door, and it was on the right end of the corridor. But—still capable of self-protective denial—he decided to check the other end just to be sure.

Moving from one end of the passageway to the other, he randomly peeked into several of the small rooms along the way. He wanted to be sure he was not overlooking any means of escape. He decided he was not; the only way out was to go up or down the stairs.

But when he arrived at the end of the hall, he discovered he had no access to any stairway.

Then his tentative panic became acute.

He pounded on the stone wall, moaning in frustration. Yet even in his despair he maintained the presence of mind not to let the candle flame go out. He needed the light. Needed it like a medicine. Somehow he sensed that permitting complete darkness would be like an invitation to the insanity he felt was so very near. Thoughts of madness crowded his fragile mind, signaling, taunting . . .

For the first time in many years, Harrison Allen sat on the floor and cried.

"I can't get out," he said over and over in a tiny, quavering voice.

Beside him the flame from the candle stub danced, throwing jittery shadows on the stone walls. A bit of sanity hidden deep below his hopelessness and defeat began to respond to the severity of his situation. Soon the tiny candle would be gone; he would be in complete darkness.

And then what?

There was no water, no accessible food supply. Shouting for help was pointless; on either side of him thick stone walls and acres and acres of uninhabited island meant no one would hear him scream.

Was this all some kind of joke? No, of course not.

Could someone have left him here to die? Probably not. At least not exactly. There was no reason to have brought him here if murder had been the plan. He was reasonably sure that his captors —whoever they might be—would arrive soon. Perhaps they'd bring food and an explanation. Perhaps they would be willing to bargain . . .

Or—and this might be a better idea—he should prepare for their arrival. At the same time, he'd prepare for his escape. After all, as he had learned long ago, the best defense is a good offense.

But whatever his plan might be, there was one nagging, unsettling phrase that continued to command his attention. It was like a persistent echo trapped inside his head.

A woman's voice. An old woman.

He could almost hear her!

In some hazy, elusive memory he recalled a conversation in which an old woman had stated . . . "The wrong and the right of it don't matter. First thing I gotta think about is the fam'ly."

What had she meant by that? What had she been talking about? God! Why couldn't he remember anything?

Slowly, reluctantly, Harrison began to rise to the challenge. For more than three decades he had successfully avoided many things. But never before had he come close to facing anything like this. This time he could not avoid it. This time there was no easy dodge or escape.

With no stretch of the imagination, Harrison knew he was a prisoner. There was no room for denial.

So what was he going to do about it?

With sustained concentration his thoughts began to clarify and focus. He needed a weapon.

Taking the remaining inch of candle, he began to look into the tiny rooms, searching for anything that might inflict pain, cause damage.

When he opened the door on the left side of the corridor—at about the middle of the building—he was startled to find himself walking into a well-lighted room. Candles, dozens of candles, lit the tiny chamber. They provided a warm, intimate glow.

Slowly, as the door opened wider, it revealed a sturdy three-legged table in the center of the room. On it Harrison could see two cups, a steaming teapot, half a loaf of dark bread on a plate. Beside the table, back against the wall, two army-type cots were pushed together, side by side. They were covered with an inviting thickness of homemade quilts.

From where she snuggled below the colorful quilts, her black eyes looked out and met the terrified eyes of her lover.

Jenny Snowdon rose to meet her husband.

Instantly, with scalding clarity of thought, Harrison Allen understood everything.

He backed out of the door. The piece of candle dropped from his hand and went out. The blanket slipped out of his grip.

He ran naked through the darkness to the far end of the corridor. He pounded on the locked door to the stairway.

A scream froze in his throat as the unyielding door tore the skin from his fists.

He wasn't a man anymore; he was a force. He was unstoppable.

The door wouldn't budge.

The last fragments of Harrison's sanity escaped with an explosion of vomit and uncontrollable screams.

Behind him, in the dark passageway, the scratching sounds of clawlike toenails inched toward him on the granite floor.

A hand touched his shoulder.

An arm embraced him.

The Monster   19

Far from the towering gray and silent walls of the ancient monastery, below the cloud-heavy, lightless sky, the ever-changing swells of the great lake throbbed to an ageless rhythm.

Beneath its perpetual, imperceptible tide, in the cold, uncharted channels north of Friar's Island, a dark, serpentine form roved silently through shadowless depths. Zeuglodon, plesiosaur, or great eel, it knew itself not by name but by sensation. Its route through the frigid waterway was guided by reaction, never by design. In the dimness of its animal brain, it knew—as well as it could know anything at all—that the waters around it were growing colder with each new darkness. And, as the temperature fell, its appetite diminished, leaving safe the small fish that frolicked nearby and fled whenever it came too near.

In a sightless, soundless recess of its primitive brain, there was a faint call, a summons, like the faraway sounds of its mother, who had died so long ago. Her tired, parasite-ridden body had drifted slowly, like a gyrating log, to the sunless depths.

And the animal was alone.

The faint call—irresistible, persistent—would guide the obedient creature among the Champlain Islands, urging it north, away from the lake and the coming of ice, then across meaningless borders to faster-moving Canadian waters. There its hunger would return. There it would feast, gaining new strength to complete its long migration to the sea.

DIANE FOULDS

AUTHOR'S NOTE

Like many authors, I have two first novels: the first written, and the first published. My first published was *Shadow Child*, but this is the first book I ever wrote.

I began it around 1983 or '84. At that time I wanted to create a scary story like many I had enjoyed over the years. A long-time affection for such writers as Bram Stoker, Sir Arthur Conan Doyle, Arthur Machen, and especially New Englander H. P. Lovecraft is evident and acknowledged.

I began reading Lovecraft when I was in the fifth grade. I remember the immediacy each tale took on when I realized it could be happening right here in Vermont. Right in the woods behind my house.

In writing this book I wanted to create what might be called a "Vermont Gothic." I tried to include as many traditional Gothic trappings as I could: menacing and mysterious characters, remote and desolate landscapes, weird family relationships, lots of shadows, and of course spooky old buildings, dark passageways, and darker secrets.

Even in my literary naiveté I knew I was championing an outdated form. I tried to compensate by devising a modern and recognizable protagonist with just the right amount of 1980s angst.

Without pontificating too much about the metaphorical implications of Harrison Allen's seemingly pointless journey to Friar's Island, let me just say that the book's original title was The Monster Hunter. It is about a man who goes looking for a monster he doesn't find; who finds a monster he isn't looking for; and whose odyssey is a search for self—a monster hunt of its own.

I chose Vermont's Champlain Islands as the setting because they comprise a magical world, unlike anywhere else in the state. My first visit to Isle La Motte suggested the microcosm that became Friar's Island.

The cycle of speculation about the Lake Champlain Monster is very much on the level. However, I felt that in dealing with legitimate folklore—or, possibly, unproven fact—it would have been irresponsible of me to ruin the integrity of the myth by "solving the problem." So the monster remains undisturbed.

I should probably close by saying that any resemblance to the real Vermont, and any similarity between Harrison Allen and myself are coincidences too astonishing to be believed.